Also l

HOLIDAY NOVELS

Merry Ex-Mas

My Phony Valentine

ROAD TRIP ROMANCE

A Cross-Country Christmas

A Cross-Country Wedding

STAND-ALONE NOVELS

The Happy Life of Isadora Bentley

Things Left Unsaid

Hometown Girl

NANTUCKET

If For Any Reason

Is it Any Wonder

A Match Made at Christmas

What Matters Most

HARBOR POINTE

Just Look Up

Just Let Go

Just One Kiss

Just Like Home

LOVES PARK, COLORADO

Paper Hearts

Change of Heart

SWEETHAVEN

A Sweethaven Summer

A Sweethaven Homecoming

A Sweethaven Christmas

A Sweethaven Romance (a novella)

COURTNEY WALSH

For Jeannie.
You are so very missed.

Chapter One

Emmy

I have a secret.

Not the kind of secret that could land me ten to fifteen years in prison, or one that Dr. Phil would announce if my parents revealed that they found me in an abandoned basket at the circus.

Although *that* would be one heck of an episode.

It would also explain my affinity for peanuts.

It doesn't matter what kind of secret it is. . .it's a secret I don't want getting out.

I've gotten pretty good at hiding it.

I fly under the radar. I blend in by not sticking out. I'm the girl at the party nobody remembers was there.

Who am I kidding? I don't go to parties. I wish someone would invite me to one so I could politely decline.

I stay home and read. A *lot.*

Pajamas > Party.

I've actually grown quite accustomed to this simple, small-town life. My days are predictable, each one basically the same—I go to work at my bookstore downtown, making lattes and pushing my latest favorite books on just about everyone who walks through my door. I test my baked goods on the regulars, which is how I knew I had too much lemon in my lemon blueberry muffin recipe. And at night, I come home, make myself a simple dinner, and devour whatever latest romance novel has caught my attention.

Except on certain days when I don't repeat my routine.

Those are the days when I find I can really be myself. Say what I want. How I want. When I want.

I have an alter ego. Like Batman, but not Batman.

Every Thursday, between 7 p.m. and 9 p.m., I enter my secret world. On the days I don't read, you'll find me here, in a little makeshift studio in my basement.

It's not hidden behind a bookcase—*I wish! That would be so cool!*—but it is hidden nonetheless.

Like the Bat Cave, but not the Bat Cave. I'm basically a superhero.

My superpower?

Romance.

More accurately, romance novels.

I know every trope, every second plot point, and every inciting incident.

I can describe the nuances of Francesca's passionate affair with a photographer of bridges, I can argue every position of Laurie, Jo, and Amy's love triangle, and always thought that Noah got the shaft from Allie when he went off to war.

I put the cover of *The Notebook* in my "People Almost Kissing" category, along with *The Last Song* and *Nights in Rodanthe.*

If only my own love life looked like that.

I'd kill to be almost kissed. In the rain. By a guy with a beard.

But it doesn't happen for me.

No beards. No rain. No kisses.

Which is why my romantic advice podcast is a secret. Who wants to take advice from a nearly thirty-year-old whose relationships last about as long as a phone battery?

Nobody. That's who.

Most days I feel like a fraud, sitting behind this microphone in my basement, and signing on as the host of my podcast, *The Hopeful Romantic*. Listeners write in via email, and I choose a few questions to answer each week.

There are days when I ask myself what business I have telling anyone how to make a relationship work, considering my track record. But the truth is, I'm good at solving these quandaries. For some unknown reason, when presented with a question about what is going wrong between two people, I seem to come upon the answers easily.

I credit my deep love of romance novels for this superhuman ability. I've been swiping them off of my mom's shelf since I was nine years old.

Not all of them were exactly age-appropriate, which is another line-item up for discussion with my therapist.

The downside is that those same novels ruined me for the real thing.

Fictional men are always better than the real ones.

Always.

Probably because they're written by women.

For instance, take a young twenty-something who pines after her hot neighbor then finds out he's a long-lost descendant of some Latvian monarchy but he doesn't want to inherit his kingdom and be forced to marry some tart to bridge the divide between two warring nations, but instead forgoes wealth, realm, and rank to knock on his neighbor's door and confess his love?

Only to find out he's *still* rich by default and whisks her away to their new castle?

And call it *The Earl Next Door*?! Take my money.

And maybe it's not realistic, but this kind of *sweep me off my feet* romance is what I'm waiting for. I won't settle. I learned a long time ago that there's no sense in giving my heart away. I'm waiting for the guy who will convince me to take a risk on him, and that guy is only going to convince me with grand romantic gestures.

The podcast started as a fun experiment. I had a knack for solving the problems of my lovelorn friends—and a few strangers who overshared at my bookstore—and I decided to conduct a little experiment.

What if my advice could help?

In the early days, I made up the questions myself. I'd write a question that seemed like something a person in a legitimate relationship might ask, and then, I'd provide the answer.

How was I supposed to know that people would actually start listening to *The Hopeful Romantic*? That this silly little idea I had would turn into something that led to advertising deals and provided me with the money to give my bookshop the facelift it deserved?

I couldn't have predicted the way people would grab onto it. Somehow though, *The Hopeful Romantic* hasn't seeped into my real life. Around the people of Harvest Hollow, it's like the podcast doesn't even exist. And that's just how I want it. Because the second I'm found out is the second I become a laughingstock and the podcast goes up in flames. After all, I haven't exactly had success when it comes to romance.

Sure, there have been boyfriends. They just don't seem to stick around. Or more to the point, I seem to push them away. I know what I'm waiting for, and I won't settle.

I want Mr. Darcy clenching his hand after helping Elizabeth into the carriage. Or Ryan Reynolds bursting into my workplace to profess his love for me after faking our engagement. Or Harry telling Sally that he wants the rest of their lives to start as soon as possible.

Holding out for that is the only way to keep myself from getting hurt. Because being the one who loves first or who loves more is *not* going to happen again. I learned that lesson the hard way.

It's Podcast Thursday, which means it's also Pajama Thursday.

I splurged and decided to try one of those mud masks because I noticed two parallel lines forming in that space at the top of my nose, right between my eyebrows.

So far, all it's doing is making it difficult to make any kind of facial expressions.

Which, in turn, is making it difficult to talk into the mic and not sound like an emotionless robot.

I'm halfway through recording and seriously contemplating pausing to peel my face when I smell something strange.

Smoke.

Harvest Hollow has a no burning ordinance, and since I'm a stickler for the rules, I'm instantly on alert. Which of my neighbors is breaking the rules again? Can't we have one nice day where someone isn't burning leaves? Last weekend, my neighbor was burning a pile of treated wood, releasing chemicals into the air for all of us to breathe.

The distraction is enough to make me forget what I'm talking about. I make a note of the time, which I'll send to my editor (a guy I found online named Ripper who I've never met but I've concocted a whole romantic backstory for him anyway). Usually, I turn in a pretty clean recording, but between the face mask and the smoke, poor Ripper is going to earn his money on this episode.

Thankfully, it will help with the impending experimental surgery for his estranged son he just recently reunited with.

Or so I've told myself.

I clear my throat and refocus on the question I was answering. What was I saying?

Right. Girl loves guy, guy *wants* to love girl, but guy seems unable to take a leap without his mom interfering. . .it's a situation straight out of (*un*)*Attached*, and in that novel, the guy attached at the hip to his mother was *not* the hero.

"I have to say, *Fed Up in the 312,* that you're right to be concerned. A man who asks his mom to do his laundry at the age of thirty-two is probably not in any hurry to become a self-sufficient member of society. Maybe this guy is showing you what you do and don't want in a relationship—"

I cough, then write down the time.

"Maybe this guy is the precursor to the real thing. The one who—"

Another cough. I pause the recording.

Is it hazy in here?

I walk over to the mini fridge in the studio and pull out a bottle of water, but as I do, I notice my eyes are starting to burn.

And the smell is thicker than it was even a few minutes ago.

But then it hits me.

There are no windows in my basement. And it's the start of autumn—too early for leaf burning.

I open the studio door and pull in a thick, gray plume of choking smoke. It fills the room and my lungs, immediately blacking out my sight and cutting off my oxygen.

My house is on fire.

My eyes go wide, and I slam the door as I struggle to breathe. I fall to the floor, gasping for air, feeling underwater but not underwater. I'm coughing, trying to remember what you're supposed to do if there's a fire in your house.

Do I run up the stairs? Is there another exit? Should I *stop, drop, and roll?*

No. My house, not me, is on fire.

What do I do?

What if I can't get out?

I push my panic down, or at least try to.

"Think, Emmy, think!" I croak as I search the space for anything helpful.

Armchair in the corner. Throw pillows. Bookshelves lining the walls. My computer. Desk. Microphone. Recording equipment. None of these things are going to help.

Now that I'm out from under my headphones, I can hear the *crack-CRACK-ssss* of fire eating away the wood walls of my home.

I need to get out of here.

I never bring my phone in the studio when I'm recording in order to prevent unnecessary distractions. The smoke, hanging in the room like a fabric fog, doesn't care.

I army crawl to the center of the room, panic wrestling out of the box I've put it in.

"Stay calm, Emmy," I say out loud. "You're smart. You can figure out what to do."

I crawl over to my laptop and flip it open. I'll send a message out on social media or try to contact the Harvest Hollow Fire Department through the internet.

I quickly switch from *The Hopeful Romantic* Facebook page over to my personal account, and that's when I hear banging.

It sounds like things are being flung around above me, stomping, sliding, footsteps.

"*Is anyone down here?*"

It's a man's voice.

I absently think that it's probably my wood-burning neighbor, Pat Grady. Under normal circumstances, I wouldn't want Pat inside my house. The man sits on his porch, shirtless, drinking beer all day and hollering at everyone who walks by. But today? Today, I couldn't be happier to have my nosy, half-nude neighbor here.

I try to answer, but I cough instead. I roll over to the door, keeping low, and kick the door with my foot. I gasp, "I'm in here!" I paw my way up to the handle but stop short of pulling it open again. I touch it. It's not burning up, but if I open it, will I get sucked out into the abyss? In my imagination, fires have arms, and they're just waiting to choke the life out of me.

"Stand back, ma'am!"

Okay, so not Pat. Pat calls me "honey" or "sweetheart." Never "ma'am."

I scoot back from the door and seconds later, there's a loud bang on the opposite side. My eyes are watering fiercely now, and I hold my arm up and cough into the crook of my elbow.

The door cracks open, breaking the frame, and there's a man, dressed in a firefighter's uniform, wearing a helmet. I can't see his face behind the mask, but I can see the bright orange glow of the flames behind him.

And all at once, a flicker of one of my favorite novels, *Paradise Bound*, races through my mind. A woman in distress, a horrible fire, and a rugged man, all set against the backdrop of the island of Bali.

Nothing like this ever happens in Harvest Hollow.

And especially not to me.

I'm feeling light-headed. Is it the smoke? Is it the way he's reaching out to me?

Under that mask, I bet he looks nothing like my neighbor, Pat.

I *hope* he looks nothing like my neighbor, Pat.

"You need to come with me," the firefighter shouts. "*Now!*"

To the ends of the earth, I think, because I'm convinced that this man is not only my savior, he's my soulmate. Here to carry me to safety.

I blink away the fume-induced stupor and focus on a horrifying thought.

Everything in this room is going to get destroyed.

I whip my head around and look at my computer. My speakers. My microphone. The external hard drive attached to my computer. I saved *forever* to buy this equipment.

And that drive has everything on it. *Everything*.

In a split second, I make the decision to forget everything else. Everything else can be replaced, no matter how expensive, but I can't leave the equipment or lose the hundreds of hours of recordings on that drive.

I scramble backward on all fours away from the firefighter, turn over, and push myself to my feet. I grab the tote bag I use for library books and start shoving things inside.

"Ma'am, we need to go."

"I just have to try and save a few things," I cough, tears stinging my eyes. If I leave, everything will go up in flames.

If I don't, then *I* will go up in flames.

"We don't have time!" he says, his tone clipped. "You have to come, now!"

"I'm coming, just let me—"

"Emmy! I have to get you out!"

Before I can pick up my microphone, the firefighter grabs ahold of me, picks me up in his arms, and makes his way through the door and up the stairs.

Wait.

He knows my name?

I try to search for a name tag, or his eyes through the plexiglass shield for anything familiar, but the smoke is getting thicker as we trudge up the stairs.

"Hold on to me, almost there," he says, pulling me closer.

I sink into the hard fabric of his coat, shutting my eyes. I can feel his form even through the girth of the thick material, and it's flexed and firm from carrying me.

I've never been carried by another human before. At least not as an adult. In other circumstances, I might like it. Being saved has its perks.

I wrap my arms up around his neck and picture myself posing for the cover of *In Heat of the Fire*, by that hack Shelly DeWinter.

Not a book I'd recommend, by the way. Page 147 is the only good part, and it's not even that clever.

We reach the top of the stairs, and I expect him to put me down, but I'm thankful that he doesn't. I cough again, into his chest, and he reaches up and pulls me closer.

"Almost out," he says.

"Fire's spread to the main floor!" Another firefighter rushes through my house, axe in hand

"Is anyone else here?" my firefighter asks me. "Any pets?"

I shake my head.

"Good," he says.

Through the haze I glimpse unwanted and invasive flames licking the walls of my stairway, and I'm about to ask him to save my favorite coral dress with the white Peter Pan collar when the whole scene fades to black.

When I come to, I'm outside, and I hear the faint sound of sirens in the distance. I'm lying on a stretcher with a plastic mask over my face, and as I start to sit up, a young female paramedic says, "Just stay still, Miss Smart. Breathe."

I try to and end up coughing thick mucus from the liters of smoke I must've inhaled.

Gross.

I frown and fuss the mask off my face. The paramedic tries

to put it back on, but I hold up my hands and say, "I'm fine, I just need a minute." I swallow as I peer around my yard. I spot my neighbor Pat, standing on my lawn, shirtless, with his wife Peggy at his side. Peggy is the town gossip, and she's got her phone pressed to her ear, and I wonder out loud, "How long I was out?"

"Not too long," the paramedic tells me. "But you're lucky that we got you out of there so quickly. It could've been a lot worse."

My vision teeters and my head lobs over to one side as another paramedic calls out, "Need to check you out."

My eyes follow his gaze to the firefighter, still wearing his mask, but it's flipped up, tilted back.

His face.

I can't focus through my watery eyes and the flashing red and blue of the emergency vehicles. He gives the paramedic a nod, then walks straight over to where I'm lying.

My romance-fueled mind is filling in every blank. It's like he's walking in slow motion. He's about to reveal himself to me. My real-life hero. And I'm about to rethink my position on fictional men being better than real ones.

He starts to pull his helmet all the way off. My heart is pounding in my chest, a literal drum.

This is the canon event. The hinge on which the story swings open.

This is the moment the reader sits forward to focus on the words.

And it's happening to me.

He walks up to me, slowly coming into focus.

There, standing on my front lawn, is Owen Larrabee.

I blink.

The man who saved my life is a grown-up version of the boy who broke my heart.

Chapter Two

Emmy

It's a hallucination. I'm hallucinating. The flames from my house leapt over my back fence and caught the neighbor's son's secret weed stash on fire, and this is the result.

"Owen?"

Is my mind conjuring him? Some smoke-induced delusion?

A cruel reminder of my foolish youth, more like.

"Hey, Em. You okay?" He's got his helmet tucked under his arm, and he's looking at me so intently, I might as well be a wet blob of clay on a potter's wheel, his hands shaping me, molding me, caressing. . .

That's enough, Emaline!

"Sir, I really need to check you out." The paramedic at Owen's side is dwarfed by Owen's flickering shadow.

"I'm fine," Owen says, waving the man off like a gnat that won't go away. He looks at the female paramedic. "Is she okay?"

He's asking about me? Why does he look so concerned? Did they forget to tell me that I'm dying or something?

"She'll be fine," my paramedic says. "But will you let Nate check you out? Please?"

He huffs. "Fine."

My mind is a jumble of questions. When did he get back to Harvest Hollow? Why didn't his sister tell me he was back? When did he grow facial hair? Does he workout every day or just most days? Does he look at everyone that intensely?

He better not be some Latvian earl, I swear.

Does he remember the day I was the one saving him?

I guess we're even now. . .

Hardly. My "saving him" turned into sheer and utter humiliation. My face flushes at the memory, and I look away.

I wish I had a Tardis or a DeLorean or a hot tub that could transport me away from this place.

Time travel is not a huge trope in romance, but I see the benefits.

"Larrabee—" the male paramedic—Nate—ushers him over to the back of the ambulance, where he sits, looking every bit the rebel he always was.

"You know him?" My paramedic asks.

"Yes. I mean. . .Kind of." I drop my head back onto the small pillow. "No, not anymore."

It hurts a little to say that. Still.

There was a time when I could've answered that question quite differently.

Per usual, though, the whole relationship was decidedly one-sided.

My friendship with Owen was never for public consumption. That probably should've been my first clue.

"He just started a few days ago," she says. "Guess saving your life is a good way to make a first impression."

Through leaking eyes, I watch as the other firefighters spray water into the second floor of my little house—and I experience an emotion I can't quite describe. It's equal parts sadness, relief, and violation.

My house.

My things.

My safe haven. The keeper of my secrets. Are they going to be able to salvage it?

I know people will probably say, "*At least you're okay—all of those things can be replaced.*" But when you're experiencing it, the weight of the inconvenience of replacing those things? The discovering of what was actually lost? The pang of pictures and keepsakes and memories reduced to ash?

Yeah, glad to be alive, but helplessly and hopelessly angry at everything else.

The heaviness of what's happening begins to settle in, and I wrack my brain trying to figure out how this happened. Did I leave my curling iron on? No. I haven't curled my hair in weeks. Did I forget to blow out a candle?

"How did this happen?" I say out loud, but the paramedic isn't standing next to me anymore. I pull myself upright on the stretcher and let my legs hang off over the side. And I watch black smoke as it billows out of a second-story window.

I start to think of everything inside. Things I can't replace. Photos. Jewelry. The little box of mementos I keep for sentimental reasons.

My books.

Oh my gosh, my BOOKS.

My entire classic romance collection. Gone.

Why do the things that are most precious have to be the most flammable?

My shoulders shake, and I start to cry. It stuffs up my nose, and since I inhaled a house full of smoke, it just makes everything worse.

I'm so dazed, I don't hear anyone come up beside me until the blanket is slipped around my shoulders. I glance over and see Owen, concern etched on his forehead.

I wipe at the tears streaming down my cheek and try to ignore the fact that in the eight years he's been gone from Harvest Hollow, he's grown up and gotten even more good-looking.

I didn't even think that was possible.

I mentally scold myself for romanticizing when my emotions are so frayed. Especially when the person I'm romanticizing is Owen.

Didn't I learn my lesson the first time?

"Hey. Look at me."

I turn, gazing into a face I had memorized in my mind so many years ago.

"I know. It's hard to watch. It feels invasive and overwhelming, and you feel helpless to stop it."

Wow. That's *exactly* how I feel. The tears don't stop, and my jaw trembles.

"They've almost got it out," he says. His voice is deep and husky. And a little brusque, reminding me again that we are no longer friends.

We're no longer anything.

I feel embarrassed all of a sudden. Like I'm sixteen all over again.

I just want him to hold me.

I wonder if he still feels misunderstood. I wonder if he still writes in that tattered journal. I wonder if he remembers. . .

"Mack didn't tell me you were back," I say, staring straight ahead.

"She's out of town," he says. "She doesn't even know yet."

I nod. My best friend, Owen's sister, is a flight attendant. She gets back tomorrow from her latest trip. I don't even remember where she is. But I do know she's had a hard time staying in touch with Owen since he left Harvest Hollow. He's not the most communicative person in the world. And that is an understatement.

I thought I was over having to hide my complicated feelings for her brother from her.

Doesn't matter. No complicated feelings here.

Only embarrassment. I need him to go away.

But he doesn't go away. He moves around in front of me. "This is a lot. But you're going to be okay." He gently hands the mask back to me, indicating for me to put it up over my nose. "Just breathe."

My pulse quickens under the weight of his gaze. Suddenly, I'm Elizabeth Bennett, feeling the passionate stare of Mr. Darcy.

I am not the kind of girl who is accustomed to attention from the opposite sex. And I'm okay with that. I've accepted it.

Although, I wouldn't complain if some guy swept me off my feet and professed his undying love for me in a gazebo in the rain.

A part of me does know that getting caught in the rain, even with Mr. Darcy, would not feel very romantic. I'd be sopping wet with mascara streaking down my face like a villain in a Tim Burton movie.

But in the novels? Totally swoony.

Doesn't matter. I don't need swoony romance novel rain. I've got my bookshop. I've got my podcast. That's enough.

The thought rolls another wave of emotion over me, and I sink my head down and cry.

Owen reaches over and puts a hand on my shoulder. A kind gesture, probably. He probably does the same for all the women he pulls out of burning buildings.

I tell myself not to confuse his attention with anything

other than what it is— professional duty. He has a job to do, and he's seeing it through.

And once he knows I'm not dying, he can take off—and out of my life—just like he did all those years ago.

Without a word.

The small crowd of people off to the side has grown, and I'm thankful to learn I'm not the only person who spends my evenings in my pajamas. One slipper hangs off my foot, and I wonder where the other one is, and if I'll have any real clothes to wear once all of this is over.

Another firefighter walks by.

"Do you know how it started?" I ask, doing my best to push aside my awkward feelings for Owen.

"Faulty wiring is the working theory." The other firefighter, who I now recognize as Owen's friend, Jace Janssen, stops beside Owen and nods at me. "I'm glad you're okay, Miss Smart." I realize that I know him. Owen's friend Jace. They grew up together, but while Owen liked to color outside the lines, Jace tended to walk a straighter, narrower path.

It would've made more sense for me to have a ridiculous crush on him, but alas, the heart wants what the heart wants. . .and my young heart really, really wanted Owen.

"Yeah," I say, eyes flicking to Owen's, then back to Jace. "Wish the same could be said for my house."

"Things can be replaced," Jace says. "People can't."

Called it.

They get pulled back into the fray, and I draw in another shaky breath.

"Emmy!" My mother's voice pulls my attention. "Emaline!" She sounds hysterical. Seconds later, I see her come through the small crowd, my dad trailing behind, clearly having been awakened from a deep sleep and dragged over here.

Odds are good that he fell asleep in his recliner watching

old reruns of *Walker, Texas Ranger*. Dad is in a Chuck Norris phase. Again.

My mom rushes over to me and takes my sweaty and sooty face in her hands. "We rushed straight over as soon as we got Peggy's call."

Peggy. Of course.

"Oh my goodness, are you okay? Are you hurt? Where does it hurt? And what's all over your face?" She pats my shoulders, as if searching for deficiencies, then rubs at the mud mask I completely forgot I was wearing. Because that's just my luck.

"I'm fine," I say, coughing.

But I'm not fine. I'm not sure how to process what's happening all around me. Or the fact that Owen Larrabee is back in town.

Or the fact that he is the one who saved my life.

When this happens in romance novels, like *Yours Sincerely*, the person who got saved now owes the other person a life debt.

But I'm not about to write fake love letters to a celebrity in hopes of him coming to a small-town 4th of July celebration—which was the somewhat far-fetched plot of *that* one.

"Peggy said they had to carry you out," Mom says. "Were you unconscious?"

"No," I say. "Not when he carried me out. I think I was taking too long. All I could save was my laptop and. . ." *And my recording equipment and external hard drive.*

I don't say it. Not even my parents know I have a podcast.

My dad comes over to my other side. "Who do we have to thank for saving you?"

I scan the scene in front of me. Paramedics stand off to the side. Firefighters scurry around my yard, bringing things out—which floods me with gratitude and hope. They're grabbing and saving what they can.

Neighbors take photos and videos and make phone calls.

By morning, everyone in Harvest Hollow is going to know that the owner of the Book Smart Bookshop downtown lost her house.

"Emmy?" Mom asks. "We want to find the firefighter who pulled you out and thank him."

"It was Owen," I say absently.

"Mackenzie's brother Owen?" Mom asks. "I thought he lived down south."

"He's back, apparently," I say.

"Well, we need to find him." Mom turns, scanning the crowd. "That boy saved my daughter. As far as I'm concerned, he is a bonafide hero."

There's a flash of a camera, and I see Jerry from the *Harvest Times* racing around in the crowd. He rushes over to me, out of breath as Mom takes off into the crowd, presumably to search for Owen.

I wish I could rush off and search for Owen and have him pick me up in his strong arms again.

Maybe without the burning destruction all around us this time.

I shake my head. History is repeating itself, all over again.

Gazing at and dreaming about him became something of a pastime in high school. And with this one, brief encounter (albeit an emotionally charged one), I'm right back there, pining away like an orthodontic schoolgirl.

If Owen was out of my league back then, he's in a whole other solar system now.

"That's cool with you, right, Emmy?"

Jerry's been talking to me this entire time, and I have no idea what he said. He looks at me, expectant, eyes wide and excited. He lifts his camera and takes a photo of the paramedics standing near the open back doors of the ambulance.

"Can't believe I was first on the scene," he says. "Saw them carry you out and everything." He shakes his head. "Nothing exciting ever happens here."

"Happy to change that for you," I groan.

"Oh, I didn't mean—" he takes a step away.

I lift a hand as if to communicate that it's fine. After all, I was thinking the same thing only a few minutes ago.

Mom rushes back over to me. "I can't find him, but I will. I have to figure out a way to thank him." She hugs me. "I'm just so, so grateful you're okay."

I tear up again.

"Me too, Mom."

She gives one more squeeze and leans back. "I'm going to bake him my pumpkin bars. Everyone loves those. It's the least I can do."

I laugh and then cough. My mom thinks the best way to someone's heart is through their stomach.

She's not wrong about the pumpkin bars, though.

"You're going to come home with us, Emmy," Mom says. "Captain Donaho said we can take you since the paramedics have cleared you and you don't need to go to the hospital. Sounds like they got you out before it got too bad."

She slips her arm around mine. "Besides, I don't think it's good for you to sit here and watch."

I scoot off the stretcher, still wrapped in the blanket and look down at my feet. "I only have one slipper."

"I'm sure I have some you can borrow," Mom says. "It's going to be okay. You're safe, and that's all that matters."

She's right. I could've died in that fire. And if it wasn't for Owen, I might've. I'd been so paralyzed when I realized what was happening that if he hadn't barged in when he did, the outcome of this whole night would've looked very different.

Owen Larrabee saved me.

Now all I have to do is not fall in love with him. Again.

Chapter Three

Owen

I have a hard time sleeping when I get back to the firehouse.

Not that I'm a great sleeper to begin with.

Lots on my mind.

I lay in the bunk and stare at the ceiling.

I didn't realize until tonight that, when I moved back home, I would know the people in the houses and businesses we were called to.

When I close my eyes to try to sleep, I replay the whole night in my head. I can still picture the flames coming out of the small craftsman as we pulled up.

Someone said, "That's Emmy's house."

Something inside me snapped.

"Emmy Smart?" I asked.

Jace nodded. "Book shop owner. She was a couple of years behind us in school."

"Yeah," I spotted the smoke coming from the second story. "I remember her."

Jace jumped out of the truck. "Really? Surprising. She was kind of a wallflower."

Not around me she wasn't.

Emmy Smart.

Not the kind of girl who should get under my skin, but for some reason, I can't stop thinking about her house and. . .her.

What if I hadn't gotten there in time?

What if we didn't find her or the fire blocked our way to her?

What if. . .?

I turn over and look at the clock. 4:43 a.m.

The next thing I know, it's light outside and someone is yelling at me.

I know that voice.

"Owen Larrabee! What the heck?"

I don't have to crack my eyes open to know it's my sister. I roll over and mumble, "Go away, Mack," even though I know she won't listen.

Younger sisters and all that.

True to form, she sits on the end of my bed, thrusting a newspaper in front of my face. "I have a major bone to pick with you." She shakes the paper. "You hardly ever respond when I call you. You didn't even tell me you were back home, and you *definitely* didn't tell me you saved my best friend's life last night!"

"Sorry," I said. "I was a little busy." I roll over on my back and rub my temples. When I open my eyes, I find her studying the newspaper.

"They're calling you a hero," she says.

I scoff. Hero. Yeah, right.

"I was just doing my job," I say, even though that's not exactly true. I wasn't even supposed to be in the house. I was assigned to help outside. I made Jace trade with me.

"They did a whole feature on you two," Mack says. "Front page and middle spread. You know the entire town is going to be freaking out over this."

Great.

"It's not a big deal," I say, not looking at the newspaper.

"I'm guessing Emmy disagrees."

I pause. She's right. Emmy would disagree.

But I got to her. She's okay.

Maybe showing up last night will make up for the way I left eight years ago.

I shake the thought away. "Have you talked to her?" Part of what kept me awake last night was wondering how she's doing. I'm relieved she wasn't hurt, but the mental and emotional toll of a house fire is not something to gloss over. And she was pretty shaken up.

"I came here first thing when I got back into town," Mack says. "I tried calling her, but there was no answer. I'm going over to the bookstore to make sure she's okay."

I nod. "Will you let me know?"

"You could ask her yourself, you know." Mack squints over at me.

"Right," I mutter.

She makes a face at me. I'm used to her faces, because even though I haven't seen them close-up in months, they're still the same faces she used to make at me when I was here.

When I was home.

"I'm still on duty," I say half-heartedly.

Emmy doesn't need me poking around her life any more than I need her poking around mine. Eight summers isn't long enough to forget everything that happened.

Thinking about it fans that long, deep-seated anger within me. Not at her, but at myself.

Nothing was ever resolved between us.

Best to keep my distance.

Mack is still standing there, making the same face. Like she's pitying me and judging me at the same time.

My sister always seemed worried I was going to try to date Emmy, or more likely, she worried I'd try to hook up with her. She made it clear what she thought of the idea—forbade it really—and said, in not so many words, that someone like her and someone like me just don't mix.

It was fine because I never looked at Emmy that way. And because I agree.

Emmy and I weren't a good fit. She was a rule-follower, and I was. . .well, not. Emmy might've been a good influence on me, but the same can't be said for me. At least not back then.

Besides, it was never like that with me and her.

"You okay?" Mack folds the paper and tucks it in her bag. "You look a little. . .moody."

I tilt my head at her.

"Even for you, I mean," she teases. She's just about the only one I let do that.

I sit up and push my hand through my hair. "Didn't really sleep."

She nods. "Do you want to talk about it?"

But she doesn't let me answer.

"That's funny. *Owen* talking. What a strange concept." She gives me a shove.

I'm getting better. At least, I think I'm getting better.

I try to prove that with, "I had a whole conversation with the lady who cut my hair. I even told her what I do for a living."

She feigns shock. "No *way*! That's a huge step! I know that small talk makes your skin crawl."

"She then told me a whole story about how her ex-husband didn't pitch in to get her kid Taylor Swift concert tickets for her birthday, so she let the air out his tires."

"Ew."

"Yeah. I almost walked out with half my hair cut."

"Would've been an improvement."

I look at her, and she's sitting there, looking like she thinks she's so clever. I soften and roll my eyes.

I love and tolerate Mack.

Mostly love.

"What are you doing back?"

I shrug. "Job opened up. Thought it might be good to be closer to home."

I don't tell her any more than that, but judging by the squinty eyes sizing me up, she knows there's more to the story.

"You think I'm not telling the whole truth."

"I *know* you're not telling the whole truth."

I press my lips together.

"You're not going to let it drop till you figure it out, are you?"

"Nope. That's what I do." She stares me down in an attempt to get me to say more.

I sit, comfortable that I'll win this little standoff.

Which I do when, after a moment, she stands. "Same old Owen," she says. "You never tell me anything."

There's a pause, and I feel the weight of the eight years of geographical distance between us. Mack never understood why I moved out of North Carolina in the first place, and she didn't have any problem telling me exactly what she thought when I left.

She seemed to think people would move past my public embarrassment, but it was more than just that that drove me away.

I needed a fresh start, away from people who'd made up their minds about me, or thought they knew me by looking at me, or judged me for my past mistakes—and there were many.

"Where are you living?" she asks.

"I'm at Mom and Dad's right now," I say.

Her eyebrows raise. "Really?"

I shrug. "It's temporary."

"They're going to drive you nuts, you know."

I offer an affirmative grunt.

"All right, Grumbles," she says, unearthing that old chestnut of a nickname that I hated as a kid. "I'm exhausted, and I need a shower. We'll catch up later." She stands and starts toward the door but stops and faces me. "Thanks for saving my best friend."

I lift my hand in a thumbs-up, she shakes her head with an eye roll, and then she's gone.

"Who was *that*?" Levi Lawrence is standing in my doorway, eyes full of Mackenzie and setting off that protective older brother thing I always have when it comes to my sister's dating life. It's stupid. I've been away too long, and Mack is an adult who can more than take care of herself. But I just met Levi yesterday, and I don't like the way he's looking at her.

"Don't worry about it," I say.

Levi puts his hands up in mock surrender. "Just going to compliment you, buddy. Every girl in town is going to want your number after last night."

"That was my sister," I say. "And I'm not looking for any numbers."

"Your sister?" Levi's eyes go wide. "Ooh, yeah, I get it. 'Off-limits,'" he chuckles. Then, after a pause, "Is she single?"

I'm about to grab the closest thing within reach and chuck it at him when I realize I don't actually know.

I've been away too long.

"Not sure." I straighten the covers and start to make the bed.

"Can you find out?" Levi asks.

I tuck the cover under the pillow. "I'm not setting you up with my sister," I say, opening the small closet on the opposite side of the room.

"Guess I'll have to find out for myself." Levi grins, then takes a step into the hallway. "Or I might take a run at your girl from last night. She had that sexy librarian thing going on."

A wave of protectiveness rises inside me. I glare at him. "Don't."

He lifts his hands. "Whoa. Got it. Message received."

Why the heck did I do that?

I try to justify it. "She's just been through a major trauma, Lawrence," I say. "The last thing she needs is some guy hitting on her."

"Look man, if you want to save her for yourself, all you have to do is say so."

I don't respond. This guy needs to take a walk.

Maybe I need to take a walk.

He starts to leave but stops. "Oh, the captain wants to see you."

I get a weird sense of déjà vu.

I frown over at him. "Why?"

Levi shrugs. "Probably wants to talk to you about you being a hero and whatever. But I wouldn't keep him waiting."

I grunt a response.

After brushing my teeth and getting dressed, I head down to the opposite end of the building where the captain's office sits. He's on the phone, and when he sees me through the glass of the door, he motions for me to come in.

I step inside and stand next to the chair opposite his desk, feeling awkward for eavesdropping on his conversation right in front of him.

"We are very proud, sir, yes." A pause. "Of course, we'd be

honored." He pauses, looks at me and smiles. "I'll let him know. Thank you, sir."

He hangs up. "First week on the job, and you already made front page news. Almost makes me want to ignore the fact that you're not clean shaven." He quirks a brow. "Almost."

I rub a hand over my chin. I know the rules. My way of bucking them, I guess. I still don't like to be told what to do.

I'll shave it. Then I'll let it grow till he says something else.

He nods at the chair next to me. "Have a seat."

I sit, but everything about this is already making me uncomfortable.

"That was the chief," he says. "He's out of town, but he wanted me to pass along his thanks and tell you we're all impressed with what you did out there last night."

"I was just doing my job, sir."

He leans back in his chair. "The whole town's talking. Center page spread of the scene in the paper. And they want to come down and do a feature on their friendly neighborhood firehouse."

"They said that?" I wince.

Captain Donoho's expression matches mine. "Must feel good to be a hero."

I look away and give a nonverbal reply.

"You might not think it," he leans back, "but to this town, you're a hero. The reporter wants to do a follow-up with you and the girl you saved—Miss—" he picks up the newspaper to search for her name.

"Smart," I say. "Emmy Smart."

His eyes flick to mine. "Miss Smart, yeah. You know her?"

"She's my sister's best friend," I say.

"That's why you barreled your way in there the way you did?" He pauses. "Or did that have something to do with what happened in Macon?"

I flinch and grit my teeth.

"Just wanted to help," I say curtly, hoping my tone signifies that this isn't a subject I want to discuss.

"Good. Then you can head down to her bookstore and check in on her," the captain says. "Take her by her house to get any important documents, see what can be salvaged, that sort of thing."

"Me?"

"You know her," he says. "Makes the most sense."

Great.

"All due respect, sir, but I think maybe someone else would be better suited to do the follow up with Miss Smart."

He frowns at me. "I disagree. If she knows you, she'll be comfortable with you—you know what kind of trauma a fire brings. She might need a comforting face."

I stare.

"Well, a face, anyways," he adds.

I do my best to conceal my feelings about this. I don't want to "check in" on Emmy, and I don't want to be the guy to take her over to assess the damage at her house. I want to keep my distance. She's like a walking reminder of the day my life fell apart.

"You've still got a few hours left on your shift," he says, defaulting to captain mode. "And I'm not asking. Expect a call or two about this whole thing in the next few days. It's not every day one of our men is photographed carrying a woman out of her burning house."

I frown. "What are you talking about?"

He pushes the newspaper toward me, and there, on the front page, is a photo of just what the captain described. Me, carrying Emmy out of her house. Her arms are wrapped up around my neck, and at the sight of it, something inside me rises. She looks so small and vulnerable.

I want to hold her and keep her safe. From everything.

"How'd they get this?" I ask, glancing up. "I don't even remember a photographer being there."

He shrugs. "Beats me. The truck was outside for a few minutes before you came out. Good chance that Jerry kid has a police scanner and showed up around the same time."

"Those things should be outlawed," I mutter.

"You know what this means, right?" he asks. "Lots of attention coming your way. And I know we haven't known each other long, but I can already tell attention isn't your thing."

He's right. It's not my thing.

"I'm no. . .spokesperson. Or whatever. You don't want me speaking in public for this station," I say.

The only reason I'm here at all is because my dad called in a favor.

Is he forgetting that?

"Oh, I don't? You trying to tell me what's best for my station? When you're like three days on the job here?" The captain bristles.

I back down. I need to keep my issues with authority in check. The captain is a good guy, and I'm not here to make waves.

He slides the paper back and taps the picture. "You proved yourself out there last night. Nobody can argue you don't know what you're doing after saving that girl."

"This town has. . .uh. . .never been very high on me, Captain," I tell him, and it's hard to get the words out without sounding angry.

His face twitches. "I know."

He does?

"And you know what they say about opinions," he adds. "Everybody's got 'em and they all stink." He looks like he has more to say but chooses not to. Instead, he tells me to go check on Emmy, then go home, and get some well-deserved rest.

I'll do as I'm told, but I won't like it.

I made up my mind when I decided to move back here that I'd keep my distance from Emmy. Let her be what she was always meant to be—my little sister's best friend.

As I stand, I glance down once more at the picture.

Looks like she's meant to be something else entirely.

Chapter Four

Emmy

I am not in love with Owen.

Let me repeat that in hopes my heart hears me.

I am not in love with Owen.

I had a momentary lapse in the wake of the fire, where I fantasized (for way too long) about his strong arms whisking me out of the burning house.

But this morning, I woke up with a clear head and clear memories of the last time I saw him.

Owen and I are not friends.

We *used* to be friends. Never more than that.

Despite my very deep, very real, very ridiculous feelings for him back then.

Now, however, we are not friends. We're just acquaintances. Who got our picture taken.

We're picture pals. At best.

And that's exactly how it should be.

Maybe Owen *might* be secretly kind and very misunderstood—but he still left town without a word, even after I—

"You're alive!"

Mack bursts through the door of Book Smart, her sleek leather bag over her shoulder, looking like the world traveler she is.

Thank God she interrupted my train of thought.

Mack is always jetting off on some adventure or another, though she swears her job is far less glamorous than it seems.

"I'm a waitress, Emmy," she told me once. "I just happen to be waiting on cranky people at thirty-five thousand feet."

The photos of her—all with the same pose— from various and exotic places in the world tell a different story, especially to me.

I've never even been out of the country, not in real life anyway. I've spent a lot of time in rural 19th century England, among other countries of the fictional variety.

And although I'd rock a bell-shaped, crinoline petticoat, somehow, I don't think that counts.

I give her some Twain. "Reports of my death have been greatly exaggerated." I'm standing behind the counter at my little shop, preparing for the morning rush.

"But. . .your house. What are you even doing here? You're already back at work?" Mack drops her bag onto the counter and throws her arms around me. She smells like vanilla and feels like home. She and I have been best friends since we were kids, and with two teeny tiny exceptions, I've never kept anything from her.

Mack knows almost everything there is to know about me.

Almost.

She doesn't know about *The Hopeful Romantic.*

And she doesn't know about my crush on her brother.

Former, I tell my brain. *In the past.*

"I think you need to give yourself the week off," Mack says.

I shake my head. "I can't sit around my parents' house. I need to stay busy. My mother made me breakfast this morning like I was just released from the Gulag. I don't want to be the center of anyone's attention."

Although, it occurs to me at that moment that I wouldn't mind having Owen's undivided attention. At least for a little while.

Nope. He is a leaver. A walker out-er. Who cares if he saved my life? I'm still supposed to be annoyed with him.

Saving my life should get him a pass, though, shouldn't it?

"What happened?" Mack slides up onto the barstool at the coffee counter and stares at me. I start making her a caramel latte.

"One of the firefighters said maybe faulty wiring?" I say, adding almond milk to the metal mixing cup. "I can't imagine what else it would be, though. There will be a report."

"If anyone would've told me ten years ago that my *brother* would be the guy pulling people from burning buildings, I would've laughed in their face."

I frown. "Why?"

She half-shrugs. "Because it's Owen! You do remember what he's like, right?"

I suddenly feel protective of Owen.

I fill the cup with a shot of espresso, trying not to reminisce. Mack holds up two fingers, so I add another shot. "I do. He was. . .complicated, that's for sure, but I always thought people misjudged him." I froth the almond milk, pour in the espresso, and slide the drink across the counter, feeling odd.

I want to defend him. *Why?*

I know it bothered him how people saw him all those years ago. A part of me wants to believe he's grown into the version of Owen I thought I knew back then.

But no. He's the guy who left.

And this isn't *Anita Brown and the Second Chance*

Romance, by Kate Bishop (that title is a little too on the nose, if you ask me), and I'm not a widower falling for a carpenter.

Guys in books who restore houses is *such* a cliché.

And yet. . .I'm a sucker for it every time.

I'm walking a very dangerous line here, and I know it. One misstep, and I'll be right back where I was all those years ago—completely smitten with a guy who would never, ever feel the same way about me.

It was a silly, schoolgirl crush, and one I needed to pack into a safe deposit box and throw away the key.

"In case you've forgotten, my brother doesn't exactly walk the straight and narrow. I don't think that's changed."

"What makes you say that?" *Did that sound nonchalant enough?*

"He's thirty-two, hasn't had a single meaningful relationship since he left Harvest Hollow, and now he's back here, living with our parents. Owen's always been kind of a disaster, you know that. I think it's gotten worse since, well, since Lindsay." She takes a drink. "Oh, wow, this is good." She takes another sip, closing her eyes to show her appreciation for the jolt of caffeine. "Also, there has to be a reason he's back here. No way a job just 'opened up.' I'm going to find out the truth."

My frown deepens.

She's not describing the Owen I know. I mean, knew.

I *knew* him. I remind myself again that I don't know him anymore.

Though, she's his sister. She knows him way better than I do, even if they've become "holiday siblings"—the kind who only see each other on holidays. She's probably right. He's probably not even the kind of guy who has a dog or a plant or anything that requires commitment.

It doesn't matter. I have no intention of finding out.

By the grace of the Lord Almighty Himself, Mack changes

the subject. But in a rare twist of fate, she moves on to something I want to discuss even less than I want to discuss her brother.

She pulls a newspaper out of her bag and lays it on the counter. "You saw this, right?"

I groan. "Yes. How embarrassing. I'm wearing one bunny slipper."

"Right, because that's what people are paying attention to when they see this huge spread with photos of my brother pulling you from your burning house. Jerry will probably win an award for this shot." She points at the one on the front page.

I can admit it—it's an incredible photo. Like something you'd see on the cover of *Time*. Not something we typically see on the front page of the *Harvest Times*.

"I think you might be wrong about your brother, Mack," I say.

She rolls her eyes.

"I'm serious. I think he's really good at his job." I wipe the counter down. "I mean, he was last night."

I just said he was "good at his job last night," and I'm going to do my best not to fantasize about what else that could mean.

"Not that I want to get in the habit of defending him, but the guy did save my life."

Whew. Nice save.

"I get it," she says. "You feel indebted to him. But that doesn't change the fact that he completely abandoned me."

"You were twenty-two."

"So?"

"All he did was move out of town," I say.

"Why are you defending him?" she asks, then squints at me, a suspicious look on her face.

I look as innocent as I can.

"Oh. Oh *no*." She's staring at me *way* too intently.

I wipe the same spot on the counter for the third time and shrug. No big deal, I'm not hiding anything, and spit out a "What?"

Her jaw drops. "You don't. . ." She leans in. "*Emmy.* Tell me you don't have some kind of, what do you call it, Munchausen's or Stockholm syndrome or something just because he saved your life!"

I stop wiping the counter.

"First, Munchausen's is when someone invents an illness. Second, Stockholm syndrome is basically Belle with the Beast. How they made that into a musical is beyond me. And third," I whip the towel over my shoulder, "I don't have *either* of them, thank you very much."

She still looks suspicious. "Don't go catching feelings for Owen. He's not the kind of guy you want to get involved with. He's all wrong for you."

"I couldn't agree more." A voice chirps in from our left. My neighbor Peggy is sitting a few stools away, eavesdropping like it's her full-time job. "No offense to you, Mack, but your brother has always been trouble."

"I beg to differ, Peg." Her sister, Meg (yes, really), is sitting on the opposite side of Peggy. "This is just like in that novel, *Burning For You.* Owen and Emmy are exactly like Rake and Jewel."

Meg might also love romance novels, but that's where our similar interests end.

"This isn't a romance novel, Meg," Peggy says. "Owen Larrabee is not the kind of guy our Emmy needs."

Our Emmy? Was I adopted by Peg and Meg and someone forgot to tell me?

"Besides, in *Burning For You,* it was Jewel who saved Rake. Further proof that Emmy is a very different kind of heroine."

Ouch.

I'm about to respond when Gracie Mitchell, one of my best customers, steps up with a smile. She's the middle school orchestra teacher and an avid reader, which makes her a kindred spirit.

"The usual?"

She nods. "And I'm glad you're okay."

I give her an appreciative smile. "Thanks."

"And for the record, the firefighter is swoony." A smile. "Like something out of one of our favorite novels."

"You too, Gracie?" I shake my head and scan the little circle of traitors. "You guys are way off-base. I'm not *catching feelings* for Owen, whatever that means. The guy's been gone for eight years. I'm not falling in love with some savior, no matter how photogenic he may be." I can practically hear the safety deposit box around my feelings slamming shut, and I picture myself throwing the key off a cliff.

"Well, that's a relief." A male voice stuns us all silent.

At that precise moment, Mack shifts on her stool, and when she does, I see Owen standing directly behind her.

I mentally feel the life drain from my body as I melt into a puddle of goo like the drenched Wicked Witch of the West.

"Owen," I say his name on an exhale and wish I could suck it back in. Owen Larrabee is here, in my shop. He's wearing black Nike joggers, a gray Appies hoodie in honor of Harvest Hollow's beloved minor league hockey team, and a pair of black cross trainers.

And he looks *so* good.

Holy heck.

My insides start to hum.

"Swoony," Gracie sighs so quietly only I can hear it. My cashier, Reagan rings her up, hands her a coffee and an apple cinnamon scone, and my *former* kindred spirit takes a seat in a nearby armchair, clearly too invested to leave just yet.

Peggy hops down off of her stool, walks right over to him and pokes him in the chest. "You deserve a medal for what you did last night, Mr. Larrabee."

Owen grunts. There's the Owen I knew.

And loved.

"I watched the whole thing, and it was very impressive." She pulls her hand back and leans in. "But you keep your distance from Emaline."

His eyes dart to mine, and I have to look away. Concurrent waves of embarrassment wash over me, and all I can picture is the fire, and the smoke, and him reaching out to me, and. . .

"I'm just here for coffee, ma'am," he says.

His voice shakes me back to reality. It's strong and sure, just like it was last night. I'll carry it like a touchstone in my pocket, even if it is coming from the one man I can never allow myself to get close to again.

Peggy is all Rachel Lynde from *Anne of Green Gables.* She's blunt and assuming and in everybody's business.

I'm still looking for her redeemable qualities.

"As long as that's all you're here for." Peggy motions to Meg and they walk out of the shop, leaving me standing behind the counter with Owen just inside the door—and Mack between us.

I'm horribly aware that my busy little shop has gotten very, very quiet. A quick scan of the tables and armchairs tells me what I need to know—everyone is watching this interaction.

Everyone is invested in the firefighter and the helpless girl whose life he saved.

What, do you want us to pose!? I yell at them in my mind.

Wait. Do you? Because I will.

My cheeks flush.

And then Mack laughs. "Oh man, Peggy is out of her mind. She obviously doesn't know anything about your dating life."

Translation: Owen would never date someone like me.

Mack motions to the stool next to hers. "I recommend the caramel latte."

Owen sits down next to her.

"Oh!" I blurt, all kinds of open-mouth-say-stuff. "You're. . .you're staying? I mean, yes. You're here. What would you like? On the house, of course. Because of the saving thing. You know. My life. And. . .all."

I can do this. He's just a guy, right? I'll give him a coffee and the key to my heart. I'll jump off the cliff to go find it.

No big deal.

I was a freshman in high school the first time Owen found me sitting on the dock at the pond that technically belonged to both of our families. The property line ran right through it, and the dock had become my thinking spot.

The academic side of school was easy for me, but the social side? Not so much. Mack made friends so easily, and every day I worried she might ditch me; but more than that, I wasn't sure how to fit in. I spent a lot of time thinking about who I wanted to be. It felt like a big decision that needed to be made and not a series of events I could allow to play out.

So, I often made my way to the dock so I could just be alone with my thoughts. It was quiet there, and there were no people to impress (or not). Just me, the pond and my books.

Always romance novels.

I'd been coming to the pond for almost a year and had never seen another person there, and then one day, I came through the trees into the clearing and spotted Mack's older brother sitting on the dock.

My dock. *My* spot.

He had a journal propped up on his knees, and he was leaning against one of the wooden posts.

Mack and I had been friends since we were little, so I'd

been around Owen over the years, but I'd never said more than two words to him, because he was intimidating.

Also, because by now I'd noticed that he was really good looking. Beautiful in this mysterious, troubled sort of way.

And because Owen hardly spoke to anyone, even Mack.

He was moody and quiet and while he wasn't the same kind of social pariah that I was, he definitely didn't fit into the social constructs of high school. If anything, he bucked that system completely.

Owen had been suspended for fighting more than once, spent more time in detention than in class, and was rumored to spend Friday night football games under the bleachers with whatever alcohol he could score.

Owen was, by all accounts, trouble.

But seeing him sitting there, writing or drawing or whatever he was doing in that journal, he looked different somehow. Quieter. Less scary.

Approachable.

Still, I froze in place, not sure what to do.

I had thinking to do, and this was *my* spot.

I walked over to the dock, aware of him watching me, and I sat down on the edge, opposite where he sat. I slowly pulled my book out of the small bag I brought with me, along with a can of Coke and a Twix bar. I opened the candy, pulled out one of the bars and offered the rest to Owen.

He stared at it for a three-count, and then, reached out and took it.

We didn't say a word to each other for the rest of the afternoon.

We just. . .sat.

We sat and let each other exist in the quiet of the summer evening, in a safe place with no judgment, no rules, and no one to impress.

But that was a long time ago.

A lifetime ago.

There's no trace of that foolish girl in the person I am today.

There's no dock. No pond. No Twix. And definitely no feelings.

So, can someone please explain to me why my pulse is racing just being in the same room as him?

Chapter Five

Emmy

"So, you're the one who saved Emmy!" My nineteen-year-old employee, Reagan, slides into the space next to me. "I saw the article online." She leans across the counter toward Owen, chin propped on her fist. "How's it feel to be a hero?"

Then, she glances at me. "How's it feel to be saved by someone who looks like *him*?"

My eyes go wide as I state in a steady, high-pitched, uninterrupted tone. "Reagan! Can you go help Mrs. Maxwell please?!"

"What? Why?"

I whip my head around. "I think she was looking for the latest Amelie De Pierre novel."

She frowns. "It's right on the front table."

"Right, but she has cataracts, so. . .go. Please and thank you."

Reagan huffs, but does as she's told. I hired her in the spring, right when she graduated high school, because despite her nosiness and her punk rock look, she is actually good at her job.

I don't prescribe to a lot of those broad-brush strokes when it comes to generation bashing, but the last three I hired who were her age had some pretty out-of-whack job expectations—and couldn't put their phones down.

Gosh, I'm turning into an old lady.

Here's hoping Mrs. Maxwell keeps her busy. The last thing I need is more humiliation.

"Ugh, I'm exhausted," Mack says. "I'm going home to sleep. Call me later?" She reaches across the counter. "You're okay, right?"

I nod absently. Mack has always been a little protective of me. I know there are a million stories about popular girls ditching their nerdy childhood best friends when high school and the clique brigade roll around, but that's not our story. Mack and I always stayed close, and she never let anyone pick on me.

And as much as I pride myself on giving advice, when it comes to my life, Mack has always been a voice of reason. Which is why I kept my feelings for Owen from her.

I knew she would not support them.

My best friend's feelings *should* be enough to keep my own in check, but as my eyes drift over to where Owen is sitting, my feelings scoff, *yeah, forget that.*

He's aloof. Gloomy, sometimes. Hard to get to know, but not unlike a walnut.

You have to crack open the outside to get to the good stuff inside.

I don't know why I'm more attracted to a brooding Heathcliff rather than a posh Edgar. Then again, it's not every day a woman compares her high school crush to the characters in *Wuthering Heights*.

A part of me wants to beg Mack not to leave me alone with her *all-wrong-for-me* brother, but another part of me knows that the odds of anything romantic happening between me and Owen are basically zero.

There's no danger of a person who looks like he could pose shirtless for a Booze and Brushes: Women Over Forty class falling for someone who looks like she was voted Most Likely to Join the Circus at their eighth-grade dinner dance.

Mack doesn't stay, despite all of my silent, mental pleading.

When the door closes behind her, I feel Owen watching me.

I try to busy myself behind the counter, doing absolutely nothing productive. How many times can I straighten the same syrups? My palms are so sweaty, if I tried to make a drink right now, the cup would most likely slip right out of my hand and spill all over the floor.

"Can I get a coffee?" he asks.

"Oh! Right, of course." If he sits there, casually drinking coffee, my entire body might catch on fire, and he'd have to save me all over again.

Then, I have an intrusive mental flash of the smoke, the fire, my things burning, eyes stinging, and I feel a slight tremor in my hand which I ball into a fist to make it go away.

I should probably pay attention to that—but I choose not to right now.

"Do you want a latte or. . .?" My voice trails off like it's decided to no longer participate in the conversation.

"Just black," he says. There's a flicker of something behind his eyes, and I want to stare into them long enough to discern what it is.

Thankfully, I pull it together long enough to muster a "Got it." I move over to the carafe, pour him a cup and set it down in front of him. "Anything else? I have fresh scones. Oh, and there are also some lemon blueberry muffins. And I always have cookies."

He sits for a slight moment. "Surprise me."

I take out an oatmeal butterscotch cookie, put it on a plate, and set it down in front of him, and as I do, I notice the Coffin Dodgers.

Four men, all friends, well into their seventies.

Ernie, Marco, John, and Mr. Ridgemont.

They named their posse themselves, not me. It was a whole thing. They felt like they needed a name for their group, and we all pitched in. I offered "The Merryatrics," which I thought was clever, but it got outvoted.

The Coffin Dodgers are as faithful to my shop as the geyser in Yellowstone, but their patronage comes at a price. All four of these men are here to A. hide from their wives, and B. tell me everything I'm doing wrong in my life and in my business.

In a very curmudgeonly, yet sweet and well-meaning way.

"I hope that's on the house!" Ernie says.

"After what this man did, you should let him have all the free coffee! For life!" John points at me.

"Good to see you cleaned up your act, Mr. Larrabee. We were worried about you for a long time." That's Mr. Ridgemont, our former high school principal.

Owen and I had very different relationships with him. He wrote me a glowing college recommendation letter. I'm pretty sure the only things he ever wrote for Owen were detention slips.

Mr. Ridgemont's first name is Barry, which is apparently how you address people when you grow up, but I'll never call him that no matter how many times I serve him coffee.

Then, there's Marco, who takes one look at Owen and grunts.

Marco was the owner of the hardware store until he sold it

two years ago in favor of retirement, which doesn't suit him at all. He's the definition of stir crazy, and now without his business to focus on, he focuses on everyone else's business.

And as it would happen, the hardware store he owned was the same one Owen and his friends vandalized during their senior year of high school.

They were never arrested or charged, but everyone in town knew—or assumed—it was them. And when that spray paint magically disappeared three days later, I knew why.

Owen squirms a little at their attention. He's not used to being praised by these men.

I get the feeling he's not used to being praised by anybody.

"I read that article," Ernie says. "Didn't they interview either of you? If I was running that newspaper, I wouldn't have printed any of it without a quote from both parties involved, and I—"

John cups his hands around his mouth and half-shouts, "You're not running the paper anymore, Ernie."

Ernie waves him off with an "Ahh, can it. Just because I'm not put out to pasture like the rest of you."

The other three men respond with a chorus of "*Moo*" and then clapping on shoulders and laughing.

I glance at Owen, who hasn't touched his cookie.

Don't they know I can't pretend not to admire him when they're all crowding around like this?

"Are you giving this man free coffee or what?" John is now eyeing me like I've done something wrong.

"I'll be paying for this," Owen interrupts.

"Oh, no, he's right," I protest. "It's the least I can do."

He half smiles and gives a nod.

"He might've saved Emmy, but that doesn't make up for everything else he's done over the years." Marco walks away.

Owen's face falls, but only slightly.

"Ah, don't listen to him," Ernie says, patting Owen on the shoulder. "You did good, kid."

"And nobody should be judged by their past," Mr. Ridgemont adds, "despite what you hear." He calls over to Marco, saying loudly, "People *can* change."

"Can I get you gentlemen anything else before you start up your game?" Scrabble, high stakes—if by "high stakes" one means who pays for coffee.

I'm hoping they take the hint and leave me alone with the firefighter and my borderline impure thoughts.

The four of them set up their custom board at the table near the window every single day. I told them they could leave everything there overnight, but they don't. Even if they're not finished with a game, they pack the tile racks on a special shelf behind my counter (Marco: "That way John won't cheat"), put a towel over the board, and vote who gets to take the bag of letters home.

And then, every day, they bring the bag back and start the ritual over again.

They eat a lot of scones and drink a lot of coffee, so I never mind too much. This is exactly how I hoped people would spend time at the bookshop when I opened it.

Books, after all, bring people together.

"We're fine, Emmy," Mr. Ridgemont tells me. He's wearing his gray cardigan with leather patches on the sleeves. Scholarly and grandfatherly all at the same time.

Unlike Owen, I never disliked the man. To me, he was always kind and encouraging. To Owen, his encouragement usually came alongside some form of discipline.

Owen got into a lot of trouble back then.

I wish I could get into trouble with Owen right now.

The thought distracts me enough that I accidentally knock

over a bottle of *Torani* Classic Hazelnut Syrup, then apologize profusely to no one in particular.

The men return to their table, and once again, I'm left standing in front of Owen, wishing we were back at the dock.

That's where talking to him always came easy. What was it about that spot that made us equals?

Out there, in the space where the yards of our childhood homes met, we weren't "rotten apple" and "bookworm." We were just two people with big feelings, trying to figure out who we were going to be.

But now, here, in the real world, under watchful eyes and opinionated people, talking to Owen isn't coming that easily. Especially with the memory of our last, eight-year-old conversation echoing in my mind.

"So," I say dumbly. "You're back."

He nods.

And. . .that's it.

As much as he's changed, he's still the same Owen.

There's still a quiet intensity behind his eyes that is uniquely him. I wonder if he's still the same misunderstood deep thinker that he was all those years ago.

And then, I casually wonder who he's sharing his deep thoughts with nowadays. . .does he miss our talks as much as I do?

He takes a drink of the coffee.

"Did you want that in a to-go cup?" I ask. "I just realized I gave you a mug and maybe—"

"Are you trying to get rid of me?"

My face heats. Yes. I am. There is no "zen" when Owen is in my orbit.

There is only me, seemingly destined to repeat my wonderful history of humiliating myself.

The day he left Harvest Hollow remains the worst day of my life.

I was so stupid. . .

"Oh! Um, no, I just thought—"

"I'm kidding, Emmy." He gives me a slight smile, and I'm pretty sure the lights in the shop flicker.

"So, what are you, um, doing here? Now?" I ask, as if English is my second language.

"Here like in Harvest Hollow?" he asks. "Or here like in your place?"

My place. Hoo boy.

My hands are cold and clammy.

Unholdable.

I inadvertently wipe them on my jeans. "Both," I offer.

Why the heck does he still make me so nervous? I'm not the awkward girl who came to him for dating advice in the tenth grade. I've grown up. Figured out who I am.

I attempt to mentally summon the version of myself that is unmoved by a man's kindness, or general good-looking-ness, but she must be off for the day.

"I'm back here because a job opened up, and I'm here, in your shop—" his eyes meet mine— "to see how you are."

I think about what Mr. Ridgemont said and wonder if it's true that people can change. The only issue is that this Owen is exactly like the old Owen.

And I liked him then, too.

The Owen I knew would've asked me how I was after something as traumatic as a house fire, just the same as he is asking now.

And he would've waited for my answer like a person who really wanted to know.

Just like he is now.

Why he chose to keep that side of himself hidden from so

many people, opting instead for vandalizing businesses, flipping the bird to the people in charge, blowing off school, and getting into fights, I have no idea.

But I got to know a different version of him. The version he didn't show people. The one who told me about his struggles, his failures, his fear, his shame.

Did he remember?

"Emmy?"

"Huh?" I realize I've been staring.

"I asked how you are."

"Oh, right, you did. Yeah. I'm fine." I wave my hand in the air, as if to say "No big deal," but Owen's look tells me he's not buying it.

Those kinds of looks aren't attractive, normally, but this one is.

I turn away because if I don't, I'll say something stupid. Like *I think I still love you.*

"Emmy, there's a woman here to see you." Reagan is back, and while she's addressed me, her eyes are focused squarely on the man across the counter.

Owen seems not to notice.

"And I think she wants to talk to you, too," Reagan says to Owen.

I spin back around, facing him. "Who is it?"

Reagan points to a woman standing near an end cap, thumbing through a book I can tell she absolutely will not buy.

I hope she doesn't crack the spine.

The woman has striking, dark hair and is wearing black dress pants and a bright green blouse. She's all hard edges, the opposite of me. I can't help it if I'm a bit gooey on the inside. If hopeless romance were a physical thing, I'm sure there would be marshmallows in it.

"She says she knows you both," Reagan says.

"From the article?"

"No, from high school."

It's only then that Owen glances toward the woman, and when he does, I see recognition splash across his face.

Then, turning back and through gritted teeth, he mutters, "It's Lindsay."

"Your ex-fiancée Lindsay?" I say, turning toward the woman who is now walking toward us.

Yep. That's her.

Perfect Lindsay Romanelli. All at once I'm the ugly duckling, sitting hopefully in the lunchroom, watching the guy I've been scribbling doodles of in my science notebook walk right past me toward the popular girl.

Which is basically what happened.

Lindsay is who got Owen.

She's also the girl who broke his heart.

Chapter Six

Owen

Lindsay. Last I heard she was living in Charlotte.

But for so many reasons, I've lost track of her over the years.

That's not entirely accurate. It's not like I've just, over time, slowly phased out paying attention.

It was more like I pushed a blasting plunger hooked up to several hundred pounds of TNT under the bridge that held all my feelings for her.

It would've been pathetic, not to mention idiotic and sad, to keep tabs on the girl who left me standing at the altar.

Seeing her now, though, the sting of that day is gone.

Surprising.

"Owen. Larrabee." Lindsay's grinning, like we're old friend.

When she reaches me, I move to stand, because I'm not sure what else I'm supposed to do. I tense as she wraps an arm around me and kisses my cheek.

The nerve.

Emmy, I notice, looks away.

"Lindsay," I say, my voice quiet.

This is not a reunion I want. Or deserve. She should leave and go back to wherever she came from.

"Didn't think I'd ever see you back in Harvest Hollow," Lindsay says.

"Funny, I didn't think I'd see you again, ever," the words are out before I can stop them.

Emmy clears her throat, but it almost sounded like a laugh.

A customer calls out to her, holding out a newspaper and a pen. If someone asks me to autograph that thing, I might consider moving again.

I sit back down and take a drink, not looking at Lindsay.

"I'm only here because of you." She sits next to me, angling her body in my direction.

I turn away in time to see Emmy glance at us as she hands the newspaper back to the customer with a smile. It probably annoyed her to have to do that, but you'd never know it by the look on her face.

Emmy is kind and sweet and good.

Lindsay, in totality, is not.

"Don't you want to know why?" Lindsay asks..

"Why what?"

She laughs. "Are you even listening to me?"

I look at her full on. "Forgive me, I haven't seen you since a gathering at a church eight years ago. Sorry if I'm at a loss for words."

Okay, so maybe not *all* of the sting is gone.

She smiles as if I just made a joke. "Oh, Owen, you always did get lost in your thoughts," she says. "You know, I spent most of our relationship wondering what you were thinking."

I frown.

She continues. "You weren't exactly an open book."

Not to you, I think.

I turn away.

So what if I have a tendency to keep most of my thoughts to myself? So what if I don't, at every waking moment, want to tell people exactly what I'm thinking?

"And not much has changed, I see," she leans back and watches me.

There were other issues in our relationship too, which I was too stupid to realize at the time. For example, I had no interest in a desk job, but Lindsay was intent on me working for her father after the wedding. It didn't matter to her that a 9-5 office job would suck the life right out of me.

But Lindsay had this savior complex, and she was convinced she could turn me into someone "respectable."

She may as well have tried to make the pope eat a ham sandwich on a Friday in March.

I guess it wasn't until the day of our wedding that she realized that—and us—would never happen.

Lindsay waves at Emmy, beckoning her away from the opposite end of the counter, and the second she returns, my insides feel off.

It's like the jocks and the band guys got invited to the same party.

No, not exactly. More like two exes.

Why does it feel like that?

I know why.

Emmy knew me better than anyone, even better than Lindsay, which is strange since Lindsay was the one I was going to marry. I never found talking to Emmy difficult. She never judged me.

These are the women I've been closest to in my entire life.

One I pulled from a fire, and the other is trying to drag me back into one.

Either way, I get burned.

"Can I help you?" Emmy asks Lindsay.

"Oh, for heaven's sake, don't be so formal, Emmy." Lindsay laughs, like they're old friends, which they aren't. Lindsay wasn't exactly a mean girl, but she never went out of her way to be nice.

Emmy's face doesn't move except for a quick fake smile. Lindsay won't be able to tell, but I can.

Funny. I still know her smiles.

"You remember me, right?" Lindsay asks, sing-songy.

"Of course!" Emmy says, mimicking her tone. Her eyes bounce to mine, then back to Lindsay, then back to mine, almost like she wants to follow my lead on how to treat her.

I raise my eyebrows in a "heck if I know" look, hoping she gets it.

She does.

"Would you like some coffee?" Emmy switches into business mode, employing a cordial but reserved tone.

"Yes!" Lindsay smiles. "How about a pumpkin spice latte?"

Emmy tucks a pencil into her apron and her hair behind her ears. "Coming right up."

She glances down at the girl who works behind the counter with a nod.

"Reagan can get that going for you," Emmy says with a smile.

Straight-forward, to the point, take charge. Not the Emmy I remember.

"Great, that'll give us time to talk."

Emmy's eyes find mine again, a quizzical look in them. As if I know what Lindsay is doing here.

"What could you possibly want to talk to me about?" Emmy half-laughs as she says this, and all at once, I see the awkward, shy girl who used to come around the house with Mack.

So, she hasn't *completely* changed.

"Owen. . .? Grunt once if you're still with me." Lindsay teases, staring at me.

I have no idea what she's playing at, and I neither have the time nor the patience for this.

"Can you just say what you want, please?"

She shakes her head and rolls her eyes. "Same old Owen."

"It's been a rough couple of days."

Lindsay closes her eyes, like she's resetting, and when she opens them, her face softens. "Right. Sorry. You two have been through a lot."

Yeah, we have. And I still have no idea how Emmy is doing, or what the state of her house is, or if she has anything but one bunny slipper to wear on her feet.

Without thinking, I lean forward, trying to see over the counter, but the angle is all wrong. "Do you have shoes on?"

Emmy frowns. "What?" She laughs.

"Shoes," I say. "Last night, you were wearing one slipper."

"Oh." She glances down at her feet. "Yeah, I mean. . .I had to wear something else, you know. . ."

I feel stupid. "Yeah, I didn't think. . .you probably couldn't go barefoot. . ."

"Yeah, I borrowed a pair from my mom." She gives herself a once-over, making a face and half-posing awkwardly. "Everything I'm wearing is my mom's. Thankfully, she doesn't dress like a grandma."

"Yeah, you look. . .it looks good. It's good."

There's a pause, and we just look at one another.

Lindsay clears her throat.

I actually forgot she was there for a minute.

Reagan brings Lindsay her drink, and Lindsay doesn't even acknowledge her. "You lost all of your clothes?"

Emmy goes still. "Oh my gosh. I don't know, actually. I have to go see what's left."

I glance down to see her slowly close her fist.

"Can I come with you for that?" Lindsay's voice is eager. And clueless.

Emmy turns to her. "What?"

I turn to her immediately after. "What?"

"Why would you. . .?" Emmy trails off.

"Oh, right! I'm sorry, I never actually explained what I'm doing here."

"No," I snap, wanting her to go away. "You didn't."

Lindsay puts a hand on my arm, like we still have the familiarity we had when we were together. I look down at her hand, and she takes it off.

Good.

"I want to do a story," she wags a finger between us, "on you two."

At first I don't understand what she's saying—but then I remember hearing that Lindsay is some kind of reporter for a station in Charlotte.

Or at least she was? I don't know. She got the job not long after she changed her mind about marrying me. Who knows if that's still where she is.

"Saving Emmy? Pulling her from a burning building? This is a big deal, Owen," Lindsay says. "When I saw the story in the *Harvest Times*, I pitched it to my producer, he loved it, and here I am." She looks at Emmy, then back at me. "I want to take a more personal angle, I mean, you two know each other, *I* know the both of you, so that makes this daring rescue all the more exciting. It's not every day you get to save someone who's practically a little sister to you."

I frown in confused disagreement and look over to see the exact same look on Emmy's face.

"So, what do you think?" Lindsay asks, as if she's asking my opinion on curtains. "It'll be great exposure for your bookstore,

Emmy." Then, to me, "And I'm sure it'll win you points with the chief."

I grit my teeth and look away, trying not to lose it.

But that's what got me here, right? So maybe in a twisted way, Lindsay has a point?

I could use some goodwill after the way I left Macon. I'm not proud of myself for losing my temper, but I do feel justified in my frustration.

Still, I want to follow Emmy's lead here. I'm going to come out looking like a hero, but who knows how she's going to feel, looking like a victim who needed saving.

"Emmy?" I say, trying—failing—to read her thoughts. "It's up to you."

"This will win you points with the chief?"

I shake my head. "Please don't do this for me."

"It *will* win him points," Lindsay says. "New job? New boss? It will go a long way to make the fire station look good, too."

"The fire station doesn't need to—"

"I'll do it," Emmy says, cutting me off.

"Beautiful!" Lindsay practically squeals.

"But you're not coming with me to my house," Emmy says. "I don't want anyone else there for that."

Unfortunately, I've been ordered to go with her, but I don't tell her that right now.

"Okay, but we can film there, right? I think we'll want to show the aftermath of the fire. We might even add a segment on fire safety." Lindsay looks at me. "Maybe you could talk people through what to do if they smell smoke, how to keep calm in an emergency, that sort of thing?"

I don't respond. I'm watching Emmy, whose strong front seems to be trembling like her balled up fist.

I realize what it is. It's trauma. And anxiety.

I stand without hesitation.

"Yeah, let's set this up for tomorrow." I say, taking Lindsay by the arm and helping her up out of her seat. "Do you have a card? I can give you a call and work out the details."

"Today would be better, Owen," Lindsay says, a little more quietly. "News doesn't wait for feelings to calm down."

The absolute gall of this woman.

"No. Absolutely not."

"But the emotion is good television," she says.

I feel the heat rise on the back of my neck, suddenly protective. "Good for. . .? Are you nuts? You want to parade her in front of a camera for what, ratings?" I feel my voice rising and I don't even care at this point.

I feel a hand on my arm.

Emmy.

"Owen, it's okay. I promise." To Lindsay, straight-toned and resolute, "Later today is fine, but I just remembered I need something from my office."

She turns and walks away, untying her apron and tossing it on the counter before disappearing into a back room.

It takes every bit of strength I have not to go after her.

And to not grab Lindsay by one arm and one foot and toss her in the river.

Chapter Seven

Emmy

I hate crying.

That doesn't keep me from doing it, though. A lot.

I'm empathetic, so I often cry on behalf of other people—or from a great scene in a book, or a father-son reunion in a Coke commercial.

Today, when I rush away from Lindsay and Owen, I'm fighting tears that are all my own.

My can-do attitude is a damp paper towel holding up a bowling ball. I'm normally all "it's fine, we'll figure it out," but something is off.

And I realize at this moment what it is.

My emotions and my things have been burned, both figuratively and literally.

My rosy attitude has been replaced with the reality that my house caught on fire and I could've died and I might've lost everything that means anything to me, and while those things are just things, they were *my* things, and being reminded of it every few minutes is shaking me to my core.

I wonder what survived.

My favorite loofa. My perfect pair of jeans. My Birkenstocks. The box of mementos—old movie stubs, notebooks, letters folded into triangles from high school—I keep under my bed. My candy stash for when I get stressed out.

Is any of it still there?

I'm not sure if I can wholly attribute this sudden burst of emotion to the frayed, post-fire state I'm in. . .or if it's seeing Owen and Lindsay together in the same place.

Lindsay's back. Owen's back.

And I never left.

It's easy to see how this could become a replay of eight years ago.

Even if he was too blind to see how wrong she was for him. Owen deserves someone who loves him just as he is. Not someone who tries to change him. And I knew back then, before he even realized it, that's exactly what Lindsay was doing.

She knew Owen was attractive and they looked great together, but she wanted to turn him into someone she could show off at office parties or family gatherings.

She waited until the day of their wedding to realize he wasn't going to ever let anyone stuff him into a box. Or a suit. Or an office.

I would never try to do that to Owen. I couldn't. I knew him, the side he didn't really show to other people, and he didn't need to be changed. Yes, he made some mistakes, but I had theories on why. I always believed what Owen really needed was a cheerleader.

Without hesitation I would've been that person.

Owen might not be the perfect man, but he was perfect for me.

And I waited until the day of their wedding to let him know.

So. Stupid.

I'm not her. All head-turning make-up and great posture.

I'm the weirdo.

I'm the girl who is more likely to spend a Friday night on my couch, engrossed up in a romance novel than going out to the bars. In fact, I can't remember the last time I went out on the weekend.

That's not something I'm looking to change.

Even if it does solidify my future as a spinster.

I like who I am. I like spending my time the way I want to spend my time. I like my pajamas and my books. And I like helping people via my podcast. I'm comfortable with who I am, and I'm not going to let this trip down memory lane change that.

"Emmy?" Owen's voice pulls me from my thoughts. I'm standing in the middle of my office, just off to the side of the back room, with my arms wrapped around myself. I hurry to wipe my cheeks dry and turn to look at him.

The second our eyes meet, concern washes across his face. "Hey. I'm sorry about. . .that. I came to check on you."

"Oh, I just needed a minute." I think I'm going to need more than that, like maybe a box of wine and a therapist.

"You always were a crier." The corner of his mouth turns up in a slight smirk.

I sniff and gesture a finger at him in a lame point. "Some things don't change."

"I'll go with you," he says, abruptly. "To look at your house." A pause. "I mean, if you need someone there. I know you said you didn't want anyone to come, but I know a little bit about dealing with the aftermath of a fire. It can mess with your head."

I hear understanding in his voice, and I wonder how his job has messed with *his* head.

Is that why he's back?

"You really don't have to do that," I say. "I'll be fine to go by myself."

He winces. "I do, and you won't be fine. Please. Trust me on this."

I sit with that for a moment. Trust him.

"Plus, my captain gave me explicit instructions to go with you."

A tiny bit of disappointment peeks up at me and waves. "Oh, you're still on the job."

He shrugs. "Technically, yeah."

That makes more sense. How silly of me to think he was here out of concern for me. He's here because he was ordered to be here. Got it.

"It's okay for you to be affected by everything that happened," he says, obviously thinking I'm back here reacting to the fire and not to my foolish feelings about him and Lindsay. And maybe I am—I don't even know anymore.

"Everyone will tell you how lucky you are, but you don't feel lucky. You feel invaded. Helpless. Grateful to be alive, but still angry that it happened. You don't know what survived, or if irreplaceable things can be saved."

He does understand. Great. The only person in the world who gets it is the one person I cannot share my feelings with.

I won't make that mistake again.

I nod. "I'm trying to stay positive, and I *am* grateful, but. . .yeah. I'm also worried about what didn't survive the fire." I feel silly for admitting this. Jace was right—those are just *things*. I escaped with my life, and that's the most important.

"I feel so ungrateful mourning the loss of *things*. It's so stupid."

"It's not."

I go on without really hearing him. "Like my worn-in

college hoodie and my super soft jeans. Do you know how many times I had to wear them to get them that soft?"

He barely smiles because Owen isn't one for smiling. Years ago, I got really good at reading his face, at hearing what he wasn't saying.

Very few people took the time to do that. It's why everyone underestimated him. Well, that and the fact that he had a temper and a *who gives a crap* attitude.

He tried so hard to buck the system. It's like he had all this potential and didn't care to use it. He put up this front that he was a tough guy with no feelings when the truth was, he was one of the kindest people I knew.

And judging by the fact that he's standing here now, he still is.

"You're not ungrateful, Emmy," he says. "You're human. And that's your home—losing any part of it warrants some sadness."

"Really?"

"Really."

I nod, fighting the tremble in my lower lip when a tear escapes. I quickly wipe it away.

I hate crying. Especially in front of Owen.

"We'll get a game plan for repairs, take pictures, get in touch with insurance. You'll feel better once you've got answers." He looks straight at me. "It's going to be okay."

His gaze pins me in place. I can't move, and I believe him.

The hopeless romantic in me wants to believe him because he's back, he's grown, and while the meet-cute was a bit fiery, there's always the middle third where our pasts get uncovered and we get closer.

The logical pragmatist in me (the little traitor) reminds me that he left without saying goodbye, that he hasn't changed, and that history has a way of repeating itself.

"You sure you have time for this?" I ask.

"Part of the job."

"Right."

"Can you leave now, or do you want to meet over there later?"

"Now is good," I say. "If we wait, my mom might show up, and I love my mom, but I have a feeling she's not the best person to do this with."

My mother will gush, and overreact, and pile on, and while she means to be helpful and understanding, it will undoubtedly make me feel worse.

"Okay, you wanna tell Reagan we're leaving?"

I have to smile. He remembered her name.

Impressive.

He turns to my jacket, hanging on a hook by the door. "This yours?"

I nod as he takes it down, then holds it open for me to slip into. I stare at him.

When I move toward him to slide my arms into the sleeves, I inhale a deep breath, like a dog locking on to the scent of a lost hiker in the woods.

I would tell myself to *knock it off already*, but it's futile. And complicated.

I want to but I don't want to. That's the problem with hope.

And my hopeful heart stopped listening the second he pulled me to safety.

Once I've got my jacket on, I turn to him.

"You ready?" he asks.

"Yeah," I exhale a big breath. "I just want to get this over with."

"My truck's out front," he says, and as we walk out into the shop, he puts a hand around my shoulder, guiding me past some people. It almost—almost—feels like we're together. Like we're more than friends. I could close my eyes and imagine we're heading out for a late breakfast, just me and my man.

But if I closed my eyes, I'd probably run into something. Best to keep my eyes open when I'm walking.

You're mad at him, Emmy. Knock it off.

I stop and tell Reagan to hold down the fort.

"You're leaving?" she asks. "With him?" Her eyebrows are raised like she's impressed by this.

"Going to look at my house," I say, hoping that puts a stop to whatever she's trying to imply.

"Okay, boss," she says. "Take your time. I'll handle everything."

I turn to go and notice people are watching. A woman standing in the fiction section raises her phone and snaps a photo. And on the opposite side of the shop, is Lindsay.

"Does she know where we're going?" I ask as Owen leads me outside and onto the sidewalk.

"I didn't tell her," he says.

"Do you want to say goodbye to her before we go?"

He frowns. "No." He says this like it's a silly thing to ask.

I silently approve of his reaction.

He points to a very nice pick-up truck parked a few spaces down the street. He pulls the door open and motions for me to get it. When I do, he closes the door behind me and walks around the front of the truck, giving me a few moments to admire him.

I've always known he's good-looking. Obnoxiously so. He won the genetic lottery, with Henry Cavill's chin and Matt Bomer's blue eyes.

But that's not the reason I fell for him.

The fact that he comes by this naturally with no Photoshop or filter really is unfair. And it's intimidating, at least for someone like me. With eight years of silence between us, I'm right back to where I was the first time I found Owen at the dock.

Awkward. Shy.

Lindsay, I noticed, had no problem treating him like he was just another guy.

How did she do that?

Who am I kidding? She did that because they are attractiveness equals. I know I'm not in their league.

Owen slips in behind the steering wheel and starts the engine. The cab of the truck fills with a scent that is so very *Owen*, equal parts sandalwood and juniper.

I'm basically high right now. And Owen is the drug.

I want to stay angry with him for the rest of my life. I should stay angry. If I'm not angry, then I will turn right back into that same lovesick girl I was all those years ago.

Maybe it's the swirling scents tilting my senses and sensibilities off-kilter, but I do what anyone would do in this particular moment.

I bring up his ex-fiancée.

"It was weird seeing Lindsay again." I state, keeping my eyes on the road in front of us.

Why must I be like this? What is wrong with me?! I feel, but don't see, his shrug. "It's whatever."

I glance at him. "Are you upset? I'd be upset. I think I *am* upset."

He shakes his head. "I'm not upset."

"Have you guys talked since. . .um. . ."

The stupid questions continue.

"Since she left me at the altar?" he says wryly. "No. Probably for the best. I had no desire to reconnect with her after that."

Good.

"Sorry," I say. "I shouldn't have brought it up."

He shakes his head as he stops at a red light on Maple Street. "It's whatever," he repeats.

All of it? Even the part involving me?

At least I have the good sense not to say *that* out loud.

The silence is a reminder that our connection was severed a long time ago, too. Owen and I were friends—good, albeit secret, friends—back then. But now? Now, we're just two acquaintances who knew each other once upon a time.

Two acquaintances who have been thrust back together through tragedy and heroics. The two of us, with a connected past, broken apart by ill-fated relationships and poor timing.

Without warning, I get a flash of a book cover. Owen and me in each other's arms, him wearing his fireman's coat with no shirt, me with my hair askew, one arm draped around his neck and the other arm alluringly arched downward with a book in one hand, and we're both set in the foreground of a house ablaze.

The title, in a script-y but readable font, reads *Forge of the Heart*.

I burst out laughing and clap my hands over my mouth. It's a horrible title.

He looks over at me, completely confused. "You. . .okay?"

I try not to giggle. "Yeah, I'm just. . .it's fine. I'm fine. Just remembered something funny."

Forge of the Heart. Good grief, it may as well be called *The Fireman's Desire* or *Slow Burn*.

Well, wait. *Slow Burn* actually isn't terrible.

It's good to know my status as a weirdo is still intact.

When we reach my street, my pulse quickens and my skin hurts at the sight of my little bungalow. The house is small—only two bedrooms—with a sage green exterior and white pillars along the front, making a little porch space that's perfect for reading.

"Well, it's still standing," I try to cover how devastated and invaded I feel as Owen parks the truck in the driveway behind my black Sentra, which I left behind last night.

"I checked before I left the station, and it's been cleared for you to go back, but only for a short period of time," he says. "So, we can grab a few things, assess the damage, but we shouldn't hang around."

"It's dangerous?"

"Could be. You'll want to call your insurance company first, and then a restoration company, before you spend any amount of time inside. The smoke damage isn't good for your lungs, even after the fire is out." He opens the door of his truck and gets out. I do the same, then meet him on the sidewalk next to the driver's side.

I pause. I'm new to trauma, and it's making my feet not work and my hands ball into fists.

It's foreign, and invading. I don't like it.

"You okay?"

"Yeah," I say.

"You're a bad liar."

I smile, in spite of the grip of sadness. To look at the house from here, it doesn't even look like anything is wrong.

I know inside it's a different story.

Owen opens the back door of the truck and pulls out a pair of boots. "Put these on."

"You have women's fire boots in your truck?"

He quirks a brow. "I grabbed them from the firehouse before I left. This too." He pulls out a mask.

"Is it really that bad in there?"

He looks right in my eyes, and it feels like he can hear me thinking. "We aren't taking any chances."

His thoughtfulness makes my breath hitch, and I look away.

If I keep staring at him the odds of getting completely lost in his blue eyes will increase exponentially.

He hasn't changed. He's always been this kind.

People just don't bother to look long enough to see it.

And *take me or leave me* Owen doesn't bother trying to prove himself.

As we look toward my house, I have a fleeting thought that even now I'd take him in a heartbeat.

That is, if I was ever given the chance.

Chapter Eight

Emmy

I slip my mom's shoes off and step into the oversized boots. They're huge. I clomp around in a little circle, and Owen gives me a look.

I pull the mask on, and I'm sure I look ridiculous.

At least my lungs will be safe.

Next, he pulls out a large, drawstring bag, like the kind I used to haul dirty laundry home from college.

"I'm going to go in first. We're going to look around, grab anything important—glasses, prescriptions, paperwork, clothes if you can find any. But remember, we can't stay in there for long, okay?"

I nod, and the mask sags behind my head, shifting askew on my face.

He reaches over and straightens it, then hands me the bag. "You can use this to carry stuff out."

This feels like a search and rescue mission. Operation Save My Stuff. I keep all my paperwork—birth certificate, passport, social security card, insurance information—in a pink binder in my desk. And I need to find my purse, assuming it survived.

I'll want my car keys and some clothes, and I really, really want my microphone. For sentimental reasons as well as practical ones.

A thought hits me, one I can't deal with right at the moment—I'm going to have to find an alternate location for recording if I'm going to keep the show up and running.

While keeping it secret.

How in the world am I going to do that?

Owen opens the front door, and I follow him inside. Even through my mask, I can smell the acrid, charred fume of smoke. The entryway looks relatively unharmed, but as I step in a little further, I can see most of the white surfaces are now gray. Some of them are black, with billowed shapes like permanent shadows.

The wall next to the staircase is caked in dark black soot, and I can only imagine what the upstairs looks like.

"My office is through there," I say, pointing down the hall. "Can I get my paperwork?"

"Course." He starts off down the hallway, and I follow close behind. Owen is careful where he steps, alert and aware of everything in the house.

My hands start inadvertently shaking, and my breath starts to fog the mask. I instinctively reach out and grab his arm.

He turns and reaches up to place his hand on mine—and I'm instantly comforted.

I didn't know it was going to be this hard.

"Hey. It's okay. If you need to take a break, or come back later. . ."

I shake my head. "No. It's. . .I'm fine. Not sure how I'll be in ten minutes, but I'm good. I promise."

It's strange. This is my home. I know that in my head, but it doesn't feel like home anymore.

I feel like my safest space in the world has been violated.

We reach the door of the office, and Owen looks around. This room is almost completely intact, barely a trace of damage.

"Oh, thank goodness. . ." I exhale a sigh, grateful that at least something in my house still feels normal.

I walk over to the desk and open the bottom drawer. I pull out my pink binder. "This is everything you'd need to steal my identity." I flip through it quickly, thankful that it's all still okay. My insurance information, credit card details, passport, bank paperwork—it's all here. I slip it into the drawstring bag.

I look around the room. "I suppose it's too much to ask to take all of the photos off the wall, huh?"

He walks over to my bookshelf and picks up a framed photo of me and Mack at our high school graduation. "You can take a few of them."

I open the bag up, and he drops it inside.

"Don't worry, none of this stuff is going anywhere," he says.

I nod, then follow him back out into the hall. I point in the direction of the kitchen at the back of the house, and he leads the way. My purse is hanging there on one of the back hooks, so I grab it and toss it in my bag. Now I have my driver's license and access to my car.

There are good things happening here, too.

I mentally tell myself this over and over because right now, I have to hold on to the good things.

I look around the kitchen. "My KitchenAid mixer looks okay."

"Almost everything in here is okay," Owen says. "I think they got it out before there was too much damage to the back of the house."

But the same can't be said for the living room. The smoke coated everything—the built-in shelves, the furniture, the walls, the ceiling. There are puddles still on the ground, intermittent drips from the floor above.

"This room is going to need some work," he says.

We stop at the bottom of the stairs, and I don't have to wait for Owen to tell me we aren't going to risk it. I can tell by the condition of the stairs, stained from water and fire, that it's not safe.

"Do you have clothes anywhere else in the house?"

"My laundry room," I say. "I think there might be some stuff in there."

"Okay, where's that?"

"Basement."

He nods, then moves toward the basement door.

I feel the overwhelming need to talk about something.

"Is it weird for you?" I blurt.

He turns. "Is what weird?"

"Being back here. At the scene of a fire. It's weird for me. I'm not sure how to feel, but I know it doesn't feel. . .right."

He pauses, hand on the doorknob. "It's different for different people. I'm more concerned about how it is for you. I know all about the emotional toll a trauma like this can take."

Thoughtful. Again.

Still.

"It is hard," I say, honestly. "I feel homeless."

He stands there, watching me, and I feel like I've just cracked myself open and offered him a peek inside.

I backtrack with, "But it's okay. I know I'll be okay."

"You don't have to do that, you know."

I frown inside the mask. "Do what?"

"Downplay this. It's a huge thing."

I shrug. "I'm not downplaying it. I really will be okay." And I will be. Someday. But I can't talk about it right now. I can't process it. I still can't even believe that this disaster zone is my house.

Owen pulls open the door to the basement, and I see a

coating from the smoke left behind on the walls. That coating is everywhere, it seems, and I have no idea how anyone is ever going to get that off. Something tells me a Mr. Clean Magic Eraser isn't going to cut it.

"Do you think they'll be able to salvage it?" I ask Owen as we start down the stairs. "The house, I mean."

"I'm not in the restoration business, but I think so," he says, reaching the bottom of the stairs. "I don't think it's going to need to be demolished."

"That's good," I say. "I was getting tired of the paint colors anyway." I force myself to smile against the way I feel. I have to find things to laugh about or I'm going to fall apart.

"Which way to the laundry room?" he asks.

"Through here." I start down the hall, stopping short outside my studio. The door is off its hinges, thanks to Owen breaking it down, and I can see the exact spot where I stood when he rescued me.

My eyes are burning, and I can't blame that on the smoke.

He stops moving.

"Sorry," I say.

"I can just go and see if I can find some clothes?"

"No, it's fine." I push past the studio and into the laundry room, thankful I was behind on housework this week. I find two full baskets of clean clothes and another one waiting to be washed. I never thought three baskets of laundry would mean so much to me, but they feel like such a gift, even if they will smell like they were hanging on a clothesline near a bonfire.

I dump the clothes into the drawstring bag, shoving them down to make room.

"Anything else?" Owen asks. "Prescriptions?"

I shake my head.

"Glasses?"

Another head shake. "I think I'm good."

He nods and starts back down the hall. As we reach my studio, I stop again, this time, taking a quiet step inside. My microphone is there, on my desk, and I think about all the hours I've spent here, bringing *The Hopeful Romantic* to life.

"What is this room?" Owen is standing behind me, looking right at my big secret and trying to make sense of it.

"Oh, just my office," I say, as nonchalantly as I can, without turning around.

"I thought your office was upstairs?"

"This is. . .um. . .my work office." I turn. "That's the beauty of living alone, you can have as many offices as you want."

I look back at my desk and then at my microphone. It's sitting there, next to my headphones—a total splurge purchase —and I want to discreetly put them both in the bag, but Owen is standing right here.

"Those look expensive, do you want to take them?" he asks.

Oh, thank goodness, I don't have to come up with some weird, convoluted lie.

I'm bad at lying anyway, so if he asks me what they're for, I don't even know what I'd say.

"What are they for?"

"Social media!" I blurt, and not quietly.

DANG IT.

I don't have to see Owen's face to know he's probably looking at me like I'm a lunatic.

"I do, uh, a lot of social media things. Down here," I say. "For Book Smart."

"Oh," he says. "Okay. Well, if it's important, I'd grab it."

"Yeah, I'll just—" I walk over to the desk, pick up the microphone and headphones and try to stuff them in the bag. When there isn't room, Owen takes the bag from me, and I give him a nod. "Okay, that's it I think."

"You must take your social media really seriously," he says.

"Yep," I say, and even though I know the less I say, the better, I can't seem to get myself to shut up. "There are always videos to make—" (it should be noted that Book Smart's social media has no videos, but I'm banking on Owen not bothering to look that up). "I'm still learning about it, but it's the curse of being a business owner. No matter how much you hate it, you have to be on the socials."

Oh my giddy aunt, I wish I'd shut my blathering mouth.

His brow furrows, but he doesn't respond.

"So. . .yeah. Ready?" I push past him to leave, hoping he follows, also hoping there's nothing else in the office to incriminate me. I'm generally pretty careful, but I never planned on having anyone else in this space.

"Will other people be in here, you know, looking around?"

"Why, is there a dead body buried under the house or something?"

Might as well be. The shock of anyone finding out that I'm the one behind *The Hopeful Romantic*, telling people how to have successful relationships, would be about the same.

Chapter Nine

Owen

We step outside, stash my stuff in my trunk, and take off the masks when my phone buzzes with a text notification.

I take it out and glance down, and immediately think, *Oh, great.*

LINDSAY

Hey, O, are you up for filming later on?

Emmy is locking her front door, and I'm wishing I wasn't the one who had to take her back here to see her house in this condition.

I might not be the best guy in the world, but seeing her take this all in is a little too much, even for me.

Emmy turns around and looks at me. There's a tension between us (I think?). Not unlike this house, there's air that needs to be cleared.

I'm not going to bring it up right now. That would most likely make everything even more awkward.

"It's Lindsay," I say.

"Oh." Emmy starts digging around in her purse.

"She wants to know about the interview."

She doesn't look up.

"We don't have to do it," I say, meaning it.

She glances at me. "I said I would."

"Yeah, but you're allowed to change your mind."

"You said it would help you, right?" she says. "With your job?"

I wish I wouldn't have confirmed that. From what I remember, Emmy has a habit of taking one thing out of a whole conversation and focusing on it.

Not that I say a lot or have a lot of conversations. But back when we were friends, she'd pull little snippets from our pond chats as proof that I was a good guy and wield those snippets like a warrior in battle.

Truth be told, I liked that she saw a different side of me. She made me think I could do anything.

I think about what brought me here. The way I messed up in Macon. Yeah. It would help to have some positive attention for once, no matter how much I would hate it. Still, I don't want her to feel obligated.

"Don't do this for me," I tell her. "I mean it. I'll survive."

She twists a silver band around on her finger, a nervous habit that dates back years.

"My store could always use good publicity too," she says. Then, with a look that makes me think this trauma hasn't stolen all of her personality, she says, "And you *did* sort of save my life."

"Yeah, well, Lindsay's a bulldozer," I say.

Emmy stifles a small laugh. "You're not wrong."

"She wants to do it today." I shake my head, partly in disgust, hating that I even have to ask.

Emmy nods. "Okay."

"Yeah?"

"It's fine." She pauses. "You can tell her it's fine. Just let me know when and where." She pulls her keys out of her purse. "I'll drive myself back to work."

I nod, but as she walks away, I realize I don't have her number. "Emmy?"

She turns around but doesn't meet my eyes. Did I imagine it, or did things between us just get even more tense?

"I need your number." I hold my phone out to her, and she hesitates for a beat, then moves toward me, types her number into my phone, and hands it back to me.

"Thanks for coming," she says, her tone clipped.

I resist the urge to ask her if she's okay and give her a simple nod instead. "I'll keep you posted when I hear back."

She starts toward the car. "Sounds good."

She gets in, starts the engine, backs out and drives away, leaving me wondering what I did wrong.

I text Lindsay back:

OWEN

Let's do it at Book Smart. Name the time.

LINDSAY

Can we do it at the house?

OWEN

No.

LINDSAY

It'll be better TV.

The nerve.

Better TV? *Better TV?* I start to slam out a response in all caps, but then stop mid-text.

Just breathe.

Calm down.

I'm not going to let Lindsay put Emmy on TV and make her cry.

Yeah, still protective of her. Not sure how to shake that.

OWEN

No. The bookstore or nothing.

Time?

LINDSAY

Fine. I'll work some editing magic, I guess.

2 PM. That'll give me time to get it ready to air tonight.

OWEN

I'll let Emmy know.

I start a new text to Emmy.

OWEN

2 PM at Book Smart work for you?

EMMY

Yep.

OWEN

See ya then.

When she doesn't respond, I head back to my truck, get in, and fling the phone on my front seat.

I want to fix things; I want to help; I want a lot of things—but just like Emmy's house, it's going to take some time.

Emmy

Owen and Lindsay, back to texting.

Because of course they are.

Maybe they do belong together. Maybe this will be a rekindling of their relationship.

Just like in *Our Hill of Stars*, the time-slip novel by Chloe Barker, when Juliette and Christopher discover that they're looking at the same night sky from the same seaside hill but in different centuries, Owen and Lindsay are connected despite time and distance, once again.

And I'm Phoebe Sutherland, the goofy, slightly unattractive, sidekick character who's in like two scenes in the book.

It's a stark reminder that I need to have clear, non-hopeless romantic eyes when looking at Owen. Between the house, the podcast, and Book Smart, I have plenty to keep me busy, and I'm glad for it.

Once I get back to the shop, I busy myself with the day-to-day operations, but also find myself fielding a lot of questions and comments, mostly of the "How are you, *really*? How scary! You could've died! We're worried about you!" variety.

My favorite is, "Oh my gosh, it could've been *so* much worse!"

As if it wasn't bad enough.

As if I want to think about all the things that *could've* been worse.

I've said those words to other people, thinking I was helping them see a more positive perspective, but now I know words like those don't help.

There were also the, "I cannot believe Owen Larrabee was the one to pull you out!" and "Is he still as hot as he used to be?" and "Wasn't he in jail?"

My customers mean well, but by the time the interview rolls around and Lindsay shows up, I want to crawl into a hole and stay hidden until hell freezes over or Leonardo DiCaprio dates someone his own age, whichever comes first.

Probably the hell thing.

Lindsay arrives early, and she and a cameraman commandeer my shop, displacing paying customers, and raising more than a few eyebrows.

People start murmuring, and I catch bits and pieces of conversation. Words like "Owen Larrabee" and "left at the altar" fly around haphazardly, putting everything that happened eight years ago right back in the Harvest Hollow limelight.

And a familiar knot twists in my belly.

Lindsay was never outwardly mean to me, but she did confront me once about my "little crush" on Owen. I was pulling out the books I needed to take home with me from school that day, and when I closed the locker, there she was, staring at me.

One pointed lecture through fake smiling teeth, and I knew my place.

She and Owen were new, but he and I were not.

But knowing they were dating had certainly put a damper on our pond chats. At least for me.

"Emmy Smart." She'd smiled at me, a smile that dripped with insincerity.

"Hey, Lindsay. . ."

"Can we talk about your *little crush* on my boyfriend?"

The way those two words belittled my feelings for Owen stung. What I felt for him was deeper than a "little crush." I really knew him, and I was convinced nobody else—not even Lindsay—could say the same.

"I don't have a crush on—"

"Let's not pretend, okay?" she said. "I see the way you look at him. And I found this." She held up a note that I'd written Owen that morning in study hall.

She shakes it slightly, like a dog treat. "Do you want me to read it out loud?"

I shook my head. I knew what it said.

Owen,

I'm bringing your favorite cookies tonight—oatmeal butterscotch. I finally perfected my recipe. Show up hungry!

—Emmy

Lindsay stared at me with a raised brow. "Care to explain?"

"It's not a big deal," I said. "I'm just—"

"Tutoring him, I know," she says, cutting me off. "And it's not like I'm threatened, I mean. . ." she gives me a dismissive shrug. "And seriously? Cookies?" She holds the note out in my direction. "Maybe don't pass my boyfriend notes in the hallway."

Owen didn't show up at the pond that night. Or for several nights after. And he never did try the oatmeal butterscotch cookies.

Watching Lindsay now, I almost feel like I'm back in high school and she's dictating my conversation with Owen. She says we can talk now, so we'll talk.

It's foolish. Silly. Misguided. Untrue.

But I feel it just the same.

Being around Lindsay brings out an insecurity I've worked really hard to get over.

Hang on a second.

I *have* worked hard to get over it.

I'm not that goofy, nerdy teenager being low-key berated in the high school hallway.

I'm a goofy, nerdy adult. And this is *my* store.

I stand a bit straighter.

The cameraman sets his camera on a tripod near the back

wall. "There's great natural light back here by this big window," Lindsay is saying, and a small crowd starts to gather.

"You look like you're going to puke." Reagan tucks a rag in the belt of her apron and stares at me.

"I just might," I say. "Man the bucket."

The door opens, and Owen strolls in.

Good grief, he looks even better in the afternoon sun than he did this morning. How does he do that?

I have to look away because my insides are humming again, and he's the reason why.

The chatter escalates, but this scene no longer has anything to do with me and everything to do with the reunion of Owen and the girl who left him standing at the altar.

It baffles me, sometimes, the small-town mentality. Harvest Hollow isn't a tiny town, yet somehow, everyone still knows everyone else's business. Besides, it's not every day someone gets left at the altar. Especially someone nobody in town was rooting for in the first place.

Harvest Hollow's runaway bride became a legend.

Owen's eyes meet mine from across the room. Then, his eyes leave mine and fall on Lindsay.

"I don't want to do this," I say under my breath, looking at Reagan.

She shrugs. "Who says you have to?"

I sit with that for a moment.

The unabashed wisdom of teenagers sometimes cuts right through all of the crap and gets right to the point.

"You're right. I don't. I know I said I would, but. . ." I stop short of saying *I don't think I can* and take a few steps back, removing my apron, then quietly, discreetly, I slip out the back door and into the alley behind the shop.

It'll help Owen, and let's face it, I do owe him—for saving my life and everything. But I just don't want to sit there, next to him, answering Lindsay's questions, watching the two of them reconnect over my tragedy.

Nor am I a huge fan of reliving it.

I don't want to keep being the fool.

And since I'm an adult, and I get to decide what I am—and am not—going to do, I get in my car and drive away.

Chapter Ten

Owen

I remember the first time I talked to Emmy.

I'd wandered down to the dock at the lake behind the house, looking for silence and solitude.

She walked up about ten minutes later.

I didn't know she'd already claimed this spot as her own.

The first time was awkward—but nice. She gave me a candy bar.

We both just sat there, neither of us saying a word. It was like she didn't expect me to, and I didn't have to.

In all the years she and Mack had been hanging out, I'd never really had a conversation with her.

But she let me sit there, in silence. She read while I wrote. I poured things into that journal that helped me sort things out in my head. Long, run-on sentences, rife with misspelled words and scratched out phrases. Haphazard thoughts that would never be judged, or graded, or seen, but somehow calmed my racing mind.

Unlike me, Emmy was smart. Really smart.

She'd probably graduate at sixteen.

I'd be lucky to graduate at all.

I wasn't proud of it, and despite what everyone said, it wasn't that I didn't try. I know that now, but somehow knowing it doesn't make it better.

I went back the next night, same thing. Just nice, undemanding silence devoid of expectation.

After three nights of consistent sitting in silence, Emmy finally spoke.

She reached into her bag and pulled out a little lunchbox. She unzipped it and pulled out a small container of brownies.

"Do you want one?" She smiled, and it caught me offguard. I'd never looked at Emmy as anything other than my sister's friend. And I didn't make a habit of hanging out with Mack's friends.

She held the glass container out to me. "I baked them. I took them out a minute early so they're warm and gooey. Nobody wants an overbaked brownie."

I reached in and took out one of the corner pieces.

She smiled again. "The corners are my favorite too."

My first word to her: "Thanks."

She set the container between us and took one for herself. Then, she nodded at my journal. "What are you writing?"

I instinctively pulled it a little closer to me.

"Oh, is it private?"

I shrugged. "It's. . .uh. . .nothing important."

"Gotcha."

She didn't press me for more information, something I wasn't used to. Most people are always trying to get me to share my thoughts or my feelings or some other garbage that I have no interest in talking about.

I nodded at her book. "What are you reading?" And then, with a smirk, "Or is it private?"

She scrunched up her face, pressing a hand to the book. "It's a re-read. *Sense and Sensibility.*"

I nodded and finished off the brownie. "These are really good."

"I know, right?" She smiled.

I reached for the container, and she slid it closer to me.

I grabbed two more.

It went on like this for weeks. Not every night, but often. Every time I needed space, I headed down to the dock.

And she was there. And somehow, she didn't intrude on my need to think.

When fall hit and it started to get a little colder, we bundled up and brought blankets. There was an unspoken agreement to share this space, because for some reason, it was safe.

And while neither of us said so, it seems we both need a safe space.

She talked a lot more than I originally thought she would, which was fine with me because I liked to listen way more than I liked to talk. Emmy wasn't some quiet little wallflower, like I thought. At least, not with me. She was spunky and witty and kind of hilarious.

She also never seemed to judge me.

We became friends—good friends.

At school, we barely acknowledged each other. Not that we were actively avoiding each other, it's just that I don't have any of the same classes as her—plus, she had her circle, and I had mine. Talking to her in public might not have been the best idea either. She would probably have teachers warning her not to fall in with a bad crowd or calling her parents.

I didn't want her to get in trouble for being my friend.

At school, we were separate.

At the dock, we were equals.

Almost. She was still *way* smarter than I was.

In the spring of my junior year, after months of covert meetings, I showed up at the pond on a regular Thursday, feeling like I just got run over by a bulldozer.

By then, Emmy could read my expressions, and vice versa. She took one look at me, frowned, and opened the small container that was on her lap and without saying a word, offered what was inside.

I nodded at it, asking a silent question.

"Banana bread with crumble on top," she said. "I'll give you a piece if you tell me why you look like that."

I made my way down the dock and sat. It was cool outside, cooler than normal, and I noticed the extra blanket she brought folded up to the side. I leaned to grab that one, but she lifted her blanket as if to say, "Here, share with me."

I scooted over, and she dropped the blanket over my legs and looked at me.

"I know you're not one to talk about your feelings or anything."

I looked away.

She tilted the container of banana bread at me, and I sheepishly took three pieces.

"Oof. Three pieces. This must be a doozy."

I smiled through my sullen expression, in spite of myself.

"I heard them call your name at the end of school," she said, then, she affects the voice of Mr. Ridgemont's secretary, Miss Landry, and said, "Owen Larrabee, please come to the principal's office."

I grunted a response.

When I didn't say anything else, Emmy looked away. "Today I had to dissect a frog in biology. Mr. Martin didn't even bring gloves for us. I had to go to the nurse's office and beg for a box. And maybe it's just me, but frog innards stink. Like really stink—"

"I might not pass eleventh grade." I blurted it out, cutting her off mid-sentence.

I felt her look at me, but I kept my eyes focused on the trees outlining the little pond. She didn't say anything. It was the lack of pressure from her that made me want to share.

She wasn't trying to figure me out, or worse, fix me.

"They called my parents in, and all they did was talk about me. About how I don't try hard enough. About how—" I looked at her—this part I hadn't shared before, not with anybody. "About how I need to accept accommodations."

She frowned, and I looked away. "Accommodations?"

"Do you remember the first day you found me here, in your thinking spot?"

She nodded.

"That was the day I found out I'm dyslexic."

Her shoulders dropped slightly. "Oh."

I felt myself getting angry. "I can't. . .read great. I look at the words and they're all jumbled up. No matter how hard I concentrate, it's like the letters jump around."

She sat and listened.

"They tested me for it a few years ago, in elementary school, but they said I was fine. Just an underachiever. Maybe I needed glasses. Maybe I needed to apply myself more."

I heard what they weren't saying. I couldn't grasp the lessons in school. I didn't read well. My spelling was bad.

I wasn't smart.

"Since then, it's been harder and harder for me to keep up," I said. "Except in woodshop. I get A's in that class."

Her eyes drifted over to the birdhouse I made last semester. She hung it in one of the trees down here by the pond. She'd actually been impressed by it; so much so that she named it, and I got to use the wood burner kit at school to etch it on the front.

Home Tweet Home. Hilarious.

But that was Emmy. Quietly funny.

Nobody had ever been impressed by something I'd done before. I wasn't used to it. Usually, all I did was let people down.

"Is there a reason you don't want the accommodations?" she asked.

I shrugged. "Don't need everyone knowing how dumb I am."

She frowned. "You're not dumb, Owen."

"There are about ten teachers at school who would disagree with you."

I'd spent most of my childhood and all of my adolescence convinced I wasn't smart. This diagnosis didn't change that. If anything, it made it worse.

She angled her body toward me and waited for me to look at her. When I did, I saw her expression was serious. "So, you learn differently than other people. That doesn't make you dumb."

I shook my head and looked away. "It doesn't matter. I'm going to have to repeat eleventh grade. I'll be lucky if I graduate."

Her brow knit together, and she chewed on her lower lip. "Do you trust me?"

I felt my forehead pull in confusion. "Why?"

"Maybe I can help," she said.

"What, like tutor the dumb kid?"

She smacked me across the arm.

"Ow! Hey!"

She looked determined. "Owen, I get that most of your life you didn't know about this, but now that you do, you can work with it. I'm not an expert, but I do work in the tutoring center at school. I've picked up a few things that will help."

"You really don't want to take this on," I told her.

"You kidding? I'm just doing this so I'm not stuck with you for an extra year." She smiled. It's a kind smile. No judgment. No opinion. Just a plan of action and a belief that I'm not a lost cause.

I fade back to the present.

Sitting here in Book Smart, I'm realizing how important her belief in me was all those years ago.

And how much I miss it now.

I'm standing off to the side, wondering where Emmy is and dreading sitting under Lindsay's watchful eye.

"Emmy's gone." It's Reagan, the teenage employee with the nose ring.

I frown. "Gone where?"

She shrugs. "Said she didn't want to do this anymore and left out the back door. Probably driving around rage singing."

"Rage singing?"

"Crank the music really loud and sing at the top of your lungs?" She says this like it's common practice. My expression must communicate that it's not because she waves me off. "You're on your own for this. Have fun with your girlfriend."

"She's not my—" But Reagan has already walked away.

I pull out my phone and text Emmy:

OWEN

You okay?

I see the three dots appear and then disappear.

"Okay!" Lindsay looks at her watch, then at me. "Where's Emmy?"

"I think it's just me."

She frowns. "That wasn't the deal."

"Well, I guess she changed her mind," I say.

Lindsay shakes her head. "Unbelievable."

"She's been through a lot."

She appears not to hear me. "She said she'd do it."

"She's entitled to change her mind." I meet her eyes, and in a moment of boldness, I chide, "Of all people, I would think you know all about that."

Lindsay's eyes dart to mine. "Do you have something to say, Owen?"

I feel heat flare on my neck and my muscles tighten in my arms. It takes every bit of self-control not to yell exactly how I feel.

In the intensity of the moment, I picture Emmy's face on the dock. The breeze off the water. The lazy calmness of the cattails, bending in the wind.

I calm down.

"No, Lindsay." I straighten. "I don't."

"Well, I don't know what to do now. The story is the two of you, not just you."

I don't say another word.

And I secretly like that Lindsay, for once, is inconvenienced. But I'm also secretly concerned about Emmy.

Chapter Eleven

Emmy

Two things are on my mind when I wake up Saturday morning.

The Farmer's Market and the Interview.

I've capitalized both in my head.

Also, both will probably have an impact on my business, but for wildly different reasons.

The interview aired last night, and today I'm up early to set up my Book Smart booth at the market. I get dressed and ready, and then come down to the kitchen to find my parents sitting at the table, each reading a section of the newspaper and drinking coffee.

People still read newspapers. It's true.

Something inside me aches at the familiarity of the scene, the way they can sit here in silence and be perfectly in sync.

My parents have the kind of relationship nobody would write about. Because it's comfortable and kind—and boring. They hardly ever fight, and over the years, they've settled into this quiet, wonderful rhythm. Even though I'm addicted to romance novels, and a part of me yearns to be swept off my feet, the truth is another part of me wants what they have.

To feel this at ease with another person? Yes, please.

Once upon a time, I *did* feel this at ease with another person. It's just that it was in a completely platonic way.

At least on his part.

"Emmy, you're awake!"

"I am," I yawn, "but just barely."

"How did you sleep? Was the bed okay? How are you feeling?" I'm used to this maternal barrage of questions.

"Good, good, and good," I muse. "Though not necessarily in that order."

My dad laughs, which I love being able to make him do, and my mom makes a face. She doesn't have time for such cleverness.

"The market is today," I say.

Mom sets her paper down and looks at me. "I'm going to help."

"Oh, you really don't have to. Reagan's coming and—"

She holds up a hand. "I want to."

I know from experience that once my mother makes up her mind, there's no talking her out of it, so I don't say anything else.

She kisses my dad on the top of his head, and then follows me out the door to my car.

"So. . ." she says once we're on our way to town.

"You're going to grill me, aren't you?"

She folds her hands on her lap. "Yes."

"There's no escape?"

"No, there is not."

"As you wish," I quip. I mentally gird my loins for this battle. Not exactly a land war in Asia, and there's no iocane powder to speak of, but it's going to be a back-and-forth worthy of Vizzini and the Dread Pirate Roberts.

"Before you start," I say. "I'm totally fine."

"Are you?"

"Yes. A little sad about my house." She starts to ask a question, but I feel what it is and add, "And yes, I called the insurance company."

Sometimes my mom forgets that I'm an adult, a business owner, and a completely independent woman.

"And Owen?"

I chew the inside of my lip and keep my eyes on the road. A good twenty seconds of silence pass.

"You ignoring me?" Mom watches me, waiting for an answer to her simple two-word question.

I raise my eyebrows and take a deeper breath.

Mom and Dad live on the outskirts of Harvest Hollow. They wanted to "spread out" and they wanted my sister, Ellie, and me to grow up with a big yard and lots of space to roam.

And lots of space for mom's gardens. My mother is the education and field trip coordinator at our local arboretum. She spends most of her time in nature, so naturally, she'd surround herself with it at home.

We're passing the big farmhouse where Owen and Mack grew up, and I notice Owen's truck isn't in the driveway.

Maybe he stayed with Lindsay last night.

Blech.

The thought sours my mood, which was borderline rancid to begin with.

Mom is the only person in the world who knew the truth about my former feelings for Owen. She's been a sounding board, a shoulder to cry on, and the voice of wisdom over the years.

But I'm not a kid anymore.

And there are some things about Owen and me that even she doesn't know.

"I'm not ignoring you," I say, stalling. "What was the question?"

"How are you doing with the fact that Owen is back in town. . .and the fact that he's the one who saved your life?"

"*Tech*nically, he didn't save my life," I say. "I was perfectly capable of walking up the stairs by myself. He just, you know, kicked down the door, and. . .led the way." I decide to finish it off with a bit of the ridiculous. "He probably just wanted to play the part of the hero. I bet he called the newspaper himself to make sure they got that money shot."

"Yeah, that sounds like him." Mom rolls her eyes. "It's okay to have feelings about all of this, Emmy. It's a lot to process."

"I really don't have any feelings, Mom," I lie.

"Well, we all know *that's* not true."

I tilt my head at her. "I'm great. I'm lucky. It's a lot, yes, but I'm working through it. They don't have to bulldoze my house, and I still have my bunny slippers. What more could a girl ask for?" I really was grateful when one of the firefighters located my other slipper and gave it to my dad before we went home that night. It's the little things, I guess.

"Oh, good! So, you won't mind if I invite Owen for Sunday dinner tomorrow?"

My heart springboards into my throat. "Nope."

"Totally fine with you?"

I muster a half-nodded "Yep."

"You're sure?" she asks, because she knows me well enough to know I'm not telling her everything.

I glance over at her. "I'm sure. Invite him. Throw him a party. Let's make tomorrow Owen Larrabee Day! I'll show up with a big cutout sign of his face on a stick."

"You are impossible."

I shake my head. "Honestly, Mom. I'm fine. Invite him. Really."

"Okay. I just wanted to make sure."

We arrive at the Harvest Hollow Farmer's Market, which is in a downtown pavilion one block over from Maple Street. Years ago, it was held in the parking lot of the United Methodist Church, but it got so big, the city raised money for the Harvest Market Pavilion to be built. It's not completely weatherproof, but it's been known to keep heads dry in the rain —if the rain falls straight down.

Now that it's autumn, the posts of the pavilion are decorated with corn stalks, tied on by handmade yellow, red and orange bows. There are hay bales and pumpkins on display, adding to the festive colors of the vendors who set up in rows underneath the pavilion.

There's a crisp chill in the North Carolina mountain air, making it the perfect time to bring out the pumpkin spice samples and apple crisp cups. For Book Smart, the market isn't as much a money maker as it is a conversation starter— and I firmly believe it's good to be involved in the community.

I love being out here every Saturday. It reminds me that I'm a part of something. And that I'm not alone.

I park on the street and make my way over to our little corner of the market, greeting the other familiar business owners as I do. Heather from Cataloochee Mountain Coffee waves from her end of the market. Since I serve her coffee and she serves my baked goods, we take opposite ends. On market days, I only serve plain coffee and Heather does fancy drinks and bagels. Maybe we should look at each other as competitors but we don't, and somehow it works for us. And people seem happy to support both of our businesses.

Mom stops to chat with some of her friends from work, and I spot Reagan over in front of the Book Smart book wagon.

The wagon, which is actually a refurbished VW van, is parked behind our booth. I had a local auto body place retrofit the side so it lifts up, like an awning, with fun rustic shelves and a woodsy interior. Just like at the shop, people can peruse books, order coffee, or purchase a pastry.

If I'm lucky, they'll do all three.

When I walk up, Regan stops setting up and looks at me. "That news lady was not happy with you yesterday."

I make a face. "I'm really broken up about that."

She chuckles. "Yeah, I can tell."

I shrug. "They did just fine without me."

Mom and Dad found Lindsay's interview last night and recorded it on the DVR, and even though I opted out, my shop was on TV, and Mom told me that Owen mentioned it twice.

It was thoughtful. Again. What in the world am I supposed to do with that?

"Did you watch it?" Reagan goes back to unloading the pastries my nighttime baker, Jenny, packed up. Jenny always comes in on Fridays to get ready for the market. Usually, I stay around to help her because baking is relaxing for me, but last night I left her high and dry.

Because that's the kind of coward I am.

"Nope," I say.

"Talk about tense."

Tense? There was tension? Between who?

I pause and look at her, then lean on the table, a little closer to her, and say, "Like . . .sexually tense?"

She laughs. "Why did you whisper that? No one's around. You can say the word 'sexually.' You are an adult."

Reagan is younger than me, but she's a whole lot more

experienced. And she likes to say whatever she thinks, appropriate or not.

"And no, I mean, I think they were in a fight."

My ears perk up at this, but my mom walks into the booth, so I strike my most nonchalant pose.

Turns out, leaning with one elbow on the table and having my other arm bent behind me, hand hooked on my back pocket like a Glamour Shot at the mall is *not* nonchalant.

Mom frowns at me. "What is wrong with you? What are you doing?"

I wave my hand at her. "I'm just, you know, chatting."

"Don't you need to set up?"

"Yes. I just took a little break." I hop up, ignoring Reagan's confused look and trying desperately not to read into the fact that Owen and Lindsay had *tension.* (And not the *sexual* kind.) I even whisper it in my head.

My mom's question is valid. What *is* wrong with me?

But then, I remember chapter sixteen in Samantha Kismet's *Under Locke and Key*, a standalone romance novel about an eccentric, wealthy recluse who hires a live-in nurse to care for his ailing father. Total enemies to lovers trope—she thinks he's rich and out of touch, he thinks she's a stickler for rules, but their argument in that chapter turns into a dinner table clearing make out scene.

Maybe their tension led to a deep heart-to-heart. Which maybe led to a make out session behind my shop. Which maybe led to. . .the reason Owen's truck wasn't in the driveway this morning.

My brain is a traitor.

"Speak of the devil."

I follow Regan's gaze across the pavilion and see Owen, wearing jeans and a navy blue T-shirt with an open flannel button-down over it. He's wearing a backwards baseball cap, and I'm pretty sure he should be named "Sexiest Man Alive" by every single magazine in the world. Even *Popular Mechanics* and *Bird Watchers Monthly*.

"Crap!" I duck down, pretending to busy myself with the bins underneath the table and stay down there until Owen passes by.

What is he doing here? Do the firefighters have a booth?

And then, my worst nightmare happens.

My *way too friendly* mother starts shouting his name and waving at him. At the sound of the crazy woman, Owen stops and turns around. I know this because I have a perfect view of his boots, and I see them change direction.

I'm still squatting, and my quads are not strong enough for this. If this takes too long, I'm going to fall over.

"Owen Larrabee, you wonderful boy," Mom gushes.

Reagan glances at me, eyebrow raised in a silent question.

I frown a silently loud answer.

My thighs are already burning. I really need to get myself to a gym. You never know when you're going to need to stay still in a deep squat.

"Mrs. Smart."

"Please, call me Jeannie." I imagine her holding onto his arms in that motherly way she does when she wants to be sure she has your attention.

I imagine him nodding. Looking away. Trying to escape an actual conversation. Talking never was his strong suit. Except. . .he used to talk to me. My heart squeezes at the memory.

"It's so good to run into you like this," she says. "Emmy and I were just talking about you in the car."

"You. . .um, you were?"

My cheeks are all ablaze. I mime slapping my hand to my forehead and beg for a quick death.

"Yes, she's just—" Mom pauses. "Emmy?"

Double crap.

"Where is she?"

I glance up, from my spot low to the ground, in time to see Reagan pointing at me. It's like someone told me to go play hide and seek but forgot to come find me. I pick up a bag of coffee beans and stand, blowing a strand of hair off my forehead.

Mom, who is applying for the title of Captain Obvious, makes a production of this. "What were you doing on the ground?"

Owen watches me, the slightest trace of amusement behind his eyes.

I hold up the bag of coffee. "Dropped this."

Mom looks at me like I'm one step away from being hauled off in a straitjacket, and I force myself to smile. I shove the bag of coffee in Reagan's hand and lean toward her. "Traitor," I whisper.

She responds with a smile.

"Honey, did you see? Owen's here!"

"Yes, Mom, he's six-foot-two and kind of hard to miss." I give Owen a quick nod of acknowledgement. "Hey."

"Hey."

"I was just telling him we wanted to invite him for dinner," she says. "To thank him for saving your life."

"Oh—" the fake smile freezes on my face. "Right! Dinner!"

"I'm making goulash," she says. "Everyone loves goulash."

"Maybe if everyone were British orphans in the 1830's," I mutter.

I glance at Owen and see him turn away. Was that a smile?

My mother frowns.

I point at the both of them, double pointer fingers. "I should —" but my brain shuts off before finishing that sentence. I point at them again, and then walk over behind the Book Smart book wagon and force myself to inhale the longest, deepest breath I've ever taken.

I wonder if there's a paper bag around here because I might hyperventilate, and nearly dying twice in the same week is just a little bit too much excitement for one girl. I close my eyes and hold my arms over my head, shaking out my hands. I inhale again—this time even more deeply.

"Is this some new sort of meditation?"

Owen's voice from behind me stuns my mouth shut, arms up, mid-breath. I spin around to face him without putting my arms down, like some lunatic sloth.

His eyes jump to my raised arms, and I quickly drop them to my sides.

"No," I say, because I'm a whiz with snappy comebacks.

"So, you're hiding," he says.

"I'm *working*," I say.

"You're avoiding me."

"No, I'm not."

"You were squatting on the ground for like a minute and a half."

"Picking up coffee."

"In a bag."

I stick out my chin.

His eyebrow quirks.

I look away. "Fine, yeah, I'm avoiding you."

"Why?" he asks.

Does he really have to ask?

I sigh. "I just feel. . .stupid."

"Because I saved you from the fire?" he asks, totally guessing wrong, thank goodness. "Don't."

"Oh, okay, well since you said so. . ." I roll my eyes.

He gives me a smile. A real one. Those are hard to come by with Owen. This is also doing things to me.

But then the smile fades, leaving us swimming in that same tense awkwardness as before. If Reagan were describing *our* tension, I dare say it would also not have the word "sexual" attached to it.

This is just me being weird.

"Look, Emmy, maybe we need to clear the air," he says.

Then he just stares.

I stare back.

He takes a breath. "I'm not. . .I'm not good at, you know. . ."

"Talking?" I cut him off, smiling.

He nods at me. "Yeah. That."

I nod back. "I know."

He looks around, as if it's hard for him to kick off the conversation. "So. . .um. . .the day I left, things got a little. . ."

Oh no, that's the air he wants to clear?

". . .strained between us, and—"

"Nope, all good!" I cut him off again. "Water under the bridge, you know?"

He stares again.

"It's great! You're coming for dinner, apparently. I'll make a pie. It will counteract the effects of the goulash. We are *totally* fine." And yet, I'm still out here acting like a weirdo.

"You're sure?" he says. "Your mom's inviting Mack and my parents. I think it's turning into a whole thing."

"She's really proud of her goulash. Be ready to gain fifteen pounds."

He smiles at that. "Okay," he says. "Then, I guess I'll see you tomorrow?" More of a question than a statement.

"Yes! Tomorrow! Great! Can't wait!" I'm sure my smile looks more *One Flew Over the Cuckoo's Nest* than "demure woman" but I'm working with what I've got.

He hesitates, as if to make sure the conversation is truly over, and then leaves.

Reagan comes up beside me and follows my gaze. "You hate to see him go, but you love to watch him walk away."

I slowly turn toward her. "Are you finished?"

"I've never seen you so flustered, Emmy." She grins. "I'm just getting started."

Chapter Twelve

Emmy

Being back in your childhood bedroom is kind of like a dating app for garden gnomes.

It's weirdly familiar, but everything is smaller.

It echoes coziness.

That night, after the market, with my parents out at bingo night, I'm back in my bedroom, surrounded by my *Gone with the Wind, Jane Eyre,* and *Wuthering Heights* posters.

As I look at them, I think, *Wow, I was a real catch in high school.*

Some parents turn their grown children's rooms into guest rooms or man caves or hobby rooms, but mine left ours alone.

Maybe because it felt like a museum already.

In stark contrast, my sister Ellie, who now lives in the Midwest and who almost never comes home, will forever be represented in this house by the sprawling collage of photos she taped to her wall and ceiling in high school.

Ellie.

Always the social one. Two years younger than me and much more popular, Ellie's room is like a shrine to social life.

Did I mention the Shakespeare art print I framed and hung over my desk? *Line up, guys!*

But I understand why everyone loves my sister. I love her, too. She's fun and goofy and always optimistic.

Now, safely alone with no chance of running into Owen, my nerves finally settle.

I sit down at my desk, open my laptop, and log in to my podcast email. I sent a message to Ripper to let him know we may need to take a break this week, but I didn't tell him any more than that. I find his simple reply waiting for me now:

All good. Here when you need me.

I begin to sort through the emails my virtual assistant, Lily, sent over. She's learned which questions make great podcast topics and having her go through them first saves me a lot of time.

"What have you found for me today, Lily?" I say out loud, scrolling subject lines for anything that catches my eye.

I read the first few emails. A woman whose boyfriend stole her identity but is now back on her doorstep wanting a second chance. A woman whose husband falls asleep at 7 p.m. every night, putting a damper on their love life. A woman who is dating a twin and is wondering if it's okay if she secretly marks him with a Sharpie to make sure they're not swapping.

Yikes.

I scroll through a few others, then stop on one that has promise.

Dear Hopeful Romantic,

I'm dating a great guy. He's funny and has a good job, and we're having a great time. There's just one problem—he isn't very romantic. I've tried bringing it up to him, but he doesn't seem to get it. His idea of romance is letting me pick the movie and the restaurant and the time and the day.

He's perfected the "whatever you want" response. Is it too much to ask him to pick?

I know you've said before to hold out for the guy who will dance with you in the rain, but there's no chance with my current boyfriend.

Am I missing out on "great" waiting for "perfect"? How would I know if this is the wrong guy who just happened to come along at the right time?

How do I know if I should walk away?

Signed,

Hopeful and Heartfelt in Hoboken

I glance over at my microphone. I hadn't planned to do any recording right now, but with my parents out, this might be the best time. I'm not sure when I'll get another chance.

I click over to the recording software on my laptop and connect my microphone to the USB interface. Thankfully, there's a format shift on the pitch correction plug-in, which allows me to alter the tone and vibe of my voice. I could sound like an eight-year-old girl or a sixty-year-old smoker.

Just on the off chance that someone local subscribes.

I draw in a breath, find my podcaster voice and then, I'm ready to go.

"Hello and welcome to *The Hopeful Romantic*, where we analyze, digest, and discuss all things romance. Today's episode is brought to you by *Glow Up*, the Botox-free and easy way to get the extra plump your face deserves.

"All right, let's get right to it, because today's question is one I'm sure many of you will be able to relate to. It comes to us from Hopeful and Heartfelt in Hoboken."

I read the letter, and then I pause to take a drink of water.

"Friends, you all know I love romance. I mean, look at the name of this podcast. I want to find adventure and romance, like Outlander Claire finds with Jamie on the Scottish hillsides. Like Julia Roberts, I want the fairy tale—okay, maybe not her profession, but the fire escape scene? Flowers and a public profession of love in the streets? Absolutely!

"We all want to be swept off our feet. It's why romance novels, rom-coms, all of them, are so popular. Is it unrealistic? Maybe. But that doesn't necessarily mean we can't hope for it. We want the romantic hero to walk out of our dreams and straight into our lives. And I, for one, don't think we should apologize for wanting that. We yearn for the guy who shows up with chicken soup to take care of us when we're sick, like Tom Hanks in *You've Got Mail*. We want our guy to write us love letters and kiss us in the rain or ask us to slow dance in the middle of the street. That's what I'm holding out for, and I won't apologize for it.

"If you're dating a perfectly fine guy, steady job, polite, and not leading some clandestine double life, but who will also never ask you to go stargazing in the back of a truck because he thinks it's stupid—what is the rest of your relationship, and life together, going to look like? No spice? No spark? No feels? I'm not sure you'd want to live in a relationship without those. Don't you deserve someone who occasionally cooks you dinner and brings you flowers—or better yet, coffee—just because?

"The answer, of course, is yes. I know it's a high expectation. I hear that a lot from subscribers, it's like every third email is about that very thing.

"But you have to believe you're worth it. Because I don't want to see you, or anyone for that matter, stuck in a relationship without romance. So, Hopeful and Heartfelt in Hoboken, ask yourself, what kind of relationship do you *really* want? If there's no room for boomboxes held over your head or the delivery of a thousand of yellow daisies, maybe it's time to move on."

I click off the recording and think it over. It's a high standard. I know this. Ninety-five percent of guys aren't going to chase down an airplane already taking off on the tarmac just to return the dried flower that you gave him when he was eight.

But the last five percent? That's what I'm holding out for. If he's a unicorn, well, then, I'm going unicorn hunting.

If the novels I've devoured over the years have taught me anything, it's that a good man will, every once in a while, slow dance in the street.

I hear the door downstairs. I'll have to finish this episode later. I stash my equipment away and go to bed thinking about romantic gestures, hoping that one day my patience will pay off and I'll be swept right off my feet.

Oddly, all I can think about is Owen.

The least romantic person ever.

He's a main factor in why I'm so adamant about my Five Percent Guy in the first place.

I literally want the exact opposite in every way. I want someone communicative and open with his feelings. Someone who loves romantic gestures. Someone who isn't afraid to make a fool of himself for me.

Tonight's letter reminded me of that.

Owen might be handsome, stupidly so, and he might make a gooey mess of my insides. But that's just attraction. Never mind that it's a strong motivator and a little too demanding. Owen is not my perfect match, my soulmate, or my future.

Which is why he should stay in the past.

Where he belongs.

My mom's always had an open kitchen policy, meaning, her dining table always has room for one more chair. She has a gift for hospitality, and she loves to entertain. But she isn't fussy about it. Her mantra is, "Come as you are, and there will be food."

A flaw, though, is that she thinks goulash is acceptable to serve to other people.

I can't prove it, but I have visions of her grabbing every leftover in the kitchen (Pasta? Broccoli? Hamburger? Skittles? You betcha!) dumping them out on the counter, then holding a huge bowl under the lip and using her arm to scrape everything into it.

Sunday afternoon, after church, with my recording off to Ripper and my nerves properly rested, I go through the motions of baking the pie I promised. As I chop up apples and sprinkle cinnamon, I am constantly shoving the words "baked with love" out of my mind.

There is no love here. Only pie. And duty.

Duty pie.

But in spite of my many reminders, I feel myself getting nervous. Because yesterday, Owen brought up The Day That Shall Not Be Named.

Right out there.

In broad daylight.

As if it's a topic to be discussed on the street.

Doesn't he know we don't rehash our most embarrassing moments? We slowly back away and never speak of them again.

What in the world do I do if he brings it up again?

Promptly at 5:30 p.m., there's a knock on the door and my stomach decides it's the best time to become a gymnast and perform an Olympic floor routine.

"They're here!" Mom practically shouts this on her way to the door, shooing my dad out of his recliner as she does.

Seconds later, Mack comes into the kitchen, and I use every ounce of my energy to keep from watching the door for Owen.

This whole "conflicting feelings thing" going on inside me is not my favorite. Why can't I just move on? He's not my person!

I hear his voice in the entryway, chatting with my dad about some football game. Probably the one blaring from the television. I force myself to focus on Mack.

"Back at home!" She grins at me. "You and Owen both. Never thought I'd see the day."

"That makes two of us."

"You could've stayed with me," she says, grabbing a corn chip and dunking it in my mom's homemade queso.

"Now you tell me," I groan. But the truth is, I don't mind staying with my parents. There's something instantly cozy about being here, and it's nice to not be alone.

Mom walks back in, a trail of people following behind. I spot Owen and quickly look away, busying myself with the chopping of the vegetables, a task I loathe but begged for in hopes of calming my nerves and occupying my hands.

Turns out using a knife when you're nervous isn't the best idea.

I set it down and open the refrigerator. I pretend I need something out of it, but really, I just want to cool down. My face is on fire.

"You're right on time," Mom says. "Dinner is all ready, and Emmy's pie is happily baking in the oven."

"It smells wonderful, Emmy," Mrs. Larrabee says.

I close the fridge, empty-handed, and face her. "Thank you."

"You've become quite the little baker, haven't you?" she says.

Mack reaches over and pinches my cheek. "Aw, quite the little baker."

Her mom takes this for what it is—Mack making fun of her—and shakes her head, smiling. "Oh, you two. I was paying her a compliment. I had a pumpkin scone the other day at Book Smart, and it was to die for."

"Thank you, Mrs. Larrabee," I say pointedly at Mack. She responds by clasping her hands in a mock "*my hero*" pose—to which I respond by throwing a towel at her face.

Something inside me settles. This is my place. These are my people.

I glance at Owen.

Except for him.

"Let's head into the dining room!" Mom says. "Dinner is ready."

"I haven't had your mom's goulash since we were in high school," Mack says as she picks up a big salad bowl. "It's my favorite."

I frown, trying to hide my disgust but failing. "Really?"

"Comfort food, Em. It's the good stuff."

There's a basket of bread on the counter, and I go to pick it up at the same time Owen grabs the basket from the other side.

I have a scene flash in my mind from *Lady and the Tramp*, only it's Owen and me eating the opposite ends of a dinner roll.

I think something might actually be wrong with me.

"I thought I'd help," he says.

"Oh! It's okay," I say, my hand still clutching the basket as if it is the only thing keeping me from collapsing into a pile on the floor. "I got it."

After all, hasn't he done enough? I mean, he did save my life and everything.

He lets go and smiles as we make our way to the dining

room. I see that the only two chairs left are right across from each other.

I freeze in place like a giant block of cement, and Owen steps forward and pulls out the chair next to Mack, motioning for me to sit down.

It's a simple, old-fashioned gesture that catches me off-guard. How am I supposed to keep my feelings in check if he's going to do things like that?

Mack grabs my arm. "Here, sit."

As I do, Owen slips the chair in closer to the table, and then takes the seat directly across from me.

Which means every time I look up, I'm going to get an eyeful of Owen.

Great.

In *The Sweeter Side of Beeville, Texas*, an overwrought Amish romance by Jordan Wynter, the heroine Sarah Sutter (a beautiful but restless girl, also a talented baker) tries to bring the hero, Jarmuth Hartzler, back into the spiritual fold by recreating all of his late mother's recipes.

Unfortunately, with the first recipe in the tattered, hand-bound book—that would be Mara Hartzler's Friendship Bread—she accidentally includes chopped nuts, to which ol' Jarmuth is severely allergic.

Wacky Amish hijinks ensue, and his face puffs up like a chipmunk trying to eat a grapefruit.

Please, Oh Lord of the Amish People, don't let this be like that.

Chapter Thirteen

Owen

Why am I here again?

I'm sitting at the table wondering just that, listening to my parents talk to Emmy's parents and noticing that Emmy is doing her level best to avoid making eye contact with me.

It's comical. I look up and she looks away.

I tried to clear the air with her yesterday. I thought it needed to be said, to make sure things weren't weird. Even though actually saying anything never comes easily to me.

She shut me down. Fast. Message received.

The way I see it, two things can happen: 1. we have an honest conversation about the day I left, figure stuff out, and move on, or 2. we spend the rest of our lives avoiding each other.

Like she's doing right now.

There's a lull in the conversation and Emmy's dad, Rob, who is sitting at the end of the table, sets his fork down and picks up his glass of water. "So, Owen. . ."

He pauses, as if waiting for the attention of the room, which I hate to say, he has.

"Back in Harvest Hollow."

"Yes, sir."

"We're awfully glad you are. Especially Emmy—am I right, kiddo?"

Emmy's eyes widen, then drop to her lap. I see her mom catch her dad's eye. She fires a sort of nonverbal warning shot, and her dad turns back to look at me.

"I just meant because you pulled her out of that fire," Rob says. "You basically saved her life."

"Technically, he didn't," Emmy mumbles without looking up.

"She's right," I say. "Technically, I only carried her because she was too stubborn to come with me when I told her to."

I feel her glare at me, and I respond by taking a bite of goulash.

"This is really good, Mrs. S."

"Jeannie," she says. "I told you. You're not going to save our daughter and call me Mrs. anything. First name basis."

I nod.

"We saw your interview," Jeannie says. "You did a very good job."

"Can't believe you sat down and talked to *Lindsay*," Mack says, emphasizing her name so it sounds like it tastes bad coming out of her mouth. "You should've told her viewers what a narcissistic snake she is."

Dad laughs, "Why don't you tell us how you really feel, hon."

"Mackenzie." My mom says this like a warning. "We've all moved on."

"Whatever." Mack spits. "I don't have any intention of

pretending everything's fine when it comes to Lindsay Freaking Romanelli. And if I run into her, I'll be sure to tell her so."

"Owen has moved on," Dad says. "You should too."

Mack scoffs. "Owen hasn't moved on." She looks at me. "She's the reason he's got a three-date policy."

"A what?" My mother frowns.

"A what?" Emmy repeats, but then quickly clams up.

"Won't go out with anyone for more than three dates," Mack says. "Right, bro?"

"Mackenzie." Now I'm the one firing the warning shot.

"*What?* You do." Mack takes a bite and chews and adds, mouth half-full. "Is that some kind of a secret?"

"It's not exactly something we need to discuss over dinner," I say, my voice low.

Mack pulls a *whatever* face.

"A three-date rule?" Jeannie says, looking at me. "Can I ask why?"

"Oh, Jeannie, leave the boy alone," Rob says. "He's young, if he wants to be picky, he can."

"He's not *that* young," my mom says, doing that mom thing where she thinks she's helping and meaning well but it just comes off as embarrassing and condescending. "We could stand to make some progress in the relationship department. I'd like to have grandchildren, you know, before I'm too old to enjoy them."

Mack snickers. "Good luck with *that*."

I'm gonna kill my sister.

"Oh, I know what you mean. We would too," Jeannie says. "Sadly, I think it's going to be a while."

Do people really talk like this?

I glance at Emmy, whose cheeks have reddened three shades since this conversation started. At least I'm not alone in this verbal assault.

"You know," Mom says, looking at me. I can see by the widening twinkle in her eyes that she has conveniently removed that filter that stops her from saying the most ridiculous things. "I always thought you and Emmy would make a cute couple."

Emmy, mid-drink, spurts a mouthful back into her glass.

"Emmy?" Mack turns to our mom and repeats it. "*My Emmy?*'

"I'm sorry, Mack. I didn't realize you owned her," Mom says. "Yes, Emmy. That beautiful girl sitting beside you." She smiles.

Mack looks at me, then at Emmy, then at me again. "Are you crazy?"

"She and Owen were friends, too, you know." Mom takes a bite nonchalantly, like this is a perfectly normal conversation to have.

"Mom, Emmy and Owen were never friends." Mack scoffs as she says this, like it's the stupidest thing she's ever heard.

"Emmy is the reason your brother graduated high school," Dad says.

I dare a glance at Emmy, who looks like she is playing a solo game of freeze tag.

My sister blasts me with a look I can only describe as "accusatory." "Is this true?"

I shrug, honestly surprised Emmy never told her. But then, knowing Mack's opinion of me and how wrong I am for "nice girls" I suppose it does make sense.

Then, to Emmy: "So, wait. This is blowing my mind. You were, what, like, his tutor?"

Emmy squirms a bit, and says, "Well, yeah, he needed help, so. . ."

Mack looks around the table in disbelief. "How did I not know this?!"

"She was his friend," Mom says. "And she was a good influence. She's the reason Owen cleaned up that spray paint on Marco's hardware store after the boys had their stupid spray paint party. She's the reason he didn't get arrested."

Mack holds up her hands as if to hit pause on this whole moment. "*What?!*"

I really don't understand why this is that big a deal.

Mack narrows her eyes and looks at me, then at Emmy. "So, you guys were like. . .real friends?"

Emmy looks at me. I raise my eyebrows and shrug.

"Owen needed help with a few classes, and I was there," she says. "That's all."

Mom looks up and frowns.

Mack softens a bit, coming down from DEFCON 1. She's *so* dramatic. "You never told me," Mack says to Emmy. "Why didn't you tell me?"

Mack and I have always had a true brother/sister relationship, complete with the teasing and the overprotectiveness and the late night heart-to-hearts. But she's possessive, and with my pre-Lindsay track record and my many—and historic—horrible choices, she never wanted me near Emmy.

But we're all adults now. Surely, my sister isn't actually offended by this?

"I asked her not to," I say, after a long pause. "Nobody wants to admit they need a tutor. Least of all me. You think I wanted to announce to everyone that I was stupid?"

Emmy looks at me, and though she says nothing, I see the gratitude—and the chastisement—in her eyes. Emmy never let me call myself stupid. That hasn't changed.

Our friendship was hard to navigate back then, and while neither of us ever said so, somehow it felt best to keep it a secret.

Mack stares at me for a moment, then finally says, "Well, that's dumb."

"Yeah," I say. "I know that now. Didn't know that then."

There's a pause, and then my sister shakes her head. "At any rate, Mom, you're still nuts if you think these two would make a good couple. It's like you don't know either one of them at all."

Mom waits until she has my attention, then says, "Or maybe it's like I do know them both perfectly."

Mack wraps a protective arm around Emmy. "Emmy is definitely not a three-dates-and-out kind of girl."

Mom touches her nose and says, "Bingo!"

"I'm going to go get the pie!" Emmy stands, but when she does, she knocks her full water glass over and the cold, wet drink spills across the table.

I jump up out of my chair, but not quick enough, and the water lands right in my lap.

Emmy gasps, Mack busts out laughing, and I stand there, looking like I just wet myself.

"Oh my gosh! I'm so sorry!" Emmy's cheeks are a new shade of bright red, as others from the table jump up quickly to move plates out of the way.

"Oh, Emmy!" Jeannie says. "You always were the clumsy one."

At that, Emmy's face falls. "I'll go get a towel." She rushes off to the kitchen.

And because I don't love standing in a room with people staring at conspicuous places on my body, I decide to follow her.

I find her standing in the kitchen, her back to the door, her arms over her head, shaking her hands. She seems to be doing the same deep breathing she was doing at the market.

"You really have it out for me, don't you?" I ask, my tone light.

She spins around, dropping her arms. "What? No! It was an accident, I—"

I hold up a hand. "Emmy, I'm joking."

"Oh." She frowns. "Well, it's not funny." She pauses, then looks away as she points down. "You look like you wet your pants."

I smirk. "It's kind of funny."

Slowly, a smile crawls across her face. "Fine. Kind of."

I smile back at her.

She tosses me a dish towel.

"I think it's a little late for this," I say. "The damage is done. There's water dripping down my—"

"Hey, Whoa! I don't need to know that," she cuts in, and then, her eyes find the tile floor. "And I'm sorry for what I said in there."

"What did you say in there?"

She shakes her head. "No. About what I *didn't* say."

I stare. I'm not sure what she means.

She looks up. "I didn't say out loud that we were friends."

Ah.

I shrug. "No big deal."

But then, she gets quiet. "We were friends, weren't we?"

I hold her gaze for several seconds, but before I can answer, Mack walks into the kitchen.

"I came to save you, Emmy," she says. "From *Three-Date Owen*."

Emmy laughs, softly, and looks away.

"I'll get the pie," Mack grabs an oven mitt. Then, to me, she says. "Grab the ice cream. Jeannie said she got cinnamon yesterday from Scoops." She picks up the pie and walks back into the dining room.

We're alone again.

"Emmy. I'm not—" I start, but she holds up a small spatula, cutting me off.

"She forgot this."

And she leaves the room so quickly, I don't have time to tell her that Mack's wrong about me.

Which is probably for the best, since I'm not actually sure she is.

Chapter Fourteen

Emmy

Well, I never want to do that again.

"That was wonderful," Mom says as she opens the dishwasher to start loading the dirty dishes.

"Uh, no. It wasn't," I say.

"What? Why?"

"It was totally embarrassing!" I drop onto the stool on the opposite side of the counter and let my head fall into my hands.

"Apart from the spilling of the water on—"

"I beg you not to finish that sentence," I say.

"*Apart* from that. . .I think it went wonderfully."

"Mrs. Larrabee thinking Owen and I would make a good couple? And saying it out loud?" I groan.

Mom starts rinsing dishes. I should be helping her, but I feel spent. Maybe the trauma is catching up to me. "I think you're being a little melodramatic." She files a plate into the dishwasher and looks at me. "Unless your feelings for Owen are back. . .?"

I glare at her. "Mom."

"I don't know," she says, a bit sing-songy. "Sexy firefighter pulling you to safety," Mom says with a sigh. "Nobody would blame you if your romantic imagination was working overtime about *that* one."

"Mother." I put my hands on the counter in front of me. "First, ew. You're my mom and he's. . ." I stall. "He's. . .Owen. He showed me his true colors the day he left town."

"Yet you're the one who downplayed being friends tonight at dinner."

"I apologized for that," I say.

"Sounds to me like you have some unresolved feelings you need to sort out," Mom says.

"I'm going to go for a walk." I stand. "Unless you want my help."

Dad walks in with a stack of dishes. "She's got me. You go."

"Thanks," I say. "And thanks for dinner. With the exception of my utter humiliation, it was really nice."

My dad sets the dishes on the counter, then steps into the space behind my mom and wraps his arms around her.

"And. . .that's my cue," I say, walking away before I see anything I can't unsee. My parents have gotten used to living alone, and I definitely don't want to witness any of their newfound frisky freedom.

I pull on a sweatshirt and step out onto the porch. It's cool, and the sunlight is fading, but I need to clear my head. Mostly I need to have a very deep, very pointed conversation with myself.

About. . .things.

And. . .people.

Well, person.

Because my heart is not obeying.

I step off the porch and inhale. The air in the mountains is crisp and cool, and it instantly calms my nerves. The leaves have started to turn, and I'm struck by how the earth beautifully lets go of the things that need to be reborn.

I also briefly think that, if trees were alive like people, how horrified they'd be that humans basically rake their hair into piles and burn it.

Letting go of dead things doesn't seem to be my forte.

I walk out behind the house and stand, looking out through the stretch of yard.

How long has it been since I've visited the pond?

In college, I always took time down there when I visited home. But after Owen left, I stopped going. Soon after, I bought my own house, and my spot became a thing of the past.

Now though, I'm curious. Pulled, almost. I take a step, then another, and begin to make my way across the yard.

As I walk through the familiar stretch of trees, and a deep, peaceful calm washes over me, I realize I missed this too.

There really is something about being home.

My calm is shattered the second I step out of the trees and see Owen, sitting on my dock, just like he did all those years ago.

He must've heard my footfalls, the cracking twigs underneath my feet, because when I spot him, he's already looking at me.

I freeze, like a psychotic deer, one foot kind of up in the air.

He tilts his head slightly, and I slowly put my foot down.

I instantly want to turn and run the other way, but then he stands up, almost like he expects me to take my spot on the opposite side of the dock.

Just like we used to.

"I can go," I say.

He shoves his hands in his pockets, and I see a flash of the high school version of him. Moody. Hurting. Broken. Misunderstood.

A tingle rushes down my spine at the memory, and I'm struck by how easy it is for me to conjure those same feelings I had all those years ago. They're *right there* on the surface, and if I give them even an ounce of attention, they'll grow like dandelions in a meadow.

Which is to say fast. And all over.

"You can stay," he says. "This was always your spot first."

I walk over, slowly, and when I reach the dock, I finally glance up and meet his eyes. "You can stay too."

"You sure?"

I nod.

"You're not going to push me in or anything, are you? Finish off what you started at dinner?"

"Ha ha." I sit down, begging my nerves to stop bouncing around like they're playing a game of table tennis inside my rib cage.

One simple night at this very dock, spent in silence with Owen, led to so many subsequent nights of talking.

Once, when I was in tenth grade, I was worried he was starting to suspect my crush on him, so I pretended to like a boy named Wyatt Mark. Owen teased me because Wyatt had two first names, but then he answered all my questions about how to get Wyatt's attention, which I really didn't care about at all.

His answers gave me a peek into his own brain, but doing all the things he told me to do didn't win me the reward of Owen's affection. By then, he was already interested in Lindsay. Owen had dated a lot, but it had never turned into anything.

Somehow, even I knew it was different with her.

Maybe that's why he was so invested in helping me snag Wyatt.

I made a half-hearted attempt, just because it was fun to

talk it over with Owen, but in the end, Wyatt barely gave me the time of day.

The way Owen tried to console me was sweet, but I quickly learned that being a pitiful reject did nothing to make me more appealing.

Now, sitting here next to him again, I'm filled with that same teenage angst.

I'm just shy of thirty-years-old! How about taking a mature approach to all of this?!

What would *The Hopeful Romantic* tell me to do?

Probably to wake up and see Owen for who he really is. He's not hiding it from me. He's Three-Date Owen. He's the guy who left without a word. He's moody and brooding and hardly ever talks. And not at all what I'm looking for in a relationship.

So, why can't I stop looking for the rest of the story where he's concerned?

The silence isn't as exciting as it was when we were kids. Now, it's just awkward.

"Dinner was. . .uh. . .interesting," Owen finally says.

I cover my face with my hands. "I'm so sorry, I'm clumsy, and I. . ."

"It's no big deal. I changed. It's all good."

I search his face for forgiveness, and it's right there. Like it always has been.

No judgment. No prejudice.

"It was good," he continues. "It was nice of your mom to invite us."

"Oh, she loves to entertain," I muse.

The dreaded silence returns.

Time to be an adult and have an adult conversation. Running away from him isn't going to work. Harvest Hollow isn't that big.

"You tried to talk to me yesterday."

"Yeah," he says, matter-of-factly. "You got weird."

"Me? Weird? Really?" My laugh is nervous.

I'm terrible at this.

I wince. "I'm a weirdo."

He looks at me. "Not with me, you aren't. Or. . .weren't."

Past tense.

I try to ease back into the familiarity of how we were before. "Oh, just with everyone else?" I offer.

He smiles. It's polite, like he's holding back, but it's a nice smile. A *really* nice smile.

"Why didn't you want Mack to know we were friends?" he asks.

I look away. "I guess I wasn't sure if that's what we really were anymore. I mean, you left. Without saying goodbye."

"Is that what you're upset about?"

"I'm not upset." I straighten. Apparently, that's what I do when I'm lying.

"Yes, you are."

"No, I'm not."

"You're standoffish with me, even when no one else is around."

I fold my hands in my lap and stare at them like I've never seen them before.

"Emmy. . ."

"Yeah, okay, I guess I am. A little." I glance at him, but quickly look away.

He pulls one leg up and lets his arm rest on it. "Why?"

The word hangs there, and the silence forces me to think about that day. I tried so many times to erase it from my memory but failed every time.

"You just. . .left," I say quietly. "After everything I said, you just left."

He isn't watching me now. I feel the second he looks away.

"Yeah, you. . .said a lot. That day."

I glance sideways at him. "Yeah. I did."

"I left, and you know why."

I stare out across the pond. It's still and quiet, and the sun is setting behind the trees. Soon it'll be dark.

He starts to say something and stops. It's as if he's trying to find the right words, but I know him.

He doesn't like talking about this stuff.

He says plainly, "That was the worst day of my life."

I know. I was there. I saw it all happen.

"And I hate to say it," he continues, "but you didn't help things."

"I got you out of there!" I say defensively, turning to him. "Away from everyone. Wasn't that what you wanted?"

"Yeah, of course," he says. "But in that moment. . .it wasn't about you. *Couldn't* be about you. I was trying to get my bearings, and you just. . ."

". . .told you how I felt."

He nods solemnly. "Yeah."

"And you're mad at me for that?"

"No. Not mad," he says. "But your timing really sucked."

"I didn't mean to say it then," I say. "It just. . .came out."

"Yeah, and it made things worse."

My stomach drops. "Worse?"

He turns his whole body to face me. "I didn't know how to process what had happened, let alone what you were saying." His voice is calm and kind. "You were important to me—*are* important to me—and I didn't want to hurt you. I already totally screwed up one relationship. How was I going to add another one less than an hour later?"

Ouch. Maybe adult conversations are overrated. He continues, and I notice his fists clenching slightly as he's talking about it. "I just needed to leave. You know how things are here. Everyone was going to be talking about the loser who was left at the altar," his voice starts to rise, "and I didn't want to stick around for it."

He's still emotional about it. It still hurts.

Well duh, Emmy, wounds like that never really heal.

I want to tell him he's right. I want to tell him I meant every word I said to him that day. I want to say a lot of things, but I can't. It's too hard.

Especially because I see his point.

My timing *was* terrible.

Chapter Fifteen

Emmy

Eight Years Ago

I almost didn't show up.

I'd just graduated college, and I could've just as easily sent a card. In the end, Mack persuaded me, and I suppose a part of me was, I don't know, curious. I'd been there when Owen and Lindsay started dating—maybe seeing them get married would give me the closure I needed.

It's this kind of logic that often gets me in trouble.

But it was time for me to let go of the ridiculous fantasy of Owen Larrabee.

I arrived at the church and found him out back, in the gazebo, and I won't lie. A part of me wanted to hear he's having second thoughts.

Like in *Old, New, Borrowed, You*, the cleverly penned rom-com by Kathleen Hayden—four weddings, four stories, and all of them realize that they're marrying the wrong person on the same day in four different cities.

Harvest Hollow could be one of those places, right?

While the rest of the guests filtered into the church, I made my way out back. When I reached the gazebo, he was leaning over the railing, staring out at the mountains, rising slightly above everything else in the near horizon. My heart fluttered at the sight of him in his tux, looking more handsome than anyone had a right to look. I knew from Mack that he was working on becoming a firefighter, and though we didn't visit the pond as much anymore, I'd found him there once or twice over the last few years.

Each time, I left with a renewed crush.

He made it darn near impossible for me to seriously date anyone else. The ridiculous, imaginary pedestal I'd put him on made everyone else pale in comparison.

In the back of my mind, I always knew that if Owen's feelings for me ever changed, I'd come running. Maybe that's why my relationships were always short-lived. I'd had two different boyfriends in college, but neither captured my affection—or listened—the way Owen did.

"Wow, you clean up nice," I said as I reached him.

He turned, and his face lit in a bright smile. "Emmy." He stood upright and held his arms out to me. I stepped into them, and he hugged me, giving me three long seconds to pretend the circumstances are different.

I stepped away, but he kept his hands on my arms. "Look at you, all grown up." He smiled.

"Look at you, about to be married."

"Right?" A pause. "*Married.*"

Weird. He sounded. . .I don't know. . .sad? Resigned?

I read into it.

He shrugged and dropped his hands to his sides. "It's good, you know? Feels like the right move."

"I'm happy for you, Owen," I said, and I meant it.

"Thanks."

I didn't ask him questions about Lindsay, because I didn't want to hear how in love with her he was, which made me a terrible friend. It didn't matter anyway, because his friend Jace called him inside. The ceremony was about to start.

"I'll see you in there?" he asked.

I nodded.

He looked happy. I couldn't deny it, and I didn't begrudge him a full, joy-filled life. I was just surprised that Lindsay was "the one."

I honestly thought they were a terrible mismatch.

Mack thought so, too. We were both shocked to learn that Owen, the guy who never took anything seriously, was *actually* getting married.

I guess we all grow up sometime.

Owen always did have an intense, serious, loyal way of loving people, even to a fault. I shouldn't be surprised he wants to be married and love the same person forever.

I didn't know everything would completely change ten minutes later.

Owen was standing at the front of the church, waiting for his bride to be, when I, along with everyone else, saw his best man hurry down the aisle and whisper something in his ear.

I knew in that moment I'd never forget the look on his face.

Eleven minutes later, the pastor stepped forward and announced that there's been a complication, and things would have to unfortunately be postponed.

Because five minutes before that. . .Lindsay left.

She left.

She left Owen standing there, in front of all their friends and family, looking lost and embarrassed and hurt.

The chatter started almost immediately. Owen's parents stood abruptly, looking around, his dad storming off in one direction, and his mom coming up to his side.

I watched as misery washed over him.

No book I've read, no novel I've lived in, could ever describe the feeling of actually watching it happen.

To someone you care about.

He met my eyes, his on fire with hurt, jaw steeling against the rage of emotions washing up, and I stood, motioning with my head in the direction of the exit. His nod was so slight, I almost missed it, but he slipped out the side door and met me in the parking lot. Without a word, he got in my car, and I drove off, leaving the church in the rearview mirror.

I sped down the highway in the direction of the only place I could think to go.

The dock.

We got out of the car, made our way there, and I sat. Owen paced. He pressed both heels of his hands to his eyes, trembling with hurt.

I waited.

After a long few moments, he shook his head and spoke. "I should've known this would happen."

"What? Why?" I asked.

He pushed his hand through his hair, laughing ruefully. "We had a fight. Last night. About my job." He moved his hands excitedly, emphasizing his words. "She honestly thought being a firefighter was like, a hobby or something." He turned toward the water at the end of the dock and shouted to no one, "It's not a hobby, Lindsay!"

I didn't know what to say, so I just let him get things out.

"And what does she do? She sets up an interview at her dad's company. In an *office*. An office!" He faced me. "Like someone like me could ever work in an office."

I frowned, choosing words carefully. "Why isn't she okay with you being a firefighter? It's one of the bravest jobs you could have."

He spun and walked down the dock. "Right?" A pause. "Who knows why she's not okay with it. Because she's Lindsay." He said her name like it had air quotes around it. "And honestly, this isn't the first time. We've been having issues. Arguing a lot. Disagreeing on everything." He slumped to a sitting position, and I had a thought that I didn't want him to ruin his tux.

He loosened the bowtie, then put his head in his hands. "Maybe the signs were there all along."

"Owen, she's an idiot."

He half-laughed, and I wondered if he was trying to keep from crying. I moved toward him and took his hands. In all the years we'd been coming here, I'd never touched him before, but it felt like the right thing to do.

He needed to know this wasn't his fault.

"She is," I said. "She doesn't deserve you."

He didn't let go of my hands.

"Yeah, well, I don't think that's how her dad sees it."

"Then he doesn't know you either."

He let out a breath. "Emmy, you know I'm a first-class screw-up, right?"

I squeezed his hands. "No. You aren't. Yeah, you've made some mistakes, but haven't we all?"

"You haven't."

"Yeah," I said. "I have. They're just. . .different kinds of mistakes."

"Well, I appreciate it, but I think you're being nice."

"No," I said, suddenly feeling like it was my duty to make him feel better, to get him to see that if Lindsay didn't realize what she had then she didn't deserve him. "I'm not. I'm being honest. You're the kindest, most thoughtful person I know. The way you've helped me over the years—"

"Uh, switch that around, I think you were the one who helped me."

"I helped you pass classes. You helped me in other ways. We're even." I looked up at him. There was hurt in his eyes, and I wanted to go hunt Lindsay down and tell her she was the worst person in the world for making him feel like this.

And then drive over her with my car.

Owen was a lot of things, but when it came to his relationship with her, he'd only ever been all in. He was loyal and dedicated and completely smitten.

One would think that would've quelled my crush on him, but it didn't.

And nothing was quelling my runaway mouth.

"Owen, how can she not see what I see?" The words were out before I could stop them. "I would kill to have you look at me the way you look at her. The way you take care of her and put her first. You're so thoughtful and attentive and kind. I've seen it for years—everything you have to offer another person. And she's just throwing it away, like she has no idea what she has."

His forehead pulled.

Without thinking, I spoke what I'd been feeling for years now.

"I'm in love with you."

He blinked, went to speak then stopped.

I didn't. I ripped the bag wide open, and the cat was free to roam.

"I am. I have been for years. I love being around you. I love our conversations. I love spending time with you, and when I don't see you, I miss you. A lot. You're more than a friend to me, and I know, it doesn't make sense, and I haven't said anything because, you know, I'm me and you're you and there really wasn't a good time to talk about it, and then there was Lindsay and—"

The only reason I stopped talking was that I'd run out of breath.

I should've turned and run the other way. My cheeks should've been on fire at this admission. I should've been horrified and embarrassed and ready to hide. But I wasn't.

Instead, I felt free. Finally—finally—Owen knew.

"Emmy. . .what?" He stood, and then took a step back, hand up, palm facing me. "Why are you telling me this now? Why now?"

I stood too, emboldened. "Because I want you to know that Lindsay's wrong."

"But—" He spun around, looking lost. "I—"

"Owen." I summoned all the courage I'd lacked all these years and said it again. "I love you."

He turned back to me, and for the second time that day, I'dl never forget the look on his face.

It looked scared.

"I gotta go."

I blinked. "You. . .what?"

Instantly, it hit me. I'd ruined everything.

What have I done?

I panicked. "Owen, I'm sorry, I didn't mean to blurt that out like that. . ."

He didn't say anything else. He just held up his hand to say *stop,* shook his head and walked away.

He left.

Panic washed over me. *What have I done?*

My dock. His altar.

I turned and faced the water. Alone.

I'm such a fool.

I stood, and as the tears fell, I wished I could take it all back.

Emmy

Present Day

But I can't.

I can't change what I said or when I said it. And now, eight years later, even with the understanding that I screwed up that day, instead of saying I'm sorry, I stupidly dig in my heels and choose stubbornness and pride over humility.

"You should've at least said goodbye," I say. Because that's also true, right?

But even as I say it, I know I shouldn't. That day wasn't about me, so why do I keep wallowing in it?

"Are we going to argue now? About which one of us was more wrong?"

"No," I say. "It doesn't matter anymore. Look, we haven't spoken in eight years. Your own sister didn't even know we were friends."

"Yeah, why is that?" he asks.

"Because you never told her," I say.

"Neither did you."

I pause.

"Fair point," I concede, turning away. "But there was no way I was going to tell anyone, especially her. What would that have done to you, telling everyone that you were friends with one of the biggest nerds in the school?"

He laughs.

"You know that was never how I saw you, right?"

I face him, which is a mistake, because the way he's looking at me now—that trademark intensity behind his eyes that I used to see in my dreams—instantly breaks down any defenses I was marshaling.

He leans in a bit closer, and I think how nice he looks with facial hair.

"*Never.*"

I angle slightly back. "It's true. I was a nerd. Correction," I hold up a pointer finger. "I *am* a nerd. And proud of it. I think it's one of my best qualities."

"Well, good," he says. "I'm glad you're happy with who you are. You should be. But I still didn't see you that way."

It's gone this far, I might as well speak aloud the question pinballing around in my head. "Then. . .how did you see me? Like another little sister?"

He pauses, looking at me, almost as though he's trying to work things out in his head.

"Emmy. We were. . .friends. I thought of you as a friend. A good one. Maybe the best one."

That hits my heart. His best friend.

But not more than that.

"My only friend, at times. Is that bad?"

"I should get back before it gets dark." I stand and start down the dock because somehow my cheeks are flaming again, and my humiliation has only gotten worse. I *am* proud of being a "nerd," but it does sting sometimes knowing it cements my place in people's lives.

"Emmy," he says.

I stop and look at him.

"Are we still?"

"Still what?"

He takes a step closer. "Friends."

He looks so earnest when he says it, I almost think he missed talking to me as much as I missed talking to him, though likely for entirely different reasons.

"Yeah," I say. "Of course."

He breathes out, almost like a sigh of relief.

Was he worried I wouldn't be his friend anymore?

"And you'll stop being a weirdo?"

I press my lips together. "No promises."

He smirks, that full smile always just out of reach. "For what it's worth, I am sorry I left that day. Without saying anything."

I go still. I believe him. "And I'm sorry I told you—" I can't even say it. It's so embarrassing. "You know."

"Yeah, I know." He nods. "Can I walk you home?"

I scrunch up my face at him. "Friends again, huh?"

He shrugs and doesn't say anything.

Classic Owen.

Friends.

Well.

It's a start.

Chapter Sixteen

Owen

"Captain wants to see you."

Jace is at the door of the firehouse when I arrive.

"Again?" I frown. "Why?"

"Probably wants to pin a medal on you or something." Jace smirks. "You're making the rest of us look bad."

I drop my bag off in my room, then head into the captain's office. I find him sitting at his desk, wearing reading glasses and working on the computer.

He looks up and takes off the glasses. "Larrabee."

"Sir."

"Sit."

I do as I'm told.

"Did you check on the girl?"

"Emmy?" I prop my leg on my other leg at the ankle. "Yes."

"And?"

I doubt he wants to know about our little chat at the pond, but it's the first thing that comes to mind. Emmy caught me off-guard last night.

There's something refreshing about a woman who likes herself.

I'm guessing that's not what the captain is asking.

"She's good, I think."

"I stopped by the house yesterday," he says. "Once her insurance comes through, which should be pretty quick, she can get the restoration process started. It could've been a lot worse."

I nod, trying not to picture it worse. It's odd, but it hurts way more than it should, thinking about something happening to Emmy.

"Listen, there are a few traditions we have here that I want to make sure you know about."

I frown because the captain sounds serious, and traditions don't seem like serious business. "Okay."

"One of them is the annual fireman's calendar."

I stare in disbelief.

"That can't be a thing."

"Unfortunately, it is," he says. "You'd think it would've gone out of style, but it's still a big moneymaker for the department."

I can see where this is going, and I don't want any part of it.

"It's all done in good taste," he says, preempting my refusal.

"So, what, they take pictures with our shirts off or something?"

"No," he says, laughing. "Have you seen Rigsby's midsection? I think the only letters of the alphabet that guy knows are K, F, and C."

I stifle a laugh. It's true.

"No, son, no half-naked firemen on my watch." A pause. "They want to take your picture with the girl."

I stare in disbelief for a second time

"You're kidding."

"I'm not."

"Captain, all due respect, but no."

He chuckles and leans back in his chair. "I thought you might say that, so we sent Clemons over to talk to her about it."

Clemons, as in, the only female firefighter in Harvest Hollow.

Also, one of the best.

"*I* don't want to be in this calendar," I stew. "Even if Emmy agrees."

"Sorry, but there's no way around it," he says. "It's for the good of the whole department."

I lean back in my chair. "There have to be rules against this."

"Nobody's trying to turn you into Magic Mike over here," he says. "And it was my wife's idea, so I don't really have a choice."

I frown. "Your wife is in on this?"

"She heads up the committee that handles fundraising and community involvement—and the calendar," he says. "She thinks the whole town will get behind a spread with a local business owner and her real-life hero. I think they're going for romance or some nonsense. Probably put you both on the cover."

I put my head in my hands and groan.

"It's what sells. Whattaya gonna do?" He shrugs.

"If you think I'm going to. . .ride a horse, or stand in some stupid pose or whatever, you've got another thing coming."

"I'll pass that along to Liz," he says, with a smirk. "But you should know she almost never listens to a thing I say when it comes to the calendar."

I shake my head. I'm starting to regret moving back here.

Donoho chuckles. "There's something else I've been

thinking about." His face turns serious again. "You know we could use a new lieutenant."

"Nah," I say. "I tried that once. Didn't go my way."

He eyes me. "I read the file."

"Then you know I'm not lieutenant material."

"Says who?"

"Everyone in Macon?" I say this harshly—harsher than I want.

He sits back in his chair, and I feel like he's sizing me up.

"I hear things," he says. "Including things about your former captain."

I frown. "Oh?"

"Baker? Yeah." He shakes his head. "Guy's a class-A jerk. Probably deserved the punch you threw."

He. . .what? He's on my side?

"Punches," I say.

He folds his arms. "Even better."

"That's not how the chief saw it." I have no interest in reliving this.

As if last night's rehashing of the humiliation of being left at the altar wasn't enough.

"Talk me through it," he says. "Your side."

I sigh.

"Humor me. It's a slow morning."

"You have my file," I say.

He nods.

"So, you know—"

"I know about the learning difficulties, yes." He studies me.

I pause. I don't like talking about this stuff.

I give my head a slight shake. "Baker knew about it too, apparently."

"And. . .?"

I grit my teeth, and I can feel my muscles tense.

"I overheard him talking about another guy at the station. Some kid, just a probie, who'd asked for accommodations. He was diabetic and needed a service animal."

Donoho nods, seemingly getting it.

"Well, our station had a 'no pet' policy. Baker said the guy was a snowflake, that he should just keep a candy bar in his pocket."

Donoho snuffs. "Not surprised."

"He then said he was going to make things purposely difficult for him." I stand because I'm getting angry all over again. "Harder. On *purpose*. Just because this kid needed some extra help. He said he didn't want 'lazy firefighters.' Said he was going to have the other guys do the same." I look away. "What kind of stupid—"

He cuts me off. "And because of that, you didn't ask for the accommodations you needed."

My eyes flick to his, resigned. "Nope."

"And you failed."

I pause and sit. "Yep."

I mentally kick myself, the way I do every time I think about this whole stupid situation.

"I. . .needed them. I can't read so well. I needed time taking tests. Changes in the way I got the study materials. Hearing it, not reading it, things like that. So. . ."

I hold up both hands in a *here's what I did* pose.

Donoho sits forward in his chair. "You told him you needed accommodations."

"Yep."

"And that didn't go so well."

I laugh ruefully. "Nope."

Another pause.

"He asked me if I think there should be a special ed wing

on the station house. I told him it's not any different than a wheelchair ramp for a person with a physical disability."

I ball up my fists. It's taken me years of grappling with this to accept it, and Baker set me back—way back—tapping in to all the old garbage I'd had to sort through after my diagnosis.

"Then he said he didn't want a—" I look away at the memory. It wasn't the first time someone had used the R-word around me. Or to describe me. And I don't even have to say it for Donoho to get it. I see the knowing in his eyes. ". . .to be lieutenant."

Donoho's jaw drops a bit. "He said. . .*what*?"

I grit my teeth and look away.

"He didn't say much after that. And I never did re-take the test."

I hate talking about it. I hate that I lost my temper, and I hate that there are idiots in this world who think like Baker.

But I don't hate feeling his teeth through his cheek slam into my fist.

"Man. I knew Baker was old school, but. . ." the captain says. "I didn't know he was like *that*."

"Yeah, well, it's more common than you think," I say, thinking of all the ways I've been judged in my life.

"Well, you won't get that kind of treatment here."

I look up.

"I've got a dyslexic kid," he says. "So, I get it. More than most."

"You do?"

The captain nods. "And as far as I'm concerned, Baker got what he deserved. Plus, I'm more than willing to let you test with the accommodations you should've had in the first place."

At that, I pull my shoulders back and sit up a little straighter.

I gave up any delusions of a promotion because I assumed that mark on my record would take me out of the running.

"You. . .you'd do that?" I ask.

"Yep. I think you'd be a fool not to try," he says. "And I think we could use someone like you in a leadership position. No reason you can't work your way all the way up, Larrabee. You've been at this long enough, and the guys respect you already. Especially after last week." He leans forward and folds his hands on his desk. "You'll think about it then?"

I nod. "I'll think about it."

"Good." He stands.

I stand. "Thanks, Captain."

He nods, and I walk out into the hallway, feeling like someone just gave me back my life. The first person I want to tell is Emmy.

I mean, we're friends now. . .again. . .right?

I realize I'd like to have Emmy back in my life.

I walk down the hall and into the common area where Rigsby's cooking, Jace is setting out plates and silverware, and a few of the other guys are gathered at the table around a small Bluetooth speaker.

I start to say something, but all three of the guys at the table shush me before I get a word out.

I frown and look at Jace, who shakes his head. "They're obsessed."

"With what?" I say, as the sound of a woman's voice fills the space.

"Welcome to *The Hopeful Romantic*, where we analyze, digest and discuss all things romance," the older woman's voice says.

I stand there, dumbfounded.

"Are they serious?"

"As a heart attack," Jace says.

"I can't wait to hear what she says about this one," one of the guys says.

"Blister, shut up, will you?"

I lean over to Rigsby.

"Blister?"

He smiles, nodding in their direction. "It's Pearson's nickname. 'Blister.' Because he only shows up when the work's all done."

Ah. Clever.

"Blister is convinced this lady on this podcast saved his marriage," Rigsby says. "They listen so they can try to figure out what women really want."

Levi, who is leaning against the counter, pipes up. "I already know what women want." He wags his eyebrows in a way that makes it clear he absolutely does not know what women want.

"It's not rocket science," I say.

"Says the guy who hasn't had a serious relationship in eight years," Jace says.

Fair point. I grab a banana and walk over to the table as the woman finishes a letter from some poor lady in Hoboken.

"This is for real?" I ask. "You're really all into this?"

A collective and forceful "Shhh!"

I hold up my hands in apology, then peel the banana. I'm sure I can find better things to do around—but then, something stops me. The voice coming through the speaker—it's familiar, somehow.

I walk back toward the table, and I find myself wondering who could possibly hold the guys' attention like this.

"Who's this woman?" I ask.

"Nobody knows," Pearson says. "She's anonymous."

"But she gives really good advice," Turner says.

"What kind of advice?" I ask.

"Relationship advice," Pearson says.

I listen as this Hopeful Romantic responds to the letter she just read.

"We all want to be swept off our feet. It's why romance novels, rom-coms, all of them, are so popular. Is it unrealistic? Maybe. But that doesn't necessarily mean we can't hope for it. We want the romantic hero to walk out of our dreams and straight into our lives. And I for one, don't think we should apologize for wanting that. We yearn for the guy who shows up with chicken soup to take care of us when we're sick, like Tom Hanks in *You've Got Mail*. We want our guy to write us love letters and kiss us in the rain or ask us to slow dance in the middle of the street. That's what I'm holding out for, and I won't apologize for it."

"Is she serious?" I scoff.

"Shhhh!"

She goes on with a whole list of things her perfect man will do. Stargazing in the back of a pick-up truck? Playing a song underneath her window? A grand gesture? I'm starting to understand why this woman is still single. Her perfect man doesn't exist.

I glance over at the others. Turner is actually taking notes.

"Are you guys for real?"

"Listen. I know it sounds crazy. But this stuff *works*, Larrabee," Pearson says. "It saved my marriage."

"Come on," I prod. "There are more important things in a relationship than making out in the rain."

"Have you ever made out in the rain?" Jace pointedly asks.

I get defensive. "Well, no, but. . ."

"Don't knock it until you try it."

He crosses his arms over his chest and looks at me. "She could probably help you get out of your little funk."

"I'm not in a funk."

"Have you dated anyone seriously since Lindsay?"

"Who's Lindsay?" Pearson asks.

"*Nobody*." I shoot Jace a look. "And no, I haven't. By choice. Women are nothing but trouble."

"You're crazy," Levi says. "I love women!"

There's a collective "we know" on a groan.

"Oh!" Pearson picks up his phone and starts scrolling around. "You should listen to Episode 115. Lonely in Larkspur."

Turner says, "Ooh, yeah, that's a good one."

"You have them memorized?" What is wrong with these guys?

"It'll help. I swear," Jace sounds convinced.

I frown. "I didn't ask for help. And I'm not lonely."

Pearson looks up and stops scrolling. "Well, you will be with that attitude."

I shake my head, stand, and head out of the room. "You guys should get back to work."

My phone buzzes, and there, in the firehouse group chat, is a link to Episode 115.

I'm not going to listen to that.

Chapter Seventeen

Owen

Okay, so, maybe I listened to a few.

Or ten.

I spend the better part of my shift listening to that idiotic podcast.

It's called *The Hopeful Romantic*, and after subjecting myself to multiple episodes, I'm more convinced than ever that whoever this woman is, she's never going to find what she's looking for.

After Episode 115, I go back to the beginning, Episode 1, and I'm in awe of how many people are actually willing to send in relationship questions to a perfect stranger who never seems to tell her listeners what her credentials are.

Still, there is something about it. Something addictive. Something I can't quite pinpoint.

So, I listen.

While I'm washing the trucks. While I'm out for my morning run. While I'm lifting weights. Throughout my entire shift, I've got this woman chattering on through my AirPods about what women really want, about how to be a good partner, about holding out for a certain kind of guy—all based on the supposed wisdom of classic (and modern) romance novels.

And, after an assumption and a quick search on Amazon, I'm not surprised to find out that 95% of romance novels are written by women.

Women writing about ideal men for women without asking the men.

Shocker that they're getting it all wrong.

She—the woman on the podcast—and the rest of them are describing a guy that I'm pretty sure doesn't exist.

By Wednesday evening, when my shift ends, I've gotten through almost three-fourths of the total episode list.

I'm packing up my bag when Jace pops his head in. "Bunch of us are going to DeLucca's to get a drink. You in?"

"Sure, I'll go." I could use a distraction. Between the podcast and the planning for this fireman's calendar, I need a good, old-fashioned night out with the guys.

But the second we arrive, I have second thoughts.

Because there, sitting at the bar, is Lindsay.

Fantastic.

"What's she doing here?" Jace asks.

"No clue." We sit down at the other end of the bar, and Lindsay and her friend look up. I glance at her, and she waves at me.

"Who's that?" Levi asks.

"Nobody," I say.

"His ex," Jace says at the same time.

"Dang, Larrabee. A hot sister, a hot damsel in distress, and now a hot ex. Tell us your secrets." Levi hasn't stopped staring at Lindsay since he sat down.

I have a feeling Levi would hit on a potted plant if it had blond hair and a pulse.

We're there for maybe three minutes when another woman

walks over. A short, brunette with a high ponytail. "You're that guy." She's looking at me, angled sideways at the bar so her front is facing my left side.

I glance at her. "I am?"

"Yeah," she bites her bottom lip. "The one who saved that girl." Her voice is a bit high-pitched and forward.

Not something I could listen to on a regular basis.

"Oh, right," I say. "Yeah, you got me."

"I don't. . .*yet*," she says.

I turn to her. "Uh, what?"

"I saw you on TV," she says, her eyes falling below mine. "It was so brave."

I shift uncomfortably.

She narrows her eyes and reaches across me close enough where her body brushes up against my arm. She picks up a napkin, writes her phone number on it, and slides it to me.

I look at the napkin and give her a smile.

There's a bit I can't read under the phone number.

"What does this say?"

She leans in close and whispers, "It says '*anytime*.'"

Then, she walks away, throwing a last look over her shoulder.

The guys all react like a frat house during pledge night.

The woman is cute, I guess. And I know I'm supposed to take her up on her not-so-subtle offer. Not that many months ago, I probably would've.

But that's not who I want to be. "Three-Date Owen" is getting old.

I'm not sure what's changed.

"This is what it's like for you, isn't it?" Levi shakes his head and takes a drink of the beer the bartender brought over. "Unreal."

I chuckle to myself, but my smile is short-lived because Lindsay is coming my way.

Levi rolls his eyes. "I've got no shot if I stay here with you. I'll be over there." He walks off, leaving me sitting with Jace and wishing I could get up and leave.

"Didn't think I'd see you out tonight," Lindsay says. She looks at Jace. "Hey, Jace. Long time."

He doesn't even look at her as he gets up and follows Levi. I'd feel bad for her if his disdain wasn't warranted. She's not going to get any love from my friends or my family.

Or me.

Still, I don't want to fight with her. Honestly, she did me a favor. We really were a wrong fit. For some reason, I was too blind to see it. She sits down next to me, and my body tenses.

I hate that I'm not completely over it yet.

She crosses her legs and faces me, her glass of white wine in her hand on the bar. "You recovered from all the excitement?"

"What are you doing here?" I ask, a little harsher than I mean to.

"Easy, tiger. I come in peace."

A Trojan horse, more like.

"I thought I'd stick around for a few days," she says. "I have some time off, and I've just been hanging out with my family."

I don't respond.

"Owen. Come on. I don't want things to be, you know, weird between us."

I scoff, and stare straight ahead.

"It was a long time ago." She puts her hand on my arm.

I look at her hand, look at her, and she pulls it away.

"So that's how it is, huh?" she asks.

I shrug.

She flips her hair off her shoulders. "I've moved on. You've moved on. Seems like you've got a great life now."

I half nod. "Yep."

There's a moment of silence, and I almost stand and make my way to the door. I don't need Lindsay speculating on my life.

"Are you. . .dating anyone?"

I close my eyes and shake my head.

"What? I can't have a conversation with. . ."

I turn to her, head cocked.

"Are we really going to do this?"

"It's a perfectly normal question," she says.

"Not from you it's not."

Another lull.

"I'm actually surprised you and Emmy aren't together yet." She takes a drink.

That strikes me as odd.

"Emmy?" I frown. "Why would you think. . .?"

"Come on, Owen," she says. "Her crush on you? For like, years? You can't tell me it was one-sided."

I suddenly get defensive of Emmy.

"What in the world are you talking about?"

She scoffs. "It was pretty obvious."

"It was absolutely one-sided," I say, sharply. "I didn't even know about it until after you took off."

She raises a brow. "If that's true, then you were in some serious denial. She knew you better than anyone." She turns away and takes a drink. "I would've killed to have you talk to me the way you talked to her."

"You've got to be kidding me," I say. "Emmy and I were just friends."

She smiles. "I really think you believed that. You might even *still* believe it."

I feel like someone is telling me that this whole time I've had it wrong, and you go on red and stop on green.

"I think you *wanted* to be in love with me. But you weren't. Not really. We had great *physical* chemistry—"

I bristle at that comment, and it stirs something in me that is both unwanted and familiar.

"—but Emmy was the one who had your heart."

I turn toward her, realization coming over me. "Wait. Is that why you—"

"No." She flicks her hand in the air. "I mean, that wasn't the *only* reason. We just. . . wanted different things."

I turn back and face forward again, not looking at her. "Yeah." A pause. "You wanted me to work for your dad."

I feel her wince at my side. "Sorry about that."

I take a drink. "That never would've worked."

"I know that *now*," she says, amused. "I hadn't figured out how to have my own opinion yet, about a lot of stuff. And my mother can be very. . ."

"Controlling?" I blurt.

She smiles. "Yeah. That."

I go still. Are we actually having a conversation? Me and Lindsay, the woman I spent years loving and even more years loathing?

"I saw you that day, you know. In the gazebo," she says, turning her glass around in her hand. "With her."

I frown for a second and then realize she's talking about Emmy.

"At the wedding?"

She nods. "I was standing in the church, watching you from the window, and the look on your face when you saw her, the way you hugged her, the way you spoke to her—that was how I wanted you to look at me." She faces me. "But you never did."

"Lindsay, I never had feelings for Emmy," I say. "Ever."

But even as I say it, I wonder if it's true.

Was it possible that a part of me connected with Emmy in a way that I should've connected to my actual fiancée?

Emmy was so easy to talk to, but that's what made us great friends.

But Lindsay was always the one I wanted.

Right?

She reaches over and squeezes my arm.

"I'm sorry for leaving the way I did," she says. "I panicked, and I ran. It was wrong of me."

My gaze falls to her hand on my arm, and I feel. . .nothing. No attraction. No spark.

Not even anger.

Surprising.

Maybe I don't want to waste any more of my time hating Lindsay or anyone else.

"You forgive me?"

I shrug. "Sure. Yeah. Water under the bridge."

"Good." She smiles and pulls her hand away. "And who knows, maybe we can figure out how to be, you know, friends."

That might be pushing it, but I don't say so.

I'm processing all of this, trying to formulate some sort of response when I turn and catch a glimpse of Emmy just inside the door. She looks at me, then at Lindsay, and then away.

I don't have time to sort through her reaction, though, because she's with my sister, and Mack is like a bull just let out of its pen.

And Lindsay just happens to be wearing red.

Chapter Eighteen

Emmy

Thirty Minutes Ago

"I cannot believe you agreed to this."

Yeah, I'm having second thoughts too, I think to myself.

Mack is sitting at the Book Smart coffee counter with me after hours, snickering to herself about my misfortune.

On Monday, a female firefighter who introduced herself only by her last name, Clemons, gave me the sales pitch of the century. She told me I needed to do my civic duty and participate in this year's firefighter calendar—and made a really good point about being the only woman in a male-dominated profession.

I tried to tell her that what happened to me isn't the same as what she does on a daily basis—it's not like she was the one who pulled me out of my house and saved my life, it was a guy saving a girl.

She let me know that any advantage, any goodwill, any positive exposure for her profession was needed, and it certainly couldn't come from her. She said that my being pulled out of my burning house made me something of a local celebrity, and when I tried to point out there are a million other things I'd rather be praised for, she said, "But this will help us get more money. Better equipment, better facilities, that means I can do my job better."

Fair point.

"I didn't *exactly* agree to it," I say. "I feel like I was voluntold."

She shakes her head. "This is how things get done around here. She's smart."

"She was very convincing," I say.

Mack laughs, then her face turns serious. "Wait, this isn't going to be like a photo of shirtless Owen, just suspenders and fireman's pants, leaf-blower aimed at him off camera, carrying you to safety, is it?"

A flash of the cover of *Roses and Flame*, from the *Hot in Memphis* series by an author named Penelope Cryden, enters my mind. I can still remember the back cover copy, and it was a gem.

"Kevin Parker is a muscular, good looking, and fun loving firefighter from Memphis. His life is going nowhere until he meets Katherine Bishop, an uptight woman with a passion for climate change.

"When a rival tries to lie about Kevin, Katherine springs to the rescue. Kevin begins to notice that Katherine is actually rather soft at heart.

"But the pressures of Katherine's job as an airline pilot leave her blind to Kevin's affections and Kevin takes up recycling to try to get Katherine to notice him.

"Finally, when a misguided nurse, Marci Thornhill, threatens to come between them, Katherine has to act fast. But will they ever find the fiery love that they deserve?"

I actually think it was written by plugging things into a random romance plot generator. But the cover—*that* was pushing the envelope, even for contemporary open-door romance.

To Mack's question, I reply, "Good grief, I hope not."

Although. . .

"Ooh, what about making you look like a 1950's pinup girl? Because I actually think you could rock a red lip."

"You aren't very sympathetic," I say.

"Sorry," she says. "I do feel sorry that you keep getting thrown together with my brother. I wonder if his flavor of the month will get jealous by all this attention on you two."

I wipe down the espresso machine and will my voice to remain calm. "Oh? Is he dating someone?"

"Not yet, but I'm sure he will be," she says.

"Is he really like that?" I turn and face her.

She shrugs. "Lindsay did a number on him. I don't think he'll ever give the real thing a chance at this point."

My heart drops a little lower than it should at that. It's not like I had some grand delusion that Owen and I were headed anywhere, not even after our conversation at the pond. We even broached the subject of my confession of true feelings for him and. . .nothing.

Owen made it clear that we were friends. We *are* friends, and that's all we'll ever be. I might be a hopeless romantic, but I can read between the lines.

"Let's go get dinner," Mack says, standing. "I'm in the mood for Italian."

"You want to go out on a Wednesday night?"

"What do you have against Wednesdays?"

"Nothing. I think Wednesdays get a bad rap. I mean, they're not Mondays, but you still have to go all the way through a Wednesday just to wake up to a Thursday."

She chuckles. "You're so weird."

I toss the towel on the back counter. "Plus, I just started rewatching the BBC's *Pride and Prejudice*."

"Again? Good grief! Emmy, you know how it ends."

I pump my eyebrows. "It ends swoony."

"Oh, come on," Mack says. "You've seen it a million times, plus you can watch it whenever. It's just dinner. And I'll have you home at a respectable hour."

"Okay, okay. DeLucca's it is." I grin at her. "Can we get family portions, eat until we have to unbutton our pants, and take the leftovers home?"

She pinches her thumbs and fingers together, Italian-style, and shakes them at me. "Is there any other way?"

DeLucca's is an Italian restaurant and bar, the kind of local hole-in-the-wall that locals frequent and tourists avoid. Both Mack's family and my own have a long-standing tradition of eating there at least once a week.

Which is why I shouldn't be surprised when I walk in and see Owen sitting at the bar.

Some of the other firefighters are at the other end of the counter, but there, beside him, is Lindsay. She's wearing a tight pencil skirt and a red button-down (she missed the top three buttons). Her dark hair falls loose past her shoulders. She's sitting close to Owen, and as she shifts, she tosses her shiny hair behind her shoulder, like she's auditioning for a Pantene commercial.

Heck, I'd cast her. She's beautiful.

Owen's free hand is wrapped around a bottle of beer, and when he glances our way, his expression changes.

I look away.

My insides twist at the scene, but when Mack stops short and grabs my arm, I realize my feelings mean nothing in this scenario. She's going to freak out.

"Are you kidding me?" Mack takes off in the direction of the bar, and I jump to try and follow.

"Mack, it's fine, let's just—"

Shoot, shoot, shoot!

Owen spots his sister, gunning for them, and he stands up in front of Lindsay.

How chivalrous.

I look away again.

"*What* in the *world* do you think you're doing?!"

Mack has always been a hothead. Me? I avoid conflict like I avoid running.

I've gotten better about standing up for myself, but it still doesn't come naturally to me. Not like it does to her.

"Mack—"

"Hi, Mackenzie." Lindsay's tone is so chipper, even I want to smack her.

"No, sorry," Mack says, glaring, finger pointing. "You don't get to say anything. Owen, what are you doing? Have you forgotten what this snake did to you?"

"Mack, hey, come on, let's go sit," I say, trying—failing—to pull her to a table.

Owen's eyes find mine. I want to know what he's thinking, but I can't read him.

"No, I haven't forgotten, but—"

"But *nothing*. She doesn't get access to you, or us, or anyone, anymore."

Lindsay tries to interject. "I get why you're mad, and we've. . ."

Mackenzie holds up one finger to shut her up. "Sorry, the adults are talking. Maybe you should just leave."

Owen shifts his weight. He doesn't like this any more than I do.

"You shouldn't even be here, Lindsay," Mack says. "I can't believe you think you can come in here and act like—" she shakes her hand between Owen and Lindsay, stopping mid-sentence. "You know what? No. On no planet do you get to get all buddy-buddy with my brother. Not after what you did."

Lindsay turns on her stool and stands. "I'll talk to y'all later." She looks at me. "Bye, Emmy."

"You will absolutely *not* talk to us all later," Mack spits. "How about you go slither back under whatever rock you're living under now and leave the rest of us alone?"

"Mack, enough." Owen moves around his sister and nods at Lindsay, like they have an unspoken code or something.

Once she's gone, Owen turns on Mack.

"What the heck?"

"*Me* what the heck?" Mack shakes her head. "I cannot believe you!"

"I'm not an idiot. Will you give me a little credit?" he snaps back.

"If you're talking to Lindsay, then you *are* an idiot," she says, causing him to roll his eyes and turn away. "Because now that you're back and you're doing well for yourself, she's going to try and weasel her way back in. *That's what she does.* You know she got married right? And he left her? *Shocker.*"

"I don't care." Owen shrugs. "I haven't cared or wasted one minute thinking about her for eight years."

I'm quietly happy about that.

"I'm a grown person. I can make my own decisions. I didn't invite her here, she just sat down and—"

Mack scoffs. "Then you forgot what she did to you. She's

always been really good at messing with your head." She looks at me. "Come on, Emmy. Suddenly, I'm not hungry."

She storms out, leaving me standing there, staring at Owen, wishing I had the right words.

We look at one another, and we both take a breath at the same time.

"Sorry about. . .that. Talk some sense into her, will ya?" he says.

"She's just worried about you," I say.

He blows out a breath. "It wasn't even. . ." He stops, trying to find the right words. "She was just—"

I hold up a hand to stop him from telling me anything about Lindsay because the truth is, I can't let myself care about this. "It's your life, Owen. I'll talk to you later."

I walk out onto the sidewalk and find Mack standing there, stewing.

"What in the world was that about?" I ask. "Don't you think that was a little over the top?"

Mack crosses her arms over her chest. That classic Larrabee temper often gets the better of her, and she's fiercely protective of the people she loves—which is one reason I never told her about my friendship with her brother—but this was next level.

"You were *there*, Emmy," she says, voice shaking from coming off a heated argument. "You saw what Lindsay did to him."

"Half the town saw," I say. "But it's been a long time. We're all adults now. Shouldn't we move on?"

"Because of what that woman did, Owen has never been the same. *Never*." In this moment, I can see just how much she cares for him.

I do too, unfortunately.

We start walking down Elm Street, back in the direction of

Book Smart. We'll inevitably end up eating day-old pastries for dinner, which, if I'm honest, is 100% fine with me.

A pecan braid softened in the microwave. Dangerous.

She continues. "It took him a year to snap out of the funk he was in, and even after that, he was. . .just. . .*different*. Owen was always rebellious, but when he loves someone, he's all in."

I smirk at her. "Must run in the family."

"Yeah, but Em, that stopped after Lindsay," she says.

I frown. "What do you mean?"

"After her, he moved away and hardly talked to any of us anymore. He didn't call, he didn't text. He really hasn't dated anyone—won't date anyone—seriously since. *She* did that to him." She stops and looks at me. "She took my brother away."

"I don't think it's as bad as all that, Mack," I tell her. "He seems the same to me. Mostly."

"You didn't really know him, Emmy," she says. "He's different now."

I chew the inside of my cheek, pondering what I'm about to say, then decide to take a leap. "I did know him, though."

I stuff my hands in my coat pockets, remembering how it felt the last time I told someone the truth about my feelings. The timing, I realize now, was terrible, and it led to the worst rejection of my life.

Mack might be really angry with me for keeping this from her all these years. But somehow, once he moved away and she saw him less, confessing it didn't seem to matter anymore.

"What are you talking about?"

"I wasn't just his tutor," I say on a sigh.

She stops dead in her tracks.

"Emmy, if you tell me you slept with Owen, I'm going to go back to DeLucca's and maim my brother. And then I'm going to maim you. Then I'm going back to maim him again, just to be sure."

"Mack."

She glares a questioning look at me.

"*Mackenzie.* I didn't sleep with Owen."

She narrows her eyes, then slowly turns and continues walking, turning onto Maple Street.

"This is Owen we're talking about," she says. "I had to ask."

"It was never like that," I say, hoping the tinge of disappointment in my voice isn't apparent to anyone but me. "But we became friends."

"When?" Mack asks.

"High school," I say. "You know the pond out back?"

"The dock? Your spot, right?"

"Yes," I say. "One day, I went down there, and he was there."

She frowns. "Doing what?"

I shrug. "He had a journal with him. Maybe he was thinking too?"

"So, what, you guys sat around thinking together?"

I shoot her a look.

"Well, Owen doesn't talk, so I can't picture you doing anything else."

I smile, remembering that first day at the dock. "No. He doesn't. Didn't, I mean. Not at first," I say. "But eventually. . .he did. Took some food to loosen him up, but yeah."

She softly chuckles. "Classic Owen"

"Turns out he's a really good listener."

"He's *what*?"

"You really should give him a chance," I say. "I don't get why you're so hard on him all the time."

"Emmy, even though he made my parents' lives a living hell all through high school, he was a good person, you know? Despite always getting in trouble. I saw this great person who was basically choosing to be a failure. He treated people like trash. Didn't care about other people's feelings or having any kind of responsibility. You know what it's like to watch someone throw their life away?"

I never looked at it like that.

She stops walking for a moment. "He's my brother. I love him. I want him to succeed. But man, did he make some idiotic choices in life. Enter, Lindsay."

I look down. I hope I'm not one of those idiotic choices.

"I still looked up to him. Like, a lot. And when he left, I don't know. I guess I took it personally."

"So, talk to him about it," I say. "It doesn't do you any good to hold a grudge. Especially when you've both grown up."

She starts walking again, and I fall into step beside her.

"Emmy, be honest," she says, not looking at me. "Did you guys hook up?"

"No, Mack, I swear," I say.

"It's weird for Owen to be friends with a girl and not hook up with her."

"Not *that* weird," I say. "He and Lindsay started dating their senior year. And you know he was faithful to her right up until she left him at the altar. He wasn't always. . .what did you call him? 'Three-Date Owen.'"

"No, that came after Lindsay," she says. "After she left, he was a mess. We went to help him get settled in his new place, and it was like he was barely functional. It took him six months to get back into training. And he told me he's never letting himself get that serious about anyone ever again."

We're standing in front of the book shop when she says this, and I quickly hide my face in the alcove and open the door. I don't know if Mack's right or if this is still how Owen feels about relationships, but I don't want it to be true.

Even though I know he feels nothing but friendship for me.

Being a hopeful romantic sucks.

I push the door open and walk inside, leaving all but one of the lights off so nobody mistakenly thinks we're open. Mack follows me, and at her silence, I turn and find her watching—studying—me.

"You like him," she says.

"Yeah, of course," I say, my pulse quickening. "He saved my life. We're friends."

"No. Not just that. You actually *really* like him." She eyes me. "Emmy, how long have you liked him?"

I walk behind the counter, as if putting it between me and Mack is going to help keep me safe. "I don't like him."

"I can't believe I didn't see this before," she says, putting her hand to her forehead. "You totally have a thing for Owen!"

"I. . .did," I finally admit. "I don't anymore."

"Emmy! Why didn't you tell me?"

"Are you kidding? You made it clear what you thought of Owen! And I didn't want it to be weird. Plus, I didn't ever want to say it out loud because it was embarrassing."

"Why?"

"Someone like Owen was never going to fall for someone like me," I say, matter-of-factly.

Mack reaches for my hands from across the counter. "My brother would be lucky to have someone like you." She pauses. "But he definitely doesn't deserve you."

"It doesn't matter," I say, squeezing her hands. "We're friends. That's it. He made it pretty clear. And I'm glad we're friends. But you need to stop berating him, and you need to chill out about Lindsay."

"She's the worst."

I smile. "Yes. I know. But he can take care of himself."

She shrugs, and her eyes blow past me to the glass display built into the counter. "Ooh, can I have a muffin?"

I drop her hands and walk over to the display case, pull out a cinnamon crumble muffin and walk back.

"Did you really like him?" Mack asks, her tone serious.

I make an embarrassed face and nod but avoid her eyes.

I honestly thought I loved him, and a part of me wanted it to be like every book I ever read, an awkward girl ends up with a troubled guy, and both find each other against all high school odds.

"I wish you'd told me," she says, breaking off the muffin top and flipping it over, making a crumble-muffin-sandwich like I showed her years ago. "You never have to be embarrassed around me. Not even when you show horrible judgment and fall for my brother."

"Well, good thing it's all in the past. You said it yourself—Owen and I are a terrible fit. I see that now."

She takes a bite of her muffwich but doesn't respond.

Probably because she senses that I'm trying to convince myself.

Which is what I'm doing.

And I'm doing a horrible job of it.

Chapter Nineteen

Owen

I see a light on.

An hour later, as I'm walking out of DeLucca's and heading toward my parked truck, I notice a light in Emmy's shop down the block.

I stand on the sidewalk for a few long seconds.

I should just go home, but something about that light draws me in.

And maybe I want to prove to myself that Lindsay is way off base about me and Emmy. I need to make sure it's clear—not to Emmy, but to me—that we are just friends.

I walk toward the shop, and when I see her inside, alone, moving around in the shadows, I almost turn and walk away.

But then, she glances up and sees me standing there. I probably look like a creep. I lift my hand in a wave. She waves back, then comes around the counter and opens the door. She stands in front of it and looks at me.

"Hey! What are you doing here?"

Great question.

"Is, uh, Mack still here?"

Emmy leans against the door and shakes her head. "No, she just went home." I tell myself that it doesn't mean anything that I'm thinking about how pretty she looks in the dim light of the streetlamp overhead. It's a perfectly natural thing to think about any woman. Emmy's always cute, but sometimes, like right now, it's more than that.

Sometimes, she's downright beautiful.

Why have I never noticed that before?

"What are you still doing here?" I ask.

"I wasn't tired, so I thought I'd get a head start on the baking for tomorrow," she says. "Plus, I was hungry because we really didn't eat, so. . ."

"Yeah. I'm so sorry about that, didn't mean—"

She holds up her hands. "No worries. It's fine." She shoots a thumb over her shoulder. "Pecan braid. Twenty-three seconds in the microwave."

I wonder if it's more than that. I glance down at her other hand, relaxed at her side, and I hope the trauma of the fire isn't what's keeping her up late.

I stuff my own hands in my pockets, feeling like I shouldn't be standing here.

"Do you want to come in? I just baked some pumpkin spice cupcakes."

"Cream cheese frosting?"

"As if there's another kind." She smiles and steps back inside, leaving the door open behind her. With Lindsay's accusations rolling around in my mind, being here almost feels exciting.

I remind myself I'm here to prove her wrong, but so far, it's not working. All it's doing is reminding me how much Emmy meant to me all those years ago.

But I never, ever thought of her as anything more than a friend.

That hasn't changed. Even if a part of me can acknowledge that she's beautiful.

"Sit," she says. "I need you to be my taste tester."

Before I obey, I glance at her display case. There are left-over pastries from yesterday inside, and my eyes scan through what she has to offer. "You've got oatmeal butterscotch."

She smiles, and taps the chalkboard display behind her. I'm confused for a moment. It just reads: OL' BUTTERSCOTCH COOKIES. . .$2.25.

"They're still your favorite, right?"

I look at the display again.

OL' BUTTERSCOTCH.

OL.

Owen Larabee. Or maybe just ol' as in "old" as in *why am I trying to make a thing out of cookies?*

She reaches in and takes one out, sets it on a plate and slides it over to me. "But save room for the pumpkin cupcakes because I think they're quite possibly the best I've ever made." She disappears into the kitchen, leaving me sitting at the counter full of confused thoughts.

Between my sister's outburst, Lindsay's comments, and that ridiculous podcast, I think what I really need is to go off-grid for a while.

Too many women getting in my head.

Emmy's back with a whole tray of cupcakes and a small bowl of frosting. She glances at the uneaten cookie in front of me. "You didn't even taste it."

"Sorry, I'm distracted."

"Mack?"

"Yeah." I shrug. "But that's only part of it."

"Ah, Lindsay," she says.

"No, that's not—"

Again, she holds up her hand. "We can talk about anything —*except* Lindsay."

I nod. That's fine with me.

I watch her and wonder if it still stings for her to think about me and Lindsay. All those times I talked to her about my feelings, Emmy listened, like a friend. But once I found out that she had similar feelings for me, I felt like a first-class jerk.

I was hurting her, daily, and she didn't say a word.

I take a bite of the cookie, which may be a day old but is still amazing.

I'm suddenly aware that this is how Emmy and I became friends in the first place.

She's looking at me now like she did then, like she actually cares what I'm thinking. And she did that at a time when nobody else really did.

It's nice to see some things between us haven't changed.

"The captain. At the station."

She grabs a spoon. "What about him?"

"He mentioned that I should take the test. You know, to become a lieutenant." Not what I planned to talk to her about, but it's what came out. I haven't told anyone else about this.

She stops "Really? Owen, that's amazing!" She picks up a bag and fills it with frosting.

I nod.

"Are you going to do it?" She hands me the bag.

I look at it, then look at her.

"What am I supposed to do with this, eat it?"

She laughs. "No, although you could probably eat the whole thing and not gain a pound. Stupid men."

I smile.

"You're going to help me frost them."

"I have no idea how to do that," I say.

"Have you held a fire hose before?"

"Of course."

"This is nothing like that."

Now I laugh. I'm comfortable. Relaxed.

Totally the opposite of an hour ago at the bar.

She smiles with her eyes. "I'll show you." She fills another bag with frosting, then squeezes it over one of the cupcakes, a perfect circular swirl, and it's obvious she's done this a million times. "Just like that."

"Just like that?"

"Yep. It's just for you anyway," she says. "You're eating it, so put as much icing on it as you want."

I pick up the cupcake, hold the piping bag over it, and squeeze. The frosting comes out way faster than I thought it would, and it shoots a glob over the side of the cupcake and down my hand.

Emmy giggles.

"You're enjoying this, aren't you?"

"I really am." She takes the bag from me, works her frosting magic, and makes my mess look like a display model. She raises her eyebrows in a *see, it's easy* look.

I raise my eyebrows in return and proceed to eat the huge glob of icing off the side of my hand.

Another giggle.

I'm glad that things between us seem to be getting back to normal. She seems less nervous around me now, more like herself.

I like it.

Because we're friends. And we should feel comfortable around each other.

She hands me the cupcake, and nods at it. "Try it."

"You're so bossy."

She grins. "It's really good," she sings at me.

I do as I'm told, and the second I take a bite, I close my eyes to let myself enjoy the way all the fall flavors blend together. Pumpkin and spices and cream cheese frosting—it's perfection. I let out a little hum of appreciation, and when I open my eyes, I see her watching me, her smile still intact. "You're right," I say, mouth still full. "It's really good."

She lifts her hands up in a victory pose, then unwraps her own cupcake, removing the bottom and squishing it onto the top of the frosting, sandwich style. Then she takes a bite. She closes her eyes and chews for a long moment, savoring the taste. "Do you know how happy it makes me to bake a perfect cupcake?" She does a little dance, and I wonder how many people in the world get to see this side of her.

"Good thing you stopped being weird," I tease.

She finishes her dance and takes another bite. "You're going to make me weird again if you keep talking about it."

"Sorry." I pause. "Mack was pretty mad, huh?"

"She's a little dramatic," Emmy says with a wince. "But she's a Larrabee. She's got that 'don't take crap from anyone' gene."

I take that for what it is, teasing.

"She's always been like that with the people she loves. We're lucky to have her." Emmy smiles.

"Well, I don't want to be on her bad side, that's for sure. I've been there. It's not pretty."

She finishes off her cupcake, then takes a swig of water. "I told her about us being friends."

"Oh yeah?"

She nods. "I hope that's okay."

"Why wouldn't it be?"

She shrugs. "Not sure you wanted her to know." I see a twinkle in her eyes. "Might ruin your street cred."

Is she making jokes? At least her sense of humor is still intact.

"Emmy, I didn't say anything to her because you didn't want me to. Not because I cared if she knew."

Emmy frowns. "Really?"

"Yes, geez. How shallow do you think I am?"

She shrugs. "You did get engaged to Lindsay." She waits a second before busting out in laughter.

I raise a brow. "Are you finished?"

"Sorry," she says, and I don't believe her for a second. "It was clever, though. Right? I'm clever?"

"Yeah, you're a real treat," I muse, through a smile.

She keeps piping the cupcakes. "Okay, so tell me about this lieutenant thing. That sounds like a great opportunity."

So, I do.

I not only tell her that. . .I tell her everything.

I tell her about the fight at my previous station. About losing my job. About my dad calling in the favor that gave me this second chance. And about the test and why I don't want to take it again.

I tell her everything.

And it feels good to say it all out loud, knowing she won't judge me for any of it.

As I talk, Emmy stays busy, but not the kind of busy where it's obvious she's not listening, like scrolling on her phone or something. The kind that lets me talk without feeling like I'm being watched or studied or judged.

And when I'm finished, she stops moving and looks at me. "So, you're doing it, right?"

I look away.

"Failing a test because you didn't study is one thing, but failing because you didn't have the right accommodations is something completely different."

"I don't want to use the accommodations," I admit.

"Why?" She waits a few seconds, and when I don't answer, she says, "Ohhh, I get it."

"Get what?"

"You're too proud."

"Hey now."

She shrugs, like it's no big deal. "No, I get it, it's a guy thing. Guys can't admit they need help; guys want to be in control; guys don't like to feel stupid."

That's a sweeping generalization. . .but she just described all the things I hate.

Asking for help.

Being out of control.

Feeling stupid.

"Okay, so, you're right. I don't like feeling stupid." I sit back on my stool. "But I'm not proud, Emmy," I say. "I've been doing this for years."

"No, you really haven't," she says, pointing the piping bag at me. "You wouldn't accept accommodations in high school either, remember?"

I look away. She still knows me. Better than anyone else.

"It doesn't make you weak, Owen. There's a reason they exist."

"You don't think it's like special treatment?"

She frowns. "Is a ramp for someone in a wheelchair special treatment?"

That's exactly what I'd said. I hadn't told her that.

I blow out a breath. I hate that I have these "differences" at all. I'm not sure how to make peace with it when it seems to be the root of so many of my problems.

My parents made me see a therapist after my diagnosis, and she told me the reason I acted out was because I felt misunderstood. But she was wrong. It wasn't because I felt misunderstood, it was because I felt stupid.

And I knew I wasn't stupid.

I just couldn't prove it.

Emmy sets a hand on mine.

It feels different than before, knowing what I know now.

I'm not sure what to make of it.

"Doctors and therapists and people who know way more about it than us have figured out a way to level the playing field," she says. "That's all. You can't let ignorant opinions of idiots get in your head." She squeezes my hand. "You deserve to be a lieutenant. Heck, you deserve to be the captain. And whatever's a higher rank than a captain."

I smirk. "Chief."

"That! Yes!" Another squeeze.

"You really think I should do it?"

"I really do."

Her hand is still on mine. There's a single light on in the entire shop, and Lindsay's words are racing through my mind.

What if she's right?

What if I had feelings for Emmy and didn't even realize it?

It doesn't matter. Emmy is absolutely one of those girls who agrees with that lady on *The Hopeful Romantic* podcast.

The kind of girl who sets her expectations based on romance novels and nonsense.

And I'm the kind of guy who'll only let her down.

Chapter Twenty

Emmy

Cream cheese frosting. Works every time.

The conversation I had with Owen after Mack went off on Lindsay almost felt normal.

Back in the day, talking to him was easy, in spite of my feelings. And if I could keep him in the friend box in my mind, I'd be just fine.

But doing that is proving to be more difficult than I want it to be.

Like I thought it would be easy.

Real life romance is never easy, no matter what The Hopeful Romantic tells you.

I've stated very plainly (albeit anonymously) what kind of guy I'm holding out for, and Owen Larrabee doesn't meet any of my criteria.

The following night, after we close, I go home and escape into my room with my laptop to check in with the responses to the Hopeful in Hoboken episode. Ripper put it together in record time, and I didn't even have to announce a delay because of the fire.

I post the transcript for each episode on my website, and listeners can respond and engage with other listeners and with me. My VA Lily also sifts through a lot of these, but I like to keep myself in the loop as to how people are responding. Helps me know what's hitting and what to do more of. Or not.

I open the site and click on the comments as a new notification pops up.

Practical in Poughkeepsie has left a comment.

I scroll to the bottom of the comments section and find the following waiting for me:

Heard this episode by accident and had to write in. I watched as my buddies ate this up, taking notes as if your list is what every woman wants.

You call yourself The Hopeful Romantic, but these ideas aren't hopeful, they're unrealistic. Would you really choose a guy who dances with you in the street or kisses you in the rain over a guy who takes out the garbage or helps you clean up the house? What about a guy who's working on getting on his feet but who would do anything for you? Or maybe just someone who'll listen when you've had a bad day?

Thoughtfulness in a relationship doesn't always have to look like a romantic gesture, and don't you think it's more important in the long run?

Let's normalize practical romance instead of holding guys to an impossible, unrealistic standard. Nobody is going to check all those boxes, no matter what your romance novels say.

Signed,
Practical in Poughkeepsie.

I re-read the comment as another notification pops up.

Practical in Poughkeepsie has left a comment.

This guy is on the site right now. The second comment is on Episode 115. *Lonely in Larkspur.*

Don't confuse a choice to stay single with loneliness. There are a lot of reasons someone would choose not to waste time in a relationship. Maybe 'Lonely in Larkspur' is onto something. Maybe living a life without having to get someone else's OK on everything is a good thing.

Wow, this guy sounds miserable.

I start to respond when I get another notification.

Practical in Poughkeepsie has left a comment.

Whoever this person is, he's been listening to a lot of episodes, and apparently had some extra time on his hands tonight to comment on every single one.

On Episode 102: Waiting in Waukesha, I helped a man plan a big, public grand gesture to propose to his girlfriend. I'd been especially proud to do a follow-up to that episode a few months later, when he sent in photos of their engagement.

My new Internet troll doesn't see it that way.

Why encourage this kind of public display? If you love someone, why isn't a quiet, private moment enough to decide you want to spend the rest of your lives together? Does the whole Internet need to be in on it?

You're raising the bar way too high that now even high school kids feel like they have to rent a mariachi band and create a mural just to ask a girl to prom.

I get three more notifications like these before I finally get up and walk away.

Practical in Poughkeepsie.

Not a fan.

I've had critical reviews before, even a few upset listeners. But never anyone who left this many comments all in the span of thirty-five minutes. It's like he stock-piled his tirade for an unexpected moment and has chosen now to unleash his fury.

Apparently Practical in Poughkeepsie has a lot of thoughts.

I have other emails I could and probably should respond to, but these comments have gotten under my skin. I copy and paste each of them into a separate document. These will take the place of the email I usually read at the top of the show.

I open the DAW, set a new file path, and check the levels on the mic. I affix my headphones over my ears, position the microphone in front of me, and click "Record."

"Hello and welcome to *The Hopeful Romantic*, where we analyze, digest and discuss all things romance. Today's episode is brought to you by *Barely There* chemical free makeup for women who don't want to feel like they're made up.

"Today I'm going a little off script to respond not to an email, but to a series of comments that have caught my attention from a new listener who calls himself Practical in Poughkeepsie. I say 'himself' because after reading the comments, I'm pretty sure this is a male listener. And a pretty cynical one.

"First, let me start by saying, Practical in Poughkeepsie, I don't know who did a number on you, but I'm sorry. Whoever broke your heart did a very thorough job. And while you raise a few interesting points, it seems you're a little bitter when it comes to romance. Maybe for good reason. Contrary to what you think, though, there *are* men out there who will go the extra mile when it comes to love."

I read his reply to my most recent episode, and then go on,

maintaining a kind, somewhat withdrawn tone. I'm not picking a fight here, just responding, as I often do, to my listeners.

"Practicality, while important, sometimes seems at odds with what I'm holding out for—but I make no apologies for believing in romance. I've been doing this long enough to know that if you love someone enough, you'll do just about anything for them. Even dance in the middle of the street and steal kisses in the rain.

"We can all agree that love and romance, intertwined, make you do some pretty crazy things! There's a reason it's an accepted fact that love makes fools of us all."

I hit the spacebar and pause, taking a drink.

After resting for a moment, I click "Record" one more time and continue.

"You also made the point that being single is often a choice —and has nothing to do with loneliness. It's a good point. For those of you out there who feel the same, I'd challenge you to examine Poughkeepsie's theory. Are you single because you're choosing to be? Or are you single because you're afraid of putting yourself out there? If you're afraid, you wouldn't be alone. Lots of people struggle to find love after being burned one too many times. But I truly believe that we're meant for relationships. We're supposed to seek companionship. And friendship. And yes, love and romance."

I think about Owen. I think about what Mack said about how his break-up with Lindsay changed him. Practically turned him into a different person.

For a moment, without thinking, I talk about him.

"I have a friend who went through a terrible, public break-up." I decide to change the gender just for an added layer of anonymity. "She was really broken by the whole thing. Devastated, really, because the way she was treated was truly awful. She's this great person, but now keeps people at an arm's length, withdrawn, and tentative, and closed off.

"Rightfully so. She needed to give herself time to heal, to mourn, to feel all the emotions, because when you stuff those down, they'll resurface later. So, she did. She took time. Moved away, got things worked out, and grew up.

"But what my friend failed to see, even after the healing and the mourning, was that she had a whole community of people who loved her. And that she was worthy of holding out for something really great. Instead, she decided to put up a wall, vowing to never fall in love again. So far, she's stayed true to her word, and that makes me really sad. Because I know there's someone out there who would love the opportunity to go stargazing in the back of a pick-up truck with her. And yeah, who would listen when she's had a bad day and take out the garbage and do pretty much anything to make her happy."

I know because I am that person, I think as I hit the spacebar and stop the recording again.

This just took a really personal turn, and I don't like it. I'm not here to air my own dirty laundry, anonymously or not. Okay. Finish strong.

Click.

"I suppose I just want to challenge you, Practical in Poughkeepsie, to ask yourself if your negative response to my hopefulness is really about me being unrealistic, or about you being closed off. I would hate to see you miss out on something wonderful because you were hurt in the past.

"You're worth it. And someone out there thinks the same."

With that, I sign off. And while I feel a little like I've just poked a bear, I stand by my view and everything I said in my last episode.

This bitter person can look down his nose at my view. He may even think I'm being naïve. Maybe I am.

But so what? I believe in love and romance and sparks and butterflies.

But then there's just the slightest question at the back of my mind: what if I'm wrong? What if Hopeful in Hoboken was onto something when she said she doesn't want to miss out on something great waiting for something perfect?

Especially when "perfect" doesn't exist.

Not that it matters in my case. I don't even have "something great" at the moment. I only have my books. Oddly, I feel comforted by that thought.

I shut everything down and crawl into bed when a text from Owen comes in:

OWEN

Hey, sorry to bug you

Have you heard from the insurance company?

EMMY

Yeah, the restoration company is coming in next week

I have to get over there and see what I can save

OWEN

Need help?

I stare at those two words.

Even when Owen lived here before and we were good friends, we didn't actually go out and do things together. Sometimes we'd end up at the same functions, and the most we ever said to each other was hello, and oftentimes, not even that.

Why, I'm not sure. It's like our friendship back then was better as a secret.

More special that way, maybe.

In a flash my mind starts writing out a whole scenario where I walk into my charred craftsman and find Owen cooking dinner for me in the kitchen. Somehow, in this hazy fantasy, my house doesn't smell like smoke anymore. The ash and soot are miraculously gone, and his apron reads "*I Don't Just Heat Things Up In The Kitchen.*"

As I enter the room, he turns and smiles. He sets down the spatula and holds out his hand to me. I take it, and then he pulls me in his arms, our bodies pressed together and the camera in my mind cuts to an old record player, the needle dropping, scratching out *Moonlight Serenade* by Glenn Miller as we slow dance, right there in the kitchen.

The kitchen timer goes off, and it sounds a lot like a phone buzzing.

Which it is.

My phone is buzzing in my hand, forcing me back to reality.

If we're going to be friends again, I'm going to have to shift my entire way of thinking where he's concerned.

I look down at the new text message.

OWEN

You've probably got it handled

EMMY

No! I don't! Sorry. Got sidetracked

If you're free, I'd love help

OWEN

Tomorrow?

EMMY

It's a date!

I hit send without thinking.

I panic, and tap over to the message stickers, grab a giraffe 'blowing it's mind', and drag it over the top of that last text.

And then instantly wish I could erase the sticker, so I try tapping on it and dragging it, but it just turns forty-five degrees and enlarges.

And because I like to make things worse, I keep going.

EMMY

Oh my gosh, not a date

And sorry about the giraffe

And the date

You know what I mean.

<face palm emoji>

OWEN

Not a date.

I got it.

Oh my gosh. There are periods at the ends of those texts. Is he mad? Did I offend him? How should I read that?

And *why* didn't I just edit my text instead of making everything weird and awkward?

I don't know how to respond, so I just type a thumbs-up emoji.

Sigh.

I'm a winner.

Chapter Twenty-One

Emmy

If I ever need to fashionably dress for the zombie apocalypse, I'm calling my mom.

Friday morning, after sending off my latest podcast file to Ripper, I come down the stairs to find she's dressed in green cargo pants and a chambray button-down. She's got a handkerchief on her head and rubber boots up to her knees. And she's wearing a pair of work gloves.

In *Dawn's Reckoning*, the post-apocalyptic zombie romance thriller, protagonist Dawn Stevens falls for survivalist, Brock Johnson, when holed up in a supermarket, fighting off a horde of the undead.

Turns out that they went to kindergarten together, and he still has a handprint turkey she made for him folded in his survival pack. Their meet-cute was over an expired can of refried beans.

It's not the most well-written book.

I silently pray to the spirit of Jane Austen that post-apocalyptic zombie romance thrillers don't become a new genre.

We've already got Amish vampires and NASCAR romance, and those are bad enough.

Although a case could be made that NASCAR romance has some serious potential.

I frown at her outfit. "What are you doing?"

"Going to your house?"

"Wouldn't it be easier to just rent a hazmat suit?"

"Owen said we should dress for a mess," she says.

I'm sure my frown deepens. "Owen said what now?"

"In the group text," she says. "Didn't you get it?"

"No." I pull out my phone. Nothing.

"Oh." Mom, with the gloves on, carefully pours coffee into a giant travel mug. "That's weird."

I shake my head. "What's going on?"

"Well, shoot. I'm not sure I'm supposed to tell you," she says.

"I think it's a little late for that."

She hesitates a moment before saying, "Owen organized a clean-up day. At your house. To prepare for the restoration company."

"I'm meeting him over there this morning, but he didn't say anything about anyone else."

"Well, if this text is any indication, it's going to be a whole crew." She holds up her phone and I scroll back to see Owen's first text to a large cluster of numbers.

OWEN

Hey everybody, it's Owen Larrabee.

I got most of your numbers from Reagan and my mom.

You heard about Emmy's house, and I thought it would be nice if we could help her go through things to prepare for the restoration company.

I'm meeting her there at 9 a.m. Friday morning if anyone is available. Oh, and wear long sleeves, long pants and gloves.

I'll bring masks from the station.

Let me know if you have any questions.

I see a series of replies, most of them heart emojis and "Aww, Owen, how sweet!"

I glance up and find Mom watching me. "His captain probably made him do it."

She frowns. "Why would you think that?"

I shrug. "It's why he walked me through my house the day after the fire. It's part of his job."

She takes her phone from me. "It doesn't feel like this would be in his job description."

"Let's not read into it, okay?"

Because my heart can't handle it.

"I'm just saying, it's awfully nice for him to do something so helpful for you during this really hard time."

I have no idea why, but this makes me think of *Practical in Poughkeepsie*.

"Well, if there's a whole crew lined up, I'm going to go get muffins from the shop," I say, suddenly nervous. Because I know there has already been a lot of chatter about Owen saving me. And because I'm not sure I can keep my resolve intact if he's going to be this kind.

The words from that stupid comment creep back into my mind:

Thoughtfulness in a relationship doesn't always have to look like a romantic gesture, and don't you think it's more important in the long run?

In this case, thoughtfulness does feel a little like romance.

Isn't the difference between "nice" and "romantic" the motivation?

So, Mr. Larrabee, what's the motivation here?

I chastise myself for even considering it would be anything but nice.

I stop by the shop and find it nearly empty. Apart from two employees, it's like a ghost town. Even The Coffin Dodgers aren't at their usual spot. At least they won't miss the muffins I'm about to steal.

I'm the owner, I can steal whatever I want, I think.

I pack up a big box of treats, pour myself a cup of coffee, and then pour one for Owen.

Friendly, right?

I get back in the car and head a few blocks over to my street. But the second I make the turn, the memory of that night flashes in my mind. My grip on the steering wheel tightens, whitening my knuckles as I slow the car down and stop a full block away.

I barely manage to get the car in park as my breath quickens. I momentarily can't think straight. I can smell the smoke. I picture all of my things as ash. My peripheral vision darkens, and I'm frozen in the driver's seat of my car.

I think I'm having a panic attack.

I hold my breath and let it out, slowly, saying, "Okay. Okay. You're okay," over and over for what feels like an eternity. My heart is racing, and I feel like every nerve is plugged in, maxed out.

On fire.

I breathe.

I breathe.

I breathe.

The dark edges in my vision subside, my hands start to relax, and I realize that my face is wet with tears I didn't even know had fallen.

I shakily breathe as I grab a Kleenex out of my bag. My pulse is starting to calm down, and I feel strangely tired.

The whole ordeal lasted only a few minutes—but I feel like I just ran a marathon carrying a sack of hammers.

I take a minute to gather myself and wipe my eyes before purposing to get to my house.

That was scary.

I pull up to see that this "crew" Owen has assembled has descended on my house. There are cars parked all the way down the block, and people moving across the yard. I see The Coffin Dodgers standing outside, looking like they're pondering something important, which means they're probably caught up in an argument about who knows the best way to clean up a house after a fire. And no matter where they land, they'll likely all agree it's not Owen Larrabee, even though he's the trained firefighter.

My neighbors, Pat and Peggy are in the mix, along with Peggy's sister, Meg, Owen's parents, Heather from Catty's Coffee, Felicia Fudrucker, the high school principal, and a whole group of people I don't know. I can't be sure, but I *think* that might be a group of Appies hockey players over there. . .

I squint for a better look. Like everyone else in town, I'm a fan of the Appies. And I'm absolutely positive that their goal-tender, Felix Jamison is standing in my front yard. Helping clean-up *my* house.

Owen recruited hockey players for this?

No, they aren't in the big time yet, but around here, they might as well be. Harvest Hollow is very proud of its minor league hockey team. Last season, I waited too long, and I never did get tickets to see them.

But they're here. At my house. Cleaning. Because of Owen.

I mentally stumble on that thought for too many seconds.

There's a dumpster out front and a small, tented canopy off to the side with folding tables underneath.

I park in the driveway, and my parents pull in behind me. I get out of the car just as Owen steps out of my house. He's talking to a group of three other guys, including Jace.

They aren't dressed like firefighters, but this must be a service they provide.

"I hope you don't mind that I lent him your key," Mom says through my window as she walks by on her way to greet Owen's parents.

She doesn't give me a chance to respond. I reach into my backseat and pull out the box of pastries.

The Coffin Dodgers are on me in seconds, ready for free treats, and I'm starting to wonder if that—and the chance to form a peanut gallery—are the only reasons they came.

"Let us help you with that," Ernie says, taking the box from me.

"Did you leave any back at the store?" John chuckles.

"Did you bring coffee?" Marco asks.

"There's coffee under the tent," Mr. Ridgemont says. "And good morning, Emmy."

"Morning." They head over to the tables under the canopy, where some of the ladies from church are bustling around. Looks like they had the food covered, but I'm glad I could at least contribute something. There's a whole spread of bagels and donuts and fruit, along with juice and coffee.

The folks of Harvest Hollow really know how to do disaster relief.

I take a second to survey the scene, and I'm overwhelmed for a moment. They're all here for me. The weight of that doesn't escape me.

Owen spots me and separates from the others. His expression is stoic, as usual, and he's all business. He stops in front of me, and I have to take a moment to right myself. His nearness, as of late, does a number on my nerves, but it's the concern etched in his forehead that I'm really struggling with.

For me, it's not a leap to think behind "concern" is "care," and not far away from "care" is "love."

I snap open the "Friend Box" and stuff all of that inside.

"What's all this?" I ask, doing my best to keep up that *friendly* facade.

"It's a big job," he says. "Called in some help."

I look around the yard. The Coffin Dodgers are standing around a table, drinking coffee and chatting with the church ladies. Reagan pulls up in her old VW bug, and magically produces a pile of boxes and a roll of packing tape.

"I can't believe you got all these people to come," I say. "You just texted me about the clean-up yesterday. No way you pulled this together in a day."

He smirks. "It's been in the works."

He'd been planning this?

"Your captain is going to be very happy."

He frowns. "I don't think he even knows we're here today."

"Owen!" Jace is pulling more masks out of the back of his truck.

Owen looks at Jace, giving me a second to process what he just said. If the captain doesn't know, then he didn't assign this task to Owen. And if he's not doing this because it's his job, then. . .

Concern to care to love to. . .

"Setting up more masks on the table!" Jace calls out.

Owen waves at him, then turns his attention back to me. "What's wrong?"

"Huh?" I say, because I'm eloquent and have a way with words.

"Are you okay?"

I shake my head slightly and erase whatever expression is trying to give me away. "Oh, yeah. I just—thought this was part of your job."

He chuckles lightly. "We just put the fires out. We don't usually handle the clean-up."

I want to ask him why my house is the exception, but he doesn't give me the chance.

He turns toward the front door. "So, the main thing we want to do is go through and separate out what can and can't be saved. I'm going to make you get rid of all the food in there, and any clothes that look like they took a hit. You need to wear these too—" he hands me a pair of gloves— "and don't get any of the soot or ash on your skin. If you do, we need to wash it off right away."

I put the gloves on and look around. Everyone else seems to have already gotten this speech. The people moving in and out of the house are masked and fully covered.

"I told everyone they need to wait for you to go through everything first. Nobody is going to throw anything away without your say so."

I nod. I feel. . .off. "Okay."

We're standing on the front porch. It's not the first time I've been back here, but it is the first time I've been back with the intention of throwing things away. Things that only about a week ago were in perfect condition.

I follow him to the open front door. It's almost as though I'm watching someone else do this—like it's not exactly real. I can hear people moving around inside. I can hear the noise of people sifting through what's left of my things.

And then, just as a few minutes before in my car, the edges of my vision start to close in.

Oh. . .oh no.

I can hear the flames. Owen's voice, telling me we've got to go. And I can feel the heat. I draw in a quick deep breath, panicked, expecting the cloud of smoke to block my airway. It's clear, and yet I feel like I can't breathe.

Logically, I know I'm out of any danger.

But my brain isn't listening.

My gloved hand begins to tremble.

Owen says something, but I can't make it out. My ears are ringing, filled with the sound of my pounding heart.

I've been here already. This shouldn't affect me. I've walked through the house. I'm safe now. I look down at my feet, still outside on the porch, and the tremor in my hand quickens. I grab ahold of it and squeeze.

It's not helping. I can't see. I want it to stop. I try to rub it away, but it doesn't work, and now I'm gasping for air.

Owen moves toward me, takes my hand, and pulls me around to the side of the house.

He positions me with my back against the side of the house and stands directly in front of me, leaning down so his eyes are level with mine. Through the blackness of my vision, I can only see the center of his face, his eyes, and I'm trying to catch my breath, but I can't. I can't breathe, and I'm trying to see him through my tears, but it's all a jumbled up mess, and I'm afraid I might actually suffocate.

Through the haze I hear, "Slow, long, deep breaths."

I can't, *I can't,* I. . .

"Emmy. I'm here. Breathe. You can breathe."

My breath hitches, my chest spasms as I fight to do as he says, focusing on the deep breath that I desperately need.

"It's just me and you now, Emmy," he says, calmly. "Nobody else matters. Can you look around and tell me three things you see?"

Three things I. . .?

"Take your time. Focus. Three things," he repeats.

Three things. Three things. . .

"Pat. . .and Peggy's uh-ugly c-curtains."

He smirks. "That's one."

I draw in one longer breath, deeper than the hiccupping ones so far. I peer through wet, slitted eyes to my left. "My b-birdhouse."

He nods. "That's two. One more"

I bring my gaze back to his. "Y-your eyes."

"Three," he says, his voice low. "Now tell me three sounds."

I listen for a moment. My heart rate is still elevated, but the pounding has subsided.

There are people talking around the corner of the house. "Ernie. He's complaining," I say on an exhale, then listen again. "There's an. . . airplane flying o-overhead and—" I close my eyes— "a chipmunk that's going to eat my pumpkins."

"Good," he says. "Now three body parts."

At that, my eyes fling wide, and I feel my cheeks flush. Because my instant reaction is: your lips, your biceps, and your backside.

Obviously, I can't say any of those out loud.

I look down at the ground. "I think I'm okay."

He reaches down and takes off my gloves, then presses my hand into his. "How's the hand?"

I must give him a quizzical look because he says, "I noticed it the day after the fire. The tremor? It's a trauma response."

I don't say anything.

"It's perfectly normal to have anxiety after what you went through."

I take a breath. It's a good one. "I don't have anxiety."

"Maybe not, but you just had a panic attack," he says.

I stop arguing because I know he's right.

"Did you think you could reason with yourself not to have big feelings about this?" he asks.

I nod, still a little shaky. I fight an overwhelming urge to fall into his arms and have him hold me.

"Something like that. It makes me feel—"

"Embarrassed?"

"Yeah, I guess."

"Do you remember when you told me that my learning differences weren't something to be ashamed of?" he asks.

"Of course."

"Did you mean it?"

I nod. And I get his point.

But I don't want to be seen as a weak person because I can't control my emotions.

"Your reaction is okay," he says.

"Feels. . ." I take another good breath, "overly dramatic."

"Emmy." He squeezes my hand. "Your house caught on fire with you inside of it. Being emotional about that isn't dramatic. It would be weird if you didn't have a big reaction to it."

I give him a small nod, lips trembling a bit.

"And I'm following your lead here," he says. "I can tell everyone to go home and come back later if you want me to."

I consider it.

I look out from the side of the house at the dozens of people talking, smiling, helping, caring.

"No, it's okay. I. . .I can do this." He lets go of my hand, and I miss his touch instantly. Which is not what I should be thinking about right now.

Not in this situation.

"Whoa! What is going on back here?"

I turn in the direction of Mack's voice as Owen takes a step back.

She widens her eyes, suspicion all over her face.

Owen glances back at me. "Come find me when you're ready."

I nod, sad to watch him walk away.

I bring my attention back to my best friend and find her watching me, arms crossed over her chest and a very pointed expression on her face.

"You said this crush was in the past."

"It is," I say, pushing myself away from the house and slipping the gloves back on.

"That is not what it looked like."

I look away. "I had a little. . .episode."

She frowns. "What kind of episode?"

I pinch the bridge of my nose. "Like a. . .I guess it was like a. . .panic attack?"

She drops her arms to her sides. "What? Oh my gosh, Em, are you okay?"

"I'm fine now," I say. "Owen helped me."

"Helped you with a panic attack?"

"Like I told you. He's good at his job."

"Yeah, his job is fighting fires," she says. "Not coaching people through anxiety."

I shrug and start walking toward the front of the house. "Well, he learned that too, I guess. You should start paying attention. Your brother is a great guy."

I walk away, feeling a little more prepared for what I'm about to face in the immediate future.

I also feel a little less sure my love for Owen is in the distant past.

Chapter Twenty-Two

Owen

I need a break from Emmy.

I've got old men berating me about "my intentions." I've got Levi asking if I'm going to "tap that." And worst of all, I've got my own memories of that look on her face the day of the clean-up when she was struggling to take a deep breath.

I watched her try to power through it. I watched her look for a place to hide. I watched her come out of it.

I helped her come out of it.

And it felt like saving her all over again.

I need a break.

Thankfully, I'm back on shift, and when I walk in, I find the captain standing near the engine, talking to a man I recognize from my interviews. Chief Fisk.

The two of them stop talking and look at me.

"Owen," Captain Donoho says. "Come on over."

I drop my bag and walk over, extending a hand when I reach them.

"Larrabee," the chief says. "Good to see you again."

"Back from vacation," I say.

"And wanted to see you," he says.

My stomach clenches in a tight, acute form of déjà vu.

This is probably the moment when I lose my job.

Maybe Fisk didn't read my file before Donoho hired me. Maybe he's here to tell me I've got no business being here after what I did.

"Me?" I ask, not really wanting the conversation to continue.

"Got a call about you last night," the chief says. "From a friend. He told me you organized a clean-up at the house you pulled that woman out of."

I nod, a bit apprehensive about where this is going.

"Said you did a fine job of mobilizing volunteers, explaining safety procedures, and getting the job done in a timely fashion. Even said you helped get the victim through a bout of anxiety."

I hold eye contact even though I really want to look away. Who would've told him all that? I didn't think anyone even saw Emmy's panic attack. "I'm not sure I follow."

"Sounds like the makings of a good leader," he says.

My eyes flick to Donoho, who raises a brow.

"Sir?"

The chief hands over a folder. "The application for lieutenant."

"Oh, sir, I haven't made up my mind about—"

"Well, let me make it up for you, then," he says. "We'll get the accommodations set up so we can, as Donoho says, 'level the playing field.'" He watches me. "This department, heck, all our departments, could use more guys like you."

I'm about to protest, to tell him all the reasons I probably shouldn't get promoted, but something stops me. Emmy's voice in the back of my mind. My own voice right after it. She told me not to let my pride get in the way. I told her not to be ashamed of her anxiety. Here's my chance to take my own advice.

Fisk claps me on the shoulder. "It was good to see you. I'll keep an eye out for your test scores."

"Thank you, Chief," I say.

He walks out, leaving me standing with Donoho and feeling blindsided and excited at the same time. This was a dream I'd given up on, but these men didn't seem to care that I'd screwed up as recently as my last job. And they didn't seem to care that I wouldn't test like other firefighters.

It seemed like what they saw was potential.

Huh. Just like someone else I know.

"Thanks, Captain," I say.

"Don't thank me yet, you're the one who has to pass." He gives me a nod. "Get to work."

I do as I'm told, going about the business of daily life in the firehouse, avoiding thoughts of Emmy because of the complicated feelings that seem to be creeping up, and trying not to let myself get freaked out about possibly failing the lieutenant test for a second time.

Practical in Poughkeepsie has left a comment.

Practical in Poughkeepsie:

You've assumed a lot about me. That I'm cynical and closed-off because someone hurt me in the past. Maybe I'm happily married with three kids and a dog, living in the suburbs. I've listened to more than a few episodes now, and as far as I can tell, you never mention your own relationships. But you do talk a lot about Pride and Prejudice *and mention lots of your favorite rom-coms. So, I wonder, is your advice based on psychology or personal experience or is it based on fiction?*

Maybe you've closed yourself off by creating these unattainable standards for every guy you date.

Practical in Poughkeepsie

The Hopeful Romantic:

I understand your cynicism isn't going to go away overnight, but to quote the great Bell Hooks, "Cynicism is the greatest barrier to love." I really hope that one day, you know the magic of a slow dance or a kiss in the rain or maybe even fall so head over heels in love with someone that a grand gesture is the only way to let her know.

Stay hopeful!

Chapter Twenty-Three

Owen

I forgot about the photoshoot.

When Captain Donoho mentioned the fireman's calendar, I reacted and then put it right out of my mind. Which is why today, when I walk downstairs and see a photographer standing in the common area, I'm confused.

A sharp-looking woman I assume to be Liz Donoho is standing beside the photographer, and they're talking about ideas for the May spread while Jace and Clemons listen and snicker and shake their heads. From what I can tell, everybody is acting like they want no part of this project, but if I had to guess, more than a few of the guys are going to relish the opportunity.

I am not one of them.

I'm about to duck back out of the room and hide for the rest of the day when the woman glances up, sees me, and puts a hand on the photographer's arm. She stops talking.

"Owen! Owen Larrabee?" She holds her arms out as she crosses the room, and when she reaches me, she grabs onto my biceps like a grandma wanting to "get a good look." Her smile is wide. "I am so happy you agreed to be a part of our calendar! We're going to sell triple what we usually do thanks to you. And we usually sell a lot." She squeezes my arms and moves a little closer. "Our hometown hero!"

She stands back and looks me up and down. "You are just a perfect addition. I'm thinking February, since we're going to feature you and that adorable Emaline Smart. Everyone is going to eat. It. Up!" She taps my arms on each of these last three words.

"Right," I say, checking where the exits are. "When are we doing this?"

She laughs. "That's funny." She points at me. "You're funny." She starts back across the room and spots the others listening. "Don't think any of you are off the hook. Clemons, I've got a big plan for you. People need to see how fierce female firefighters really are. And you—" She points at Jace. "Jace the Ace. I'm thinking of a poker theme for you."

She gets distracted while talking to several others, and Jace walks over to where I'm standing.

"You light a fire in the garbage can. When she's distracted, I'll dump a load of coats on her, and we'll make a break for it."

I chuckle, but consider it.

"I really don't know when we're doing this," I say. "She never answered my question."

"Dude, it's today," he says. "The schedule? On the fridge?"

I stare blankly.

"It has your name on today's date and under that it says 'on location.'"

I slowly turn. "I don't even want to know what that means."

He shrugs and slaps me on the arm. "You're gonna find out, big guy."

As he walks away, I mutter, "Can't wait."

Then it hits me that Emmy will be there.

Maybe it won't be so bad.

Thankfully, for the next few hours there are calls that come in that I have to take care of.

Two minor incidents, one involving an old woman who locked herself out of her house and another involving a cat and a bucket.

I'd gladly trade my current situation with the cat.

When I get back to the station, I'm instructed to come back to the common area, and when I do, I find Liz, the photographer, and no Emmy. It hits me that I might've actually been looking forward to seeing her, because when I walk in and she's not there, I'm disappointed.

And then, Liz tells me we're going over to Book Smart for our photo shoot. "We saved the best for last." She grins. "Do you want a ride, or do you want to meet us there?"

"Emmy knows we're coming, right?"

She laughs. "Of course! We sent her a hair and makeup person an hour ago."

"Really?" I ask. "And she went for that?" Emmy is the least fussy person I know. Knowing they're going to do her hair and makeup doubles my surprise that she even agreed to do this in the first place.

"What girl doesn't love to play dress-up?" She picks up her purse and slings it over her shoulder. "So. Riding with us or. . .?"

"Thanks, but I'll drive." This feels like a situation that calls for an exit strategy.

"Don't skip out on us, Mr. Larrabee." She points at me, chuckling like she's joking, but I'd been considering faking a stomach flu or a bomb scare or a sudden emergency hip replacement ever since this morning.

But I'm not about to skip out on Emmy.

Odds are she's going to feel as awkward about this whole thing as I do—and strangely, that relaxes me a bit.

When I reach Emmy's shop, Liz is already bustling people out, switching the open sign over to closed and just generally taking charge. I step inside and Marco's standing there, eyeing me as Ernie packs up their Scrabble board.

John spots me and walks over. "Don't think we don't know what you're up to."

"I'm not up to anything," I say. "I'm here for work."

Ernie scoffs. "Your 'work' is trying to turn our Emmy into a harlot."

Mr. Ridgemont, who is apparently the only sane one of this bunch, pushes Ernie out. "Have fun!" he says, chuckling to himself because I'm pretty sure he knows that nothing about posing for photos is going to be fun. Not for me anyway.

There's a lull. And I hate small talk—but I feel like I should try to make the best of it.

"Have you, uh, ever been in a photo shoot with the captain, Mrs. D.?" I ask, as I take a seat at the coffee counter.

She gives me a "who me?" laugh of false humility. "Oh, no, Owen. I just organize. No non-firefighters in the calendar. Come to think of it, this is the first time we've ever asked someone outside the station to be a part of it!"

I don't respond. I'm not great at *chit chat.*

She nods, smiling. "But then again, we've never had such excitement here in town before."

I make a face. "It wasn't anything that anyone else couldn't have done."

"I couldn't disagree more. What happened with you and Emmy was *special.*"

Special?

"What happened was her house caught on fire, and I helped her out."

"You *carried* her out," she says. "There's a difference."

"Okay, but do we have to recreate it in a calendar?"

She narrows her eyes. "It's not what you think! This calendar is a well-loved tradition. *And* it's good for the whole department. I don't know if people actually realize how much you men and women do. Or risk. But when something happens like you carrying our local bookstore owner out of her burning house, well, it puts your job in the spotlight. And we want to keep it in the spotlight for as long as possible. This calendar will help raise money for all kinds of extra things that will help make your job easier."

"Like an espresso machine?" I ask, straight-faced.

"My husband said you had a dry sense of humor." She smiles. "I like it. I won't even ask you to smile in the photos, that's how nice I am." She winks at me as a blond woman I don't recognize pushes through the door that leads to Emmy's back room.

"Ah, Char, have you worked your magic?" Liz asks.

"She was like a blank canvas," Char muses. "She sent me out here to make sure nobody could see her. Said she doesn't want anyone seeing her 'all dolled up.'"

"She knows we're going to splash her picture all over to promote this calendar, doesn't she?" Liz sounds amused.

Emmy, I'm guessing, is not.

"Oh, she knows," Char says. "And she's not happy about it."

She's not the only one.

"I'm thinking she's going to need a little hand-holding." Char disappears back through the same door she came from, and Liz walks off to talk to the photographer, whose name I still don't know.

I spin around on the chair and glance out the large front windows of the shop.

When I lived here, this little bookstore was old and uninviting—and smelled weird. Emmy bought the business three years ago, and she must've instantly gotten to work on putting her fingerprints on it.

The books are arranged in a way that even makes me want to take a stroll down the aisles, and the addition of the locally brewed coffee and pastries was genius. There are couches and mismatched armchairs for reading, along with tables for working or chatting or, in at least one case, Scrabble-playing.

It's got a moody vibe. Cozy, I guess. And it feels like it was made by someone who put a lot of thought into it. And a lot of love.

She turned this passion she had for books into a genuine lifestyle, and it's kind of inspiring.

Emmy's done well for herself.

"Oh. My. Goodness! Look at you!" Liz's words pull me back to reality and reminds me that I'm about to *pose for photos*. Dread shocks my flesh, making my skin crawl a little.

But then, I turn back toward the door and see Emmy standing there.

I like the plain, simple version of Emmy. She's my friend, and she probably still knows me better than everyone (at least according to Lindsay). But the version standing in front of me right now is having a completely different effect on me.

Let's just say long talks aren't what's on my mind.

I stand up and try not to stare.

I absolutely fail.

Emmy is. . .stunning.

Her hair is usually pulled back, in a braid or a ponytail. But right now, it's loose and wavy, falling past her shoulders. She's wearing a simple red dress that hugs her in all the right places, and somehow her face is brighter, her eyes wider, her lips—

She's looking at me now, and I'm pretty sure she asked me a question.

For the life of me, I can't figure out what it was.

I've never been tongue-tied because of a woman. I dated Lindsay for years, and she's gorgeous, but she never rendered me mute.

"Doesn't she, Owen?"

Oh. It was Liz who asked the question. And I definitely have no idea what it was.

"Sorry, what?"

"I said, doesn't she look beautiful?" Liz's eyes are wide, as if to lead me to the correct answer.

I glance up at Emmy, whose cheeks are pink and who looks like she'd like to be put out of her misery. She meets my eyes briefly, then looks away.

I clear my throat. "Yeah. She's beautiful."

At that, she looks back at me, a trace of surprise on her face, but then she looks away.

"Okay, I'm told you two are old friends, so you won't mind if you have to get up close and personal, right?"

Emmy's eyes dart to mine and widen.

I'm not upset at all anymore about having to be here.

Chapter Twenty-Four

Emmy

Did that really just happen?

I'm Elphaba when Madame Morrible tells her that one day she might get to work with the Wizard. And while the soundtrack from *Wicked* plays on repeat in the back of my mind, I try desperately not to read into Owen's reaction or his words.

She's beautiful.

How in the world am I even supposed to react to that?

I'm not beautiful.

I know it. He knows it.

So, what the French toast?

He could've said, "Beautiful is a stretch, but I'm glad you did something with her hair." Or even, "Glad you put her in red. Now her dress matches her cheeks."

Those comments would've made him a royal jerk wagon, but they'd be honest.

I'm also still reeling over the "up close and personal" comment because *What Does That Mean* and are they going to give me free reign to explore Owen Larrabee?

Because I'm pretty sure I've got a map. . .

"All right!" Liz claps her hands together. She's one of those women who has figured out her personal style. The kind who actually wears accessories. Who buys shoes to match her outfit. For instance, right now, she's wearing dark jeans with a white top and a bright green blazer. Her earrings are the same shade of green and so are her shoes.

Who spends money on green shoes?

By contrast, I never buy a new pair of shoes unless they're versatile and sensible enough to wear with just about every outfit in my closet.

Actually, I don't really have "outfits."

I just have clothes.

Owen's wearing his uniform. A pair of navy blue pants with a tucked in navy T-shirt and red suspenders. I'm guessing this is what Liz told him to wear, and it summons all kinds of feelings inside me. Not because of how he looks in it, but because it reminds me of his job—which reminds me of the way he saved me—which reminds me of the cleanup day he organized just to be kind.

And also because of how he looks in it.

Well, crap.

There's no way around it. The crush is back. Full force. Which means I not only lied to Mack about it, I lied to myself. It not only feels like it never went away, it feels like it intensified. Back then, I wouldn't have thought it possible. . .

Now I know better.

My fingers tingle at the realization.

Liz walks over to me. "So, Emaline—"

"You can call me Emmy," I say, forcing myself to smile.

"Emmy." She clasps her hands in front of her mouth. "Adorable."

I glance at Owen. He's standing off to the side looking like he wants to do this even less than me, and all at once I'm not sure either of us is going to be able to relax.

It's also slightly disconcerting that he seems so miserable about having his photo taken with me.

"Okay, you two," Liz says. "I love that we're doing this in Emmy's bookshop—love to give a local small business a little extra exposure. What I'm picturing is the two of you in the aisle over here with bookshelves on either side of you, maybe Emmy, you leaning up against one, Owen, you with a hand on the shelf behind her, facing her? Sort of a 'stolen moment in the stacks' kind of feel?"

Nobody moves.

"Okay?" Liz's eyebrows shoot up, like she's trying to lead the witness.

Objection!

"Sure," I say. "Sounds good."

She turns to Owen. "You okay? You look like you're going to throw up." She laughs. "This will be painless, I promise."

Owen grunt-mumbles a response.

"Great." She glances at the photographer, a woman I heard Char call Godiva, but who nobody has introduced me to. They seem to be communicating, and I think they're worried. I'm worried too. When she was doing my hair, Char told me to "just relax and be natural." I don't think she realized that for me, those two things were in direct opposition to each other.

I think I'm going to be really bad at this.

We all move out of the coffee shop area of the store and toward the books, which happens to be my favorite part of my shop. Godiva has set up lighting around the space where they'll have us stand, and as awkward as this whole thing makes me feel, it's a great backdrop.

Surrounded by books, what could be better?

Owen's lips an inch from mine, that's what.

"Your shop is cool," Owen says as he comes alongside me.

Liz is chatting with Godiva to set up the perfect background for our shot, giving Owen and me a brief second alone.

A stolen moment in the stacks.

"Thanks. I *am* cool." I keep my eyes straight ahead, as if I'm driving up the side of the mountain and don't want to veer off of a cliff.

"Okay, you two," Liz turns to us. "Why don't you stand right in between—" she looks at the shelves— "thrillers and romance."

Thrilling romance. Just like *Texas Hold Me*, the enemies to lovers trope set in the 1870's.

The only problem is that Owen isn't the outlaw with the heart of gold and I'm not the Mayor of Dry Bluff's upstart daughter.

Once we're in the aisle, I realize these shelves are very close together. Too close. Someone should fix that immediately. Who owns this place, anyway?

I stand so close to the thriller section I might as well be the girl loosely draped on one of these Harlan Coben novel covers. Owen seems to be doing the same on the opposite side.

And it isn't hard to picture him as a Jane Austen hero.

Liz takes one look at us and laughs. "Okay, this is not going to cut it, kids."

I look at her, feigning innocence as if I have no idea why hugging my side of the aisle isn't going to give them the vibe they're going for.

"He saved your life," she says, emphatically. "We all saw the way he carried you out of the house, right? We're trying to give people the fantasy of, you know, what happens next."

"What happens next?" I ask, because I really want to know.

"Yes!" she says, like I've just gotten the correct answer on a game show. "Maybe he's your knight in shining armor! Maybe you start a casual friendship that leads to more, who knows? Give people a hint of romance! Can we try that?"

No response.

"Great," she says, eyes wide again. She's starting to look panicked. She turns to Godiva. "How about you try?"

"Maybe let's just take a few test shots to check the lighting," she says. Oh. She's British. Her accent is warm and wonderful. I wish I had an accent.

The momentary distraction calms me for a split second, and then I realize I have to actually *do* what they're asking.

Owen and I stand opposite each other like two people trying to win an award for best impression of a statue.

Godiva snaps a few shots, then checks the back of the camera.

"Why don't we try one standing just a little bit closer?" Liz asks.

We inch slightly closer together, but barely change the way we're standing. We're two eighth graders at their very first dance. His tie is too tight and my corsage is about to draw blood.

"Relax, you two," Liz says. "This is supposed to be fun."

We look at one another, and we must have the same expression on our faces, because we both raise our eyebrows simultaneously, then frown, then smile, then relax into a bit of laughter.

"There! See? Just like that!" Godiva snaps a few rapid shots.

Liz snaps her fingers. "Hey! Maybe that's where we go with this, more candid, more natural, less staged?"

Owen loosens his shoulders to be less tense. "Yeah, posing us maybe isn't the best idea."

I agree. "It's not like I'm some Harlequin cover model.

What, do you want me to. . ." I raise one arm and slide a palm down the books, comically popping a hip.

Click, click-click.

Owen chuckles. Wow, his smile.

Click-click.

"Take this one, for instance. . ." I grab a book titled *The Rake's Road to Ruin*, a perfectly trashy romance, where the lady's dress covers up half the front cover.

Owen makes a face. "There's no way those people are real. How do you even get in that position and not get a cramp?"

I giggle. "You have no idea how ridiculously awesome some of these book covers are."

Liz interjects, "Why don't you face each other?"

We are still chuckling, and without thinking, we turn. I still have the book in my hand.

"Now, take her in your arms, like you're going to slow dance."

"Slow dance?" Owen asks.

I quirk a brow. "What, you've never slow danced with an overly made-up woman between shelves of romance novels in a bookstore before?"

"Not lately," he chuckles. "Doesn't seem like something real people do."

"Oh, *no*," I gasp.

"What?"

"Don't tell me you're a cynic," I say.

He gives me a look like he knows I know the answer to that question because I do. Owen is my romance opposite.

Click-click, click.

"Maybe you should work on that," I say, a tease in my tone. "Cynicism is the greatest barrier to love, you know."

He pauses.

"What did you say?" His brow furrows.

"It's a quote," I tell him.

"Yeah, Bell Hooks."

Now my brow furrows. "You know Bell Hooks?"

"Not personally," he quips.

I shake my head. "Funny."

"This doesn't look like slow dancing!" Liz calls from behind Godiva.

Owen looks at me, a questioning look on his face.

I make a face back, because the mood is still light, and affecting a faux Southern accent, I fan myself, and say, "Why, Mistah *Larr*-a-bee, I would be de-*lah*-ted!"

When I get nervous, I get weird. It's kind of my thing. But I'm not prepared for how the mood immediately changes.

I'm still holding the book in my left hand, the side that's facing Godiva, clicking away, taking pictures and making comments to herself in that lovely accent. I glance up, and without breaking eye contact, Owen slips his right hand under and around on the small of my back and pulls me toward him.

I instinctively grab around his neck with my right hand, look up into his eyes, his intense eyes, and I feel like I'm floating, or dreaming, or both. I let my other hand—and the book—slowly lower. Just before I let the book drop to the floor. . .

Click!

. . .and it hits the ground.

He reaches down and off to the side, and I take my hand from around his neck. His other hand is still firmly pressing against the small of my back. I reach up and touch his shoulder, completely lost in his eyes. I dare not look away, because if I do, I might actually wake up from this dream.

I'm aware of the sound of a soft guitar echoing through the speakers as he pulls me a little closer.

Liz must've found the speaker, and she's chosen to play, of all songs, a cover of "Can't Help Falling in Love," the version from *Crazy Rich Asians.* A woman's beautiful voice begins to sing the familiar lyrics, and I beg my body to relax, even as every nerve-ending is standing at attention.

Owen's grip on my hand is firm, but loose, and we begin to sway, our bodies pulled together by an unexpected outside force. We settle into a gentle rhythm, and everything else fades away.

All at once, it's like we're the only two people in the world as the song builds and I begin to relax in his arms. I feel like I'm floating. Owen's gaze takes my breath away.

Because he's not looking at me like he usually does. He's looking at me like he likes what he sees.

And he isn't looking away.

His gaze pins me in place, conjuring feelings inside me that I buried a long time ago. His hand guides me in a slow circle, and I can't help but get swept up in the romance of it. We're held together by a single electric strand, and it sizzles and burns as the seconds tick by.

In this moment, what's happening between us doesn't feel like a put-on or a performance. It feels honest and raw and right.

He feels right.

Even though I know he is so, so wrong.

"Emmy—" His voice is low and deep.

"Perfect! We got it!" Liz claps her hands together.

The moment is severed in an abrupt snap.

I freeze as the lights change and the music cuts out and the bookstore is transformed from *romantic fantasy destination* to *place of business* once again.

I want to hit pause, then rewind. Back to the moment Owen said my name.

I try to catch my breath, wondering where it all went.

But he takes a step back and nods at me. "There, that wasn't so bad, right?"

Not so bad? It was *awesome*! It was *heaven*! It was *the stuff my dreams are made of*!

But then I look around. I see the lights, the camera stands, the people off to the side.

Like the fictional characters I idolize, like the relationships I adore on the page. . .

None of it was real.

Chapter Twenty-Five

Owen

What was THAT?

The second Liz gives me the all clear, I mumble my good-byes and dart out of the bookshop as fast as I can.

There is no way slow dancing in a bookstore is supposed to have *that* kind of effect on me. My heart is pounding out of my chest. I can feel it in my ears.

Once Emmy settled in my arms, I was done for. I couldn't look away. I don't know if Liz and that photographer are really that good at their jobs or what, but standing there with her looking up at me, seeing straight through me, time stood still.

Nothing else really mattered.

It was like. . .magic.

The kind of magic that lady on the podcast talked about.

The kind of magic I don't—or didn't—believe in.

I hope that one day, you know the magic of a sweet slow dance. That's what that Hopeful Romantic had written.

Well, guess what, lady?

I get in my truck and start the engine, but I don't pull away.

The photographer walks out of the shop, and a few seconds later, Liz follows. And then Emmy is the only one left inside.

I could make some excuse to go back in.

See if she wants to get dinner.

Or I could stop acting like a fool. This whole thing was a fabrication. Liz basically said we were creating a fantasy. The kind I'd been known to mock.

So why did it feel so real?

I get out of the car, but instead of going back into the bookshop, I walk down the street to DeLucca's. I'm not surprised to find Jace and some of the other guys playing pool in the back. I order a beer and head back there. Maybe they'll help me get my head back on straight. Because not only was that moment with Emmy tripping me up, but so was the fact that she pulled out the same quote as the podcast lady.

Or maybe it's a coincidence. Emmy *is* well-read.

I shake the thoughts away. I don't know what to make of any of it, and I don't want to dwell on it. I need a distraction.

"You survived!" Jace is holding a pool cue, waiting on Blister to take a turn.

"Barely," I groan. "It wasn't the worst thing in the world, but I'll be happy if I never have to do that again."

A waitress brings me my beer.

Jace clinks the bottle with his own. "To never having to do that again!"

I raise mine in the air and take a swig.

"Until next year!" he adds.

I wince. "I think I'll be sick that day."

"That bad?" Jace frowns.

No, that good.

"It was fine. Emmy's great. Just. . .not my thing."

The restaurant is quieter than usual, and I'm glad for it. I want the distraction, but not the noise. Not when my mind is already so loud.

"Emmy's. . .great?" Jace asks.

I try to brush it off. "Nah, it's nothing."

He eyes me. "It's not nothing, whatever it is."

"It's probably the test he's taking, right Larrabee?"

I turn and find Levi standing off to the side with Turner.

"What's he talking about?" Jace sets his bottle on the table.

I shoot a pointed look at Levi. I'm liking this guy less and less.

"Overheard the captain saying you're looking to move up. *Lieutenant* Larrabee." Levi has a big mouth. How does he even know about the test?

The chatter in the bar dulls to a low hum. I straighten.

"Seriously?" Jace looks at me. "That's awesome, man. Why didn't you say anything?"

"It's not for sure," I mutter.

"You been here, what, two weeks, and all of a sudden you're getting promoted?" Levi says, in a tone that sounds like we're facing off in the schoolyard. "Guess that's what special treatment gets you nowadays, huh?" He chuckles like he's just said something funny.

Beside me, Jace tenses.

The muscles in my body flare as I try to hold back saying what I'm actually thinking. I look at Levi, seeing him more clearly than before.

I slowly turn back to face the bar.

"Nothing to say? Nothing?" He raises his voice. "I've been here four years, and not so much as a glance from the captain. You waltz in here, save some hot chick, and now you're the freaking golden boy of the station?"

My hand squeezes tighter around my bottle.

He turns to Turner. "Heck, maybe I should pay her a visit, throw her over my shoulder, see where that gets me," he laughs.

I slam the bottle down on the counter, and beer shoots out, spilling down the sides over my hand.

I don't even feel it.

Without turning around, I say, "I think you better walk away."

Levi cracks a taunting laugh that tells me he's not going anywhere. "Come on, buddy," he says. "There's no shame in taking the easy way out." He leans toward me. "Gotta do what we can to move up in this world, right?"

Jace puts a hand on Levi's arm. "Hey, that's enough, Lawrence, come on."

I try to breathe. I try to relax.

But all I see is red.

I turn. "I said. . .walk. Away."

"Or what? You gonna come at me like you did your last captain?"

I glare.

"Oh yeah. I know all about that, everyone does. The way I figure it, the only possibility is that you called in some kind of favor to get a job back here—or you're claiming you're stupid so they'll take pity on you."

His expression shifts, and he takes a step closer.

"Either way, *it ain't fair*."

"Come on, Owen, let's get out of here." Jace grabs my arm, but I shrug him off.

My pulse quickens. I'm back in my old firehouse with Baker in my face. I'm back in grade school and some faceless bully is calling me stupid.

Levi needs to learn a lesson. And I'm happy to be the one to teach him.

I size him up, keeping my hands at my sides—which takes

every ounce of my willpower. He's not a small guy, but I've got a good twenty pounds and three inches on him.

He looks at Turner, then back at me. "Not sure I want to be taking orders from someone who's too dumb to read the test."

Levi laughs again, his self-righteous, *I'm better than you* attitude showing through, and something inside me snaps.

My left hand is no longer at my side, it's grabbing the front of his shirt. My other hand, now a fist, is cocked back and ready to swing.

I hold it there, twitching, not sure what's stopping me, so I shove both hands so hard into Levi's chest that he stumbles back into the pool table, bending in half and falling to the floor. He scrambles, then pulls himself back up.

"Okay, Larrabee. This is what you want? Is this how a lieutenant would act?" He's goading me. He wants the promotion, and I'm in the way—I don't really care at this point.

I brace myself for his charge, my heart pumping, my blood boiling, but before I can move, I hear someone call my name from behind.

I turn and there, standing just inside the doorway, is Emmy.

My breath is ragged, and I have to swallow the bitter taste of shame as it crawls up the back of my throat.

She locks onto my eyes and makes quick work of the space between us. When she reaches me, she stands between me and Levi, hands on my chest. "He's not worth it." Her eyes are so wide and focused they pull me right in.

She knows that if my temper gets the better of me here, I might not get another chance. I could ruin my shot at that promotion. All because some punk got the better of me. She doesn't say it out loud, but I can see it on her face.

I can hear the warning in her voice.

And just like I did in the midst of her panic attack, she

reaches out and takes my fisted hand between hers. "He doesn't matter."

I look up and glare at Levi, and she takes a hand and puts it on my cheek.

"Hey. . .hey," she says, then leans in and softer, "*tell me three body parts you see.*"

I blink, look down, and her eyes twinkle.

I immediately break, relax, and feel a slight smile crawl across my face.

In an instant, with one softly spoken sentence, Emmy has saved me.

Behind her, Levi makes a snide comment, then laughs that annoying laugh. And normally I would want to barrel past her and introduce him to the business end of a barstool.

But instead, I'm calm. It's odd, but Emmy has made me see this whole situation as funny.

And pathetic.

I feel sorry for Levi.

I take a step back.

"Not cool, man," Jace says to Levi.

"Really not cool." Turner walks away from Levi.

Emmy is still holding my hand, and just like in her bookshop only an hour ago, it's like the rest of the world disappears, and she is all that matters.

Levi glares at me as he takes a step away. "Good luck on your test."

I look at him, and without thinking, I say, "I might fail it, but you'll always succeed at being a total scumbag."

Emmy, still facing only me, smiles.

Levi storms through the restaurant and out the door.

I take a breath and look around. People are starting to go back to their conversations, which, I'm guessing, are all about what just happened.

"You have perfect timing, you know that?" My hand is still in hers, and she pats it and lets it go. "What are you even doing here?"

She shrugs, a soft smile dancing on her lips. "A girl's gotta eat."

She's amazing right now.

"Well, I'm buying," I tell her. "I owe you."

"You don't," she says. "That's what friends are for."

Friends.

"I'll go get a table." Before she walks away, she turns back. "Can I trust you to not go find that guy and run him over with your truck?"

I push my hand through my hair, chuckling a little. "Yeah. Yeah, I'm good."

Emmy has a way of making sense of things—of making things make sense. Like in high school when she gently explained how my vandalism hurt Marco (and the rest of the community) without making me feel completely ashamed. She made me want to clean up my own mess, just like she made me want to take the high road tonight.

How did she do that?

She leaves, and I turn to find Jace watching me. "What?"

He holds up a hand. "I didn't say anything."

"You've got a look."

"I do not," he says.

I stare at him.

"Fine, I do," he says. "What's going on there?"

"Nothing," I say.

"Well, keep her." He takes a drink. "She's like Black Widow with the Hulk. What did she whisper to you anyway?"

I just smile and raise a hand to the bartender, asking for a napkin and a new beer.

"At any rate, she makes you better."

My mom said the same thing.

She does, doesn't she? She at least makes me want to *try* and be better. Emmy sees me differently than other people. And her belief in me is convincing. Sometimes.

I take the new bottle from the bartender and shake my head. "You've got the wrong idea."

"Or you're kidding yourself." He tips his bottle at me and takes a drink. "Time will tell."

I walk away, and as I turn the corner and spot Emmy sitting in a booth against the back wall, I realize I don't need time to tell me anything.

She's amazing.

And she always has been.

Chapter Twenty-Six

Emmy

This is not a date.

This is a *post-almost-fight-after-romantic-slow-dance-in-the-stacks-for-a-calendar-photograph* dinner.

No big deal.

I briefly consider that premise for a romance trope—guy saves girl from fire, girl saves guy from fight, will they, won't they—and decide it's too far-fetched.

I don't need a menu for a restaurant I eat at weekly, but I've got one, and I'm hiding behind it because *what am I doing here*?

When I left the shop, I saw Owen's truck was still parked outside, and while I told myself I needed dinner, it's *possible* I ~~hoped~~ thought I'd run into him here.

I'm keenly aware that he's just around that corner, probably gathering himself. Maybe talking to Jace.

Maybe regretting his offer to buy me dinner.

Because while it's absolutely not, it does feel a little date-like.

When he walks around the corner, I zero in on the word *Pasta* on the menu in my hand, and then my eyes do that unfocusing thing where the words don't read like words anymore and none of them mean anything.

"Hey." He sits down across from me.

"Hey." It comes out tinny. I don't look up.

"You're studying that thing like there's going to be a quiz later."

"Maybe there will be."

"I'm sure you'll ace it."

I set the menu down. "I'm getting stuffed shells and meatballs."

"I'm getting lasagna."

"Great."

"Good."

We stare at each other.

"What was that fight about?" I finally ask. "And would you have actually punched that guy if I hadn't come in?"

"Same crap, different day." He sighs and looks away. "And yeah. I would have."

I caught enough of the conversation to fill in the blanks as to the "why" Owen lost his temper. When he was younger, I noticed a trend. Owen really only acted up when he felt stupid.

"You know he's an idiot, right?"

He shrugs. And as confident as Owen is, I see the remnant of a lot of years of believing he wasn't smart enough to amount to anything. I don't know if anyone ever said that to him. Probably, given the fact that he was always getting into trouble. If I had to guess, that guy knew just what buttons to push to set him off.

"And if you don't take that test, he wins."

He takes a drink. "Let's talk about something else."

The waitress comes by and takes our order. True to form, we order way more food than we can eat because in addition to our entrees, Owen adds garlic bread and I add mozzarella sticks. We agree to share both, but I've been known to clear a whole order of mozzarella sticks by myself.

When she walks away, he smirks at me. "Are we going to have a *see who can eat more* contest?"

"I will eat you under the table," I say. "You're out of practice."

"Big words for someone so small."

I'm still getting used to talking to Owen in public. It's strange because in my little corner of this town, people know me. And some of them remember Owen. And while pulling me out of my burning house and saving my life changed the way some people saw him, others won't ever see him as anything but trouble.

The kid who never obeyed the speed limit.

The kid who brought beer to high school football games and drank it under the bleachers.

The kid who got into fights in the hallway.

They didn't see the other side of him. And I know how that sounds. If I said these things to other people, it would sound like I'm making excuses for him—but I'm not.

If people tell you something often enough, especially people in authority, you start to believe it. You're not smart. You make bad choices. You're not living up to your potential. That's what he's been told his whole life, by pretty much everyone with varying degrees of tact.

How hard would it be to try to live in a world that's not set up to help you succeed?

Owen didn't stand a chance.

And tonight, when that stupid guy ran his mouth, I saw the hurt masked as anger behind Owen's eyes.

And, I don't know, I just wanted to take that pain away.

Which is why it makes zero sense that the next thing I say is, "Have you seen Lindsay lately? How's she doing?"

Call it self-preservation. Call it stupidity. Both things are equally true.

His expression shifts. He almost looks confused. Doesn't he understand that I have to remind myself regularly he is not mine?

"Uh, no," he says. "Why would I?"

I shrug. "Didn't know if you guys had, you know, reconnected. When you, uh, were talking the other day, she looked, you know, comfortable, and so I, um didn't know if there were sparks or. . .whatever. . ."

Mercifully, the waitress is back with our appetizers. She sets them down in the center of the table, asks if we need anything else. When we say no, she vanishes.

I load up my plate with garlic bread and mozzarella sticks and pretend I didn't just bring up the worst topic in the world.

I plow ahead with the conversational deftness of an eggplant.

"So, what's going on in sports these days?"

He frowns. "What?" He puts down his fork. "What just happened?"

"Huh?" I've made a tightrope out of the mozzarella sticks, with three inches hanging from my mouth to the food in my hand.

"You're being weird again."

"No, I'm not." My mouth is full, and I finally sever the cheese and chew, hoping it'll get lodged in my throat and I'll have to be rushed away from here in an ambulance.

But then I remember Owen is a trained firefighter and he'd be the one to save me, and all at once, I'm looking around for all the things that could cause me to need CPR.

I'm about to open my mouth and say whatever pops into my head again when there's a tapping from outside the window. We both turn and there, standing on the street, wearing a jean jacket, scarf, and the stocking hat I knitted her for Christmas, is Mack.

She motions to both of us and shrugs, as if to say: *What's going on here?*

I wave her in and smile awkwardly at Owen.

His expression is idling in neutral, and I'm trying my best not to crash and burn. I think I'm failing.

"Is this like, a date?" Mack now stands at the end of our table.

Owen goes to say something, but I cut him off.

"No!" I say, a little more forcefully than I mean to.

Wait. What was he going to say?

I blather on. "I mean, don't be crazy. We just bumped into each other again. After the photo shoot. I needed food, and he was here, and I came in, and. . ." I trail off, waving my hand like a drunk queen of a very remote island in Europe.

"Mozzarella stick?" I ask, holding one up.

I won't tell Mack about the near-fight because I don't think Owen would want her to know. He's never said so, but I think he cares a lot about what his family thinks of him, and after years of letting them down, I know he's trying to do better. He *is* doing better.

But Mack still doesn't see it. She just stares at us.

"We're having an eat-off," I say.

Her face changes.

"Without me? Why didn't you just say so?" Mack scoots into the booth next to me.

Our weekly ritual of overeating at DeLucca's had gotten interrupted last time due to the unfortunate Lindsay-sighting, so we're overdue for what we call *paralisi della pasta.*

Roughly translated, it means "pasta coma."

"You guys are not going to believe the flight I just had." Mack nabs the mozzarella stick out of my hand and takes a bite.

She does this much more gracefully than I did. There's no cheese hanging out of her mouth.

My eyes drift over to Owen's as I half-listen to Mack's story. He should be looking at her—she *is* the one talking. But he's not. He's looking at me.

Something silent passes between us, and I realize my gratitude for Mack's interruption is short-lived. How would this night have gone if she wasn't here? I love my best friend, but her timing is sort of terrible.

Before long, Jace is also at our table, sitting next to Owen and flirting with Mack. Owen and I are both quiet, though I'm guessing not for the same reason. Maybe Owen is thinking about what that guy said to him.

Meanwhile, I'm just thinking about Owen.

"Oh! Emmy, I forgot to tell you. Chad Rober was asking about you." Mack says this last part in a sing-songy tone, like it's an exciting new development.

When I don't react accordingly, she nudges my arm.

"Did you hear me?" she asks. "You remember him, right?"

Chad Rober. . .Chad Rober. . .

"Wasn't he the one who got in trouble for listing the principal's house for sale on Craigslist for the senior prank?"

"Yep. And you'll never guess, he's a high school English teacher now." She pumps her eyebrows. "And he asked about you."

"Ah," I say absently. Am I supposed to care?

She frowns. "Oh, I know what this is." She pops a bite in her mouth and looks across the table. "This is the E.S.M."

I frown. "Oh, stop it."

Owen looks at me, confused. "The E.S.M. . .?"

I roll my eyes. "The 'Emaline Smart Meter.'"

Mack talks mid-bite. "That's it. That's what's happening. It's the meter."

"Mack, there's no meter."

Both guys look confused, so I try to explain.

"She thinks that I hold every guy to some ridiculous standard. They never measure up because of the—" both Mack and I hold our hands up as measuring sticks and say simultaneously "*—Emaline Smart Meter.*"

"There's no meter!" I take a bite.

"There is. You reject every guy who shows any interest because you're holding out for someone as hopelessly romantic as you."

My stomach springboards into my throat, and I almost choke on my meatball.

"Oh?" Jace leans back in the booth. "Do you have, like, a checklist or something?"

"No," I say, a little too quickly. *Not one that's written down anyway.*

"She might as well." Mack looks at Jace. "I keep telling her she's too picky."

"She's allowed to be picky." It's like Owen has rumbled to life, and the second the words are out, I'm holding on to them as if they're a bouquet of balloons that have lifted me off the ground.

"Oh?" Mack looks at him. "You think it's smart to hold out for someone who'll—what was it you said Emmy? —who'll sweep you off your feet?"

Jace, ever the comic, smacks Owen on the arm and points at me. "Wait a sec. . .didn't you literally do that a few weeks ago?"

I feel myself blush as Owen shoots him a look.

Mack continues eating while talking. "Owen doesn't sweep people. Right, Grumbles?"

Owen snatches the half-eaten mozzarella stick out of Mack's hand and shoves it in his mouth.

"Hey!"

"He doesn't think it's smart," Jace says, nodding to Owen. "He's made that very clear after listening to—"

"All I'm saying—" Owen cuts in— "is that both of you—" he makes sure to include his sister in this proclamation— "are entitled to hold out for someone who is exactly what you want. Make sure whoever the guy is, he ticks all the boxes."

Mack takes a drink, then says, "Okay, so, if Emmy's waiting for a guy who's going to, say, take her stargazing in the back of a truck, you think that's perfectly logical?"

"No *way*," Jace says, straightening. "You've been listening to her too, haven't you?!"

Mack grins. "*The Hopeful Romantic*?"

Jace laughs. "The guys at the station are obsessed."

My cheeks are on fire. Yes, I use a voice changer. Yes, I do everything I can to be sure not to slip and give myself away. But nobody has ever mentioned the podcast in my real life before.

"I should go," I say quickly, pushing Mack so she'll get up and let me out of the booth.

"Chill, girl, what's the rush?"

I fumble for an excuse. "I just remembered my mom asked me to water her mums!"

"Oh—kay," Mack says. "Call me later then? And let me know when you hear from Chad! Maybe he's the star gazing type."

"Wait, what?" I freeze.

Mack grins. "I gave him your number!"

"Oh, no! Why?!"

"Because if you're not going to put yourself out there, I'm going to do it for you."

"Okay, sorry I have to run, night guys!" I'm about to dart out the door, shrugging my jacket on, when I realize Owen's following me. I turn. "What's wrong?"

"It's dark out."

"And. . .?"

"And I'm going to walk you back to your car."

My stomach takes a shot at the uneven parallel bars but forgets how to dismount. "You really don't have to. It's Harvest Hollow. It's perfectly safe."

"I can follow behind at a safe distance if you'd prefer it, but I'm walking you to your car."

I feel my shoulders drop. "Okay."

"Okay."

Outside, it's starting to smell like autumn. Not the start of autumn, but the whole of the season. Crunchy leaves and mountain air. My favorite season. I take a moment and draw in a chilly breath. It fills me up and when I exhale, there's a cloud from my warm exhale mixing with the cool air.

As we start back in the direction of the shop, he says, "So, holding out for another hopeless romantic, huh?"

I wrap my coat around me a little tighter. "Mack thinks I'm being ridiculous." I look at him. "Oh, and in case you didn't notice, Jace is totally into her."

"Wait. Jace? Should I go back in there or. . ." He stops and looks back at the restaurant.

I laugh and give his arm a tug. "She can handle herself."

He must decide I'm right because he starts walking again. "Do you think it's ridiculous?"

"To want someone to sweep me off my feet?" I ask. "Probably." A pause. "But I still want it." I smile at him.

He shoves his hands in his pockets.

"What about you?"

He shrugs.

This is typical of Owen, shutting down and not saying what he's thinking. Sometimes, though, when I just wait a few moments. . .

"I'm not really the, uh, romance type. Had kind of a bad experience, so. . ."

I can tell he's trying to cover his true feelings, but I don't say anything.

"At any rate, I'm more of a practical guy. Not the 'rent a billboard to profess my love' kind. Three-Date Owen, remember?"

I squint over at him. "Yeah, I remember, but I don't know if I buy it."

"Why not?"

I shrug. "You have too much to offer to withhold yourself forever. And even in high school, that wasn't who you were."

He scoffs. "People change, Emmy." We're almost back at the bookshop, and I find myself wishing I could slow down without him noticing. "I can live without romance. Give me practical every day of the week."

"Practical, huh?" I study him. Is Owen one of the guys at the station who's obsessed with the podcast? I really can't see him tuning in. He'd think it was all nonsense.

"Yeah, like, taking out the garbage, or filling her car up with gas, or staying up late so she can unload about a bad day."

Huh. So maybe he *does* listen. I narrow my eyes. "Or organizing a team of people to clean someone's house after a fire?"

He looks caught for a moment. I shouldn't have said that.

"I mean. . .yeah. Nice things. People should do nice things for. . .friends and people they care about."

Friends. Sigh.

"And you think that's better than romance."

"It doesn't matter because I took myself off the market a long time ago." He stops walking. I've never been more unhappy to see my car in my life.

"There. Got you back safe," he says.

I fish around in my purse for my keys thinking about the

movie *Hitch* and how this is me signaling to him that I want him to kiss me.

He wouldn't even have to go the ninety percent. I'd go the whole hundred.

And even though I absolutely would not be opposed to that, this really is just me forgetting that I need keys to drive my car home. Still, just the stray thought is enough to light my cheeks on fire.

"Thanks." I pull my keys out in a *eureka* fashion and unlock my car. I'm about to leave, but in a rare stroke of boldness, I turn back. "You should put yourself back on the market."

"Oh?"

"Yeah," I say. "I bet there's someone out there who could make you really happy."

"Someone practical?" he asks.

I smile. "Or someone romantic."

Chapter Twenty-Seven

Emmy

Did I just flirt?

That was too much. Too close. Too many feelings.

I'm halfway home, and I still feel the nervous energy bubbling inside of me.

Everything about my friendship with Owen is starting to take a turn in a different, familiar direction. If history is any kind of a teacher, I can't let myself get swept away in the idea of him again. I just can't.

Getting humiliated by expressing my feelings for him once was bad enough—if I do it again, I may as well check into that special kind of hospital with the padded walls.

Plus, Mack's right. I'm too picky. Maybe she doesn't realize it, but that's not the reason I'm holding out for someone as hopelessly romantic as me—not entirely.

The main reason is I haven't met anyone who makes me feel the way Owen does.

Er, did.

Continues to do.

I don't think there's a tense for something that has happened, continues to happen, and probably will happen in the future.

Maybe I need to broaden my horizons.

Sow some royal oats.

Leave the house.

What if *Practical in Poughkeepsie* was onto something with his whole idea of what's really important? What if I've been waiting for a lightning bolt when what I really needed was a cozy electric blanket that I could turn on with the flip of a switch?

Maybe someone like Chad Rober.

Maybe he's exactly who I need.

Smart. Stable. Dependable.

Is that bad?

Maybe I've been holding out for something that doesn't even exist beyond the page.

Never mind that even the briefest eye contact with Owen makes me feel like I'm sitting in a sauna.

What am I supposed to do with that?

Wait and melt?

Waiting is not only hopeless, it's idiotic.

It's time for me to admit what a part of me has always known: Owen Larrabee and I have no future together.

We were always a mismatch. At odds. Polar opposites.

Being older doesn't change that.

As if the universe can sense this shift in my thought process, my phone buzzes as I pull into my driveway and turn off the engine.

It's a text from a number I don't have saved in my phone.

UNKNOWN NUMBER

Hey Emmy, it's Chad Rober. I read the article about the fire in the newspaper.

How are you holding up?

Okay, if this happened in a romance novel, the reader would give it a two-star review for using coincidence as a plot driver.

But this is not a novel. This is real life. *My* real life.

I blink at my phone. The text is still there.

Is this a sign? A sign that it's time to move on? That I'm not destined to be the crazy Harvest Hollow cat lady at the end of the block that trick or treaters avoid?

As I stare at the phone in my hand, I think about the way Owen looked at me tonight during dinner.

There's no way I want to get hurt again. Not like before.

I've been protecting myself by keeping myself out of relationships altogether, but maybe the right answer is to throw myself into a safer one.

One where there's no danger of, you know, me falling in love.

Romance novel heroines do that all the time.

It doesn't usually work, but I'm going to ignore that for now.

My thumbs hover over my phone screen, and I finally text back:

EMMY

Hey, Chad!

Thanks for asking. I'm doing okay now.

It was pretty scary.

CHAD

Yeah, I bet

I can't even imagine what it's like to go through something like that.

EMMY

Good thing it's in the rear view mirror <sighing face emoji>

CHAD

Kind of out of left field, but I was wondering if you wanted to go get dinner sometime?

Why this question makes my ears hot, I have no idea. It's not the kind of heat I feel around Owen. It's a preemptive embarrassment because I haven't been the most successful dater.

I realize this makes my podcast hypocritical, but I liken this to, say, a basketball coach. Some of the best coaches could never play professionally in their sport, but they understand how the sport works and how to make their players better at it.

That's me. I understand how relationships work. I can even troubleshoot how to make them better. But for whatever reason, I haven't quite figured out how to make one work for me.

Maybe this is my chance.

Maybe I should give Chad Rober a real, honest-to-goodness shot. There will be no sparks or fireworks. Only good, old-fashioned dating.

EMMY

That sounds fun!

CHAD

. . .no way, really?

That's awesome!

I smile to myself at his sincerity.

EMMY

I'm free this weekend?

CHAD

Great! How's Friday?

EMMY

Perfect! Pick me up at the store?

CHAD

I'll swing by around 7!!

His overuse of exclamation points notwithstanding, he seems to be a perfectly normal human.

And that's what I'll choose.

EMMY

Looking forward to it!

I do a quick gut-check.

No butterflies.

No hum.

No bodice-ripping scenes playing in my head.

I'm perfectly calm over the whole thing. And maybe, just maybe, that's a good thing.

I can call it an experiment. I can even talk about it in my next episode.

"Practical Over Romantic: The Research and the Development."

Who knows? Maybe Chad Rober will be the one to finally take me off the market.

Chapter Twenty-Eight

Owen

The day after the DeLucca's incident, I get a text from Mack.

MACK

Hey, can you come fix a door for me?

OWEN

What's wrong with it?

MACK

It sticks. Old house.

OWEN

Be over in a little bit.

On the way to Mack's house, I swing through Book Smart for coffee, but Emmy's not there. I try to ignore my disappointment, but it's there, plain as day.

I even hang around for a few minutes after I get my drink, thinking maybe she'll show up. . .

These new feelings for Emmy might need to be put in check.

I leave, feeling like I showed up early at the amusement park only to find out it doesn't open for another hour, and head to Mack's.

Mack lives in a small craftsman that's not that different from Emmy's, all triangular roofs and exposed rafters. It's old though, and old houses need upkeep. I used to wonder why my sister chooses to live here rather than in Asheville, or Knoxville, or any other big city, but I think I've figured it out.

Mack has this strong, independent, tough exterior, but inside she's a softie.

And the most important thing in her life is her people.

Even when I was away, she tried to keep in touch. It was me who put a wall up. When I left, I cut everyone off.

I had to retreat to a corner and lick my wounds, I guess.

Somehow, I convinced myself that a fresh start meant that I needed to distance myself from the people who knew me before.

An unintended consequence of that is it included people who actually cared.

Mack doesn't talk about it really, but I know it hurt her. A lot. I've noticed the chip on her shoulder since I got back.

I park in my sister's driveway, walk up onto the front porch, and raise my hand to knock when the door opens. She's standing there in gray sweatpants and a gray hoodie, blond hair piled in a bun on top of her head and no makeup on.

"You look great," I tease. "I bet that look brings all the boys to your yard."

"Shut up," she snarks back. "It's my day off."

I walk inside and look around. It's the first time I've been to her place since I got back. She leads me into the living room, and I can't help but admire the built-in bookshelves on the far wall.

At the risk of sounding like an old man, they don't build them like they used to.

"This is the kind of house I've been looking for," I tell her. I notice a few framed photos propped among the books. Mostly of Mack in distant and exotic locations, but there's one of her and Emmy at the Harvest Festival that's probably a couple of years old and another of me and Mack when we were kids.

I kept her at arm's length, and she kept me close.

I feel like a jerk all of a sudden.

"They go fast," she says. "But you should hold out for what you want."

I glance at her. "Why do I feel like you're speaking in code?"

"No reason." She shrugs as she gives me a knowing smile. "Except that I think after years of holding out, maybe you actually know what you want."

I turn away from the photo of Emmy and shove my hands in my pockets. "Where's this sticking door?"

She plops down onto the sofa.

I stare at her. "There's no sticking door, is there?"

"Sit."

"Don't boss me, Mackenzie."

"We need to have a heart-to-heart."

I stare.

She points to the couch.

I sag my head to one side and sigh, looking at the door. I look back at her and see that I'm not going to win this fight.

I do as she says, not because I think I need to obey her but because she's insufferable when she doesn't get her way. "First, let's talk about you and Jace."

She frowns, "fake innocence" all over her face.

"Don't lie to me. What's going on?"

"Nothing," she protests, and then, after a pause, "Except. . .he's really good-looking. I've just. . .never, you know. . .noticed it before."

I'm weirded out. "Jace has been my friend since grade school."

"Well, what a coincidence. That's about as long as Emmy's been my friend."

I frown and stare.

She frowns and stares back.

"So?"

She quirks a brow. "So, are you going to ask her out, or what?"

Now it's me feigning innocence. "No," I protest. "I'm just. . .not dating right now, you know. . .with everything that's happened."

She frowns and stares.

I frown and stare right back.

"So what, that's like, forever?"

I shrug. "Not forever, but I'm not going to be any good to anyone right now."

"Why not?"

I fold my arms. "If I'd known I was coming over here for an interrogation, I would've eaten first."

"I missed you," she says, without looking at me. "And I hate that you're so different now."

"I'm not different," I say. Though, some people would argue it would be better if I was.

"You are," she says, waving a hand in the air. "You're all grown-up now."

"So are you."

"Yeah, I guess." I see the kid sister who used to hang around, waiting for me to give her some of my time. Even when

I was a jerk, Mack still wanted to be around me. I didn't always give her that chance.

"Hey, I'm sorry I cut you off," I say. "When I left."

She waves me off like it's not a big deal, but we both know better.

"It wasn't cool of me." I draw in a breath. I don't like sharing feelings, not even with people I'm close to, but I owe her. "It's part of why I wanted to come back here."

"Really?" Her eyes flick to mine.

"Really."

I sit, trying to think of the best words to say. It's at this point in talking I usually fail.

Thankfully, Mack speaks first to fill the silence.

"I *was* hurt when you left. It's like you made this decision for me, and I didn't even get a say."

I wince.

"But. . .Owen." We look at one another. "It's okay. Really."

I frown. "You mean it?

She nods.

"And to make up for it you'll let me help you with Emmy, right?"

"What?!" I scoff. "No!"

"Owen," she says. "I know you guys were close. Emmy told me."

"We used to be." I lean back on the couch.

"But, last night, I was picking up on some serious vibes."

I don't say anything.

"Tension."

I make a disagreeing grunt sound.

"She must like cavemen."

I groan. "You're seeing things that aren't there."

"I know my best friend, and I know what I saw," she says.

"I'm definitely not seeing things. I just can't believe I didn't see it back then."

I shift in my seat. This is weird, talking about Emmy. Especially to Mack.

"I know you're not telling me something," she says. "Which seems to be a trend when it comes to you two."

"Oh, stop it," I say. "You know it would've been weird."

"Not *that* weird."

"You pretty much told everyone within earshot what a screw-up I was," I say. "And you made it clear you did not want me anywhere near your friends."

"I know. I was a jerk." She looks away. "Emmy's been telling me that for a while."

"She said you were a jerk?" I laugh at that, mostly because I can't picture it at all.

"She said I wasn't giving you a chance," she says. "That you're not the guy I think you are. And she was right, I think."

Emmy said that? About me?

"I'm sorry, too," she says.

"For what?"

"For not being more understanding," she says. "You guys were smart to keep your friendship from me. I probably wouldn't have been cool about it."

"Probably not," I say.

She looks at me. "I'm trying to apologize here."

I smirk. "Sorry," I say. "Keep going."

"No, that's it," she says, faking offense. "That's all you get."

I laugh. "Okay, well, I'm glad you're cool if me and Emmy are friends, but that's all we are."

"Okay, fine. Friends." She sits forward a bit. "But why?"

I frown. "Why what?"

"Don't you think she's pretty?"

More than I want to let on. "Yeah, sure, she's fine."

She chucks a throw pillow at me. "She's more than fine, Owen. Don't be a jerk."

I hug the pillow in front of me. "Okay, yeah, she's more than fine. She's. . ." I think of her at the photo shoot, between the bookshelves, her body pressed to mine.

A slow smile spreads across her lips. "I knew I was right."

I shake the memory off and hold up a hand in protest because I can already see what's happening here, and I don't want any part of it.

She points at me. "You like her."

"Mack, I told you, we're fr—"

She cuts me off with an upheld hand. "Ah. Don't even pretend."

I feel caught.

"Level with me. There's something happening between you two, isn't there?"

I draw in a breath, toss the pillow away from me, and stretch my hands over my head. "It would never work, so it doesn't matter."

"What? Why not?" she asks.

"You said it yourself," I say. "She's a hopeless romantic. She's basically just waiting for some sappy guy to come in and sweep her off her feet in the rain on the hood of a truck."

She laughs.

"What?"

"You dope."

I shake my head. "That's not me."

"So?"

"So what? That's not me."

She narrows her eyes. "But it could be."

"No," I say. "It couldn't. Trust me. Emmy and I are different."

"Different isn't always bad," she says. "And she makes you better."

I frown. Again with that?

"Jace told me about the fight at the bar."

I sit forward, suddenly defensive. "It wasn't—"

She shakes her head. "No, that guy had it coming to him. If I'd been there, I would've punched him myself."

I go still.

"He told me that Emmy basically saved you from yourself."

I turn my head away, then look at her.

"Yeah, Emmy's always had a way of calming me down."

"So, what's the problem? What the heck are you waiting for?" Mack asks.

I think back to the day of my wedding. The day Emmy told me how she felt about me.

I don't say anything.

"What aren't you telling me?"

I hold back. I really don't want to talk about this.

"Owen?"

"I screwed up, okay?" I say it on a sigh.

"Did you sleep with my best friend?" Mack's forehead pulls in a tight line.

I make a face. "No, geez, that's where your mind goes?"

She shrugs like it's a perfectly logical question.

"Mack, come on. Good grief."

She shrugs again, then softens. "Sorry. I didn't mean to offend you."

"Emmy and I have only ever been friends," I tell her. "But I guess she had some feelings. . .and she told me about them right after Lindsay disappeared."

"What do you mean right after?"

I look up at her.

"Your wedding day?"

"Yeah."

She sits back. "Go on."

I tell Mack the whole story. I tell her about the dock, me yelling at the water, Emmy's terribly timed confession, and my even worse reaction. I tell her that I'm pretty sure I blew my chance with her before I even knew I wanted it. I tell her that I doubt she'll ever trust me after that, and really, I can't blame her. I'm not even sure I trust myself.

Mack shakes her head. "I cannot believe she never told me."

"Mack."

"Sorry!" she says. "This is not about me. I know." She goes quiet for a minute, then pulls out her phone. "I have an idea!"

"I don't want you trying to play matchmaker."

"Don't you mean 'Mack-maker'?" She waggles her eyebrows, and I roll my eyes.

"What is wrong with you?" I ask.

"I have a few days off," she says with a smile. "I need a project."

I groan because I really don't want to be her next "project."

She taps around on her phone, then messes with the volume, and in seconds, I'm listening to that blasted podcast episode again. As if the first time wasn't enough.

"I already heard this," I tell her. "The guys at the station—"

"Shhhh!"

This again?

This is the episode where The Hopeful Romantic recounts her idea of the perfect guy. I listen half-heartedly because I've heard it before, and I have *thoughts*, but my sister is eating it up.

"What point are you trying to make?"

"This woman might as well *be* Emmy," she says. "This is the kind of stuff she says all the time."

Interesting.

I pause. "Mack, you don't think this woman might actually be Emmy, do you?"

Mack frowns at me. "Emmy with a relationship podcast?" She scoffs. "No. She's never even had a real relationship. I mean, there was a guy in college. Very short-lived. And a guy a few months after—"

At her verbal halt, I frown. "What?"

"It makes sense now," she says. "Why Emmy never dates." She spins and faces me. "She's been pining for you!"

"For eight years?" I scoff. "Doubt it."

"Maybe not pining, but maybe waiting for someone she feels the same way about? I don't know, I still can't figure out what she sees in you, so maybe I'm way off-base."

I give her a pointed look and she grins at me. It's nice having my sister back in my life.

"Anyway, why would you assume Emmy is The Hopeful Romantic?" she asks. "Feels like quite the leap."

If Emmy is the podcaster, Mack would definitely know about it, right?

"Just something this Hopeful Romantic said," I tell her.

"Oh, so you *have* been listening."

I hold her gaze, debating on telling her my own secret. "I went on a little bender." And then, without thinking, I add, "I might've actually written in."

Mack lets out a laugh that's pretty much torture. "My brother, Owen Larrabee, writing in to a relationship podcast? Should I look to the East? Is Jesus coming back on a cloud?"

"This is not something we need to talk about," I tell her.

"Oh, no. We do." Her eyes are bright, and then, realization hits her. "Wait a minute, are you that guy?"

I wince.

"You're not. . ."

I can't believe I'm admitting this. I shake my head in embarrassment and say, "Practical in—"

"Poughkeepsie!" Another laugh. "Owen!"

"I couldn't help it," I say. "The stuff this lady says is so ridiculous. She's setting people up for disappointment."

Now, Mack snaps her mouth shut and looks at me.

"What?" I ask. "What now?"

"Is what she's saying ridiculous. . .or is it the way to Emmy's heart?"

"What are you even talking about?"

"I'm saying. . .if you want to win Emmy, then you should do *every single thing* on The Hopeful Romantic's list."

I think again about the slow dance in the bookstore. Yes, it was staged, but something happened. I liked the way she felt in my arms. A lot. And I haven't let myself feel that way about anyone in a really long time.

It felt good. Safe. Easy. Natural.

"What are you thinking?" Mack asks. "You disappeared there for a minute."

"I'm thinking this is crazy," I say. "And not me at all."

"No, but it is *her*," Mack says.

"Aren't you the one who gave some other guy her number?"

Mack waves me off. "Yes, but that was *before*."

"Before?"

"Before I realized that you two have this—" she shimmies her shoulders— "chemistry."

I roll my eyes. "Did you forget the part where I told you we're just friends? And that we're totally opposite? And that I screwed this up a long time ago?"

"Owen. Emmy is not a grudge-holder," she says. "I may not have seen it in high school, but whatever feelings she had for you back then, she's still got them."

"How do you know?"

"Just trust me. And I think this list is a great place to start. It's like making her the heroine of one of her favorite romance novels. She'll eat it up."

I hesitate for a few long seconds.

Then, I finally relent.

She's right. As pointless as I think romance is, Emmy lives for it. And somehow, that makes it seem less pointless and more like something worth trying.

"Fine," I say. "Let's just, for the sake of argument, say that I'm going to try. . ." I wave an abstract hand, ". . .all of this. Where do I start?"

Mack smiles.

"Flowers," she says simply. "You start with flowers."

Chapter Twenty-Nine

Owen

I have no idea what I'm doing, and I'm going to need some professional help.

As much as I don't want to ask, whoever this podcast lady is might have some answers. Plus, maybe I can deduce whether or not she *is* Emmy.

On the landing page, there's a "Contact Us" link. I click on it, and start to type, but stop. There's no way I'm using my real email. Thankfully, PracticalinPoughkeepsie@gmail.com isn't taken.

I click again, and write out some thoughts.

Dear Hopeful Romantic,

Found the "Contact Us" link.

Hopefully this doesn't go into some assistant's junk mail.

I stand by my original belief that practical is better than romantic any day of the week.

However, I'm kind of stuck. If a practical person—like me, but not me—were to become interested in someone else who is way more into romance, is it insincere for that person to do the things you suggested in an effort to win her over?

Asking for a friend.

—Practical in Poughkeepsie

. . .

I click send, and head out for a run.

When I return, I notice a new email in my inbox.

She wrote back.

Dear Practical,

First, I think it's fun that you nabbed that email address.

Second, I don't think it's a bad idea at all.

Third, I know you're not asking for a friend. ;)

Doing something because someone else would like it is never insincere, especially if your goal is to prove to her that you want to put her feelings first.

I must say, I'm glad to see you trying something new!

Funny twist, you're not the only one. I guess you got me thinking, and I'm going to give "practical" a shot just to see if you've got a point worth taking.

Who knows? Maybe we'll turn you into "The Practical Romantic!"

Signed,

Hopeful

She's going to give practical a shot? Why does my stomach sink at that? I have zero proof this woman is Emmy, and yet, I latch onto those words and for some reason, they make me far more upset than they should.

I reread the email.

Practical romantic. Two completely opposite things.

Like Emmy and me.

I crack my knuckles and write back.

Dear Hopeful,

Caught. It's me. Figured I'd give it a shot.

And you, going practical? Never thought I'd see the day.

I'm assuming this is going to end up in some future podcast.

—Practical

This time, it only takes ten minutes for an email to pop back into my inbox.

She must be a night owl. I absently wonder if I should head over to the Smart house and see if the upstairs lights are on.

Dear Practical,

Oh, it is. A bit of research, a bit of experimentation, just keeping that romance door open a sliver in case he gets a few ideas.

What romantic gesture are you starting with, if you don't mind my asking?

—Hopeful

Dear Hopeful,

Going with the flowers for no reason. I figured that's the most practical of the romantic gestures :)

—Practical

Dear Practical,

Ha. Flowers are always a good choice. And if I can be so bold, I'd find out her favorite flowers OR pick a flower that reminds you of her. And tell her why. It just adds that little personal touch.

Oh! And don't get flowers from the grocery store. Make it the farmer's market or a florist. And if you DO get them from the supermarket, take them out of the plastic and wrap them in something else. Brown paper is always a nice touch.

Good luck!

—Hopeful

Dear Hopeful,

And here I thought it's the thought that counts.

If I may be so bold, pay attention to the little things. A solid guy is better than some big, grand gesture. Focus on his strengths. He may not be charming, but is he kind? He may not be witty, but is he a good listener? He may not be romantic, but is he thoughtful in other ways?

A stand-up guy is a good thing. Even if he doesn't sweep you off your feet.

—Practical

Dear Practical,

You make a lot of sense. I'll keep it in mind on my date this weekend. Would you ever be up for an interview down the road? We can discuss practical versus romantic. I think it would make a great episode.

—Hopeful

A date? This weekend?

Maybe it's *not* Emmy.

Dear Hopeful,

Send over details, and I'll consider it. But I'm not telling anyone my real name.

—Practical

Dear Practical,

Well, good, because I'm not telling anyone mine either.

:)

—Hopeful

Emmy

After I click send, I look at the time.

12:19 a.m.

I'm not surc how I got lost in all of this back and forth, but I feel weirdly exhilarated.

Like I have a secret friendship.

Just like before.

Chapter Thirty

Emmy

Keep an open mind.

That's what I tell myself when I spot Chad standing inside the door of the shop.

Chad.

He looks. . .perfectly normal.

He's no James Alexander Malcolm MacKenzie Fraser, that's for sure. But let's be honest, who really is?

Reagan walks over to where I'm standing, which is out of sight, but with a good view of the door.

"Are you hiding?"

"No, just trying not to be seen."

"That's literally the definition of hiding." She frowns. "What's his name?"

"Chad."

She slowly nods, looking at him. "Chad?"

I slowly nod, looking at him, too. "Yep."

She turns to me. "Is this really the guy who got you back out there?" She sizes him up as The Coffin Dodgers accost him and drag him to their table. "What about the firefighter? He seems a little more exciting."

Well, *duh.*

"There is nothing wrong with a stable man," I say, trying to convince myself that this is a good decision.

"I predict you're going to be home and in bed by ten," she deadpans.

I roll my eyes. I'm already nervous enough about this date. The last thing I need is Reagan (or anyone else) weighing in.

I give myself a few more minutes before stepping out from my hiding spot and see that I'm not going to get my wish. Somehow, The Coffin Dodgers have roped Chad into a game of Scrabble. And judging by the accusations, he's already winning.

"You're cheating!" Ernie shouts. "Did you hide a tile in your shirt sleeve?"

Chad laughs, offering his shirt for inspection. John takes him up on the offer while Marco shakes his head and Mr. Ridgemont smirks. I'll never tell his secret, but of the four of them, Mr. Ridgemont is the one with the slippery fingers.

He told me once he doesn't look at it as cheating because he only does it to get a rise out of his friends.

He glances my way, meets my eyes, and throws a wink.

I wink back. Because leave it to me to have a good-natured inside joke with my former high school principal.

Perks of being a teacher's pet, I suppose.

I start toward the table, and when I reach them, Chad is putting down a Triple Word Score. I watch as he lays down a word on the right-hand side of the board, attaching his word to the "p" of "stoop."

Chad plays "paczki," the "a" falling on the triple letter score and the "i" on the triple word score. 75 points.

Not bad.

"Challenge!" John shouts.

"I wouldn't do that," Ernie says.

"Why not?! I've never heard of it!"

"Oh, and because you never heard of it, it must not exist, huh?" Mr. Ridgemont quips.

"Agree! I challenge it too!" Marco slams his hand on the table, jostling the board and causing a groan from the others.

"It's a real word," I say, peering over Chad's shoulder to see what other weird words have made it onto the board. "It's a round, filled donut."

"How do you know that?" John's tone sounds accusatory.

I shrug and tap my index finger to my temple. "My last name is Smart for a reason."

Chad stands and spins around simultaneously, knocking into the board as he does. The tiles go flying, scattering across the table and onto the floor.

The Coffin Dodgers all jump to their feet, shouting over the disruption, and I hear phrases like "You klutz!" and "That's a forfeit!" and "His score gets set back to zero!"

Chad pushes his glasses up onto his nose and gives them a sheepish smile. "Sorry about that." He looks at me. "Wow. You look really nice."

The Coffin Dodgers stop talking and glare at him.

"Emaline," Mr. Ridgemont says. "Is this boy here to. . .take you out?"

"On a date?" John frowns.

"Well, he's better than the vandal," Marco says.

"Even if he is a palooka," Ernie says.

"Pssh. Another made-up word." John plops back down.

"All words are made up." Ernie also sits.

Mr. Ridgemont kneels to pick up the Scrabble tiles and Marco takes a step toward Chad.

"Emmy is special," Marco says. "If your intentions aren't honorable, speak now."

Chad's eyes go wide.

I grab onto his arm and tug him toward me. "Okay! Great! Thanks, guys! We're fine, gotta go!"

"I'm serious, Emmy," Marco says. "I want to hear him say it!" He points a finger in the air, and I shake my head at him.

They remind me of Statler and Waldorf on *The Muppet Show*, if they had two brothers.

I lead Chad to the door, and step outside. I realize I'm still holding onto his arm, so I drop it, a little more abruptly than I mean to. "Sorry about them. For some reason they're all really protective of me."

"Oh! Yeah, no problem. It's nice," he says.

And that's all he says.

I follow him over to the white Ford Taurus parked in front of the shop, and he holds up a hand and runs in front of me. He opens the car door, and once I'm inside, he closes it, giving me a moment to take a few deep, calming breaths.

I do another gut check.

No sparks. No embers. No flickers.

I remind myself, that's not what I'm after.

I'm after practical.

And judging by the car and the khakis and the loafers, that's exactly what Chad Rober is. Practical.

Is it a little troubling that he's not wearing socks with those loafers? Yes.

Is it a deal breaker? I'm going to say no for now, but I reserve the right to change my mind.

We'll see how much it bothers me. All I can picture is sweaty feet.

He slips into the driver's seat and pats the steering wheel. "This is Babs."

"Who is? Your car?"

"Yeah," he says, like this it's perfectly normal for a grown man to give his car a nickname. "Does your car have a name?"

"No," I say. "It never occurred to me to name it."

"I can help you come up with one." He starts Babs, puts his blinker on, and carefully pulls away from the curb. He pulls up to the stop sign and brings Babs to an alarmingly slow stop. There are no other cars at the intersection, but he takes a painstakingly long time checking each corner before stepping on the gas again.

"Do you like music?" I ask, hopeful for a distraction.

"I listen to video game soundtracks mostly," he says. "You can open my Spotify and find my playlist. I can send you the link too."

"Oh, that's okay," I say. "I'm more of a country music lover."

"Oh." He says this like I've just confessed that I like to eat raw meat. "Why?"

"I like the stories," I say. "I've always liked stories."

"Book shop," he says. "Right."

And that's all he says.

And I remind myself again to keep an open mind.

But as we drive in the direction of the restaurant, I can't help but think of the way it felt when Owen walked me to my car the other night. Or the way it felt when I was in his arms during the photoshoot. Or the way it felt when he helped coach me through my panic attack the day of the clean-up.

And as much as a part of me wants to put all of those feelings in a little box and bury it in my backyard, the truth is, a bigger part of me wants to take them out and relive them over and over again.

Owen

There are flowers on the seat of my truck.

Not just any flowers. *Emmy's* flowers. Sunflowers. I walked into Blooms after work today and had to endure an unauthorized game of Twenty Questions with the older woman behind the counter. She wanted to know who the flowers were for, if it was a special occasion, and how I wanted the recipient to feel when she got them.

If her questions were a test, I failed, because I pretty much just mumbled "They're just for a friend," followed by "I'm in a hurry," and ending with "Do you have brown paper to wrap them in?"

It was obvious by the look on her face she was feeling pity for whoever I was going to give the flowers to, but she stopped talking, so I guess that's a win.

Now I'm sitting outside of Book Smart, waiting for Emmy to flip the sign over to "closed," and the flowers seem to be looking at me with their big brown faces. If I walk in there and hand her this bouquet, she won't be able to misinterpret anything.

I'll be crossing the friendship line.

Is this a horrible idea?

I feel like I'm about to lose my nerve, so I open the door to my truck and step out onto the street. I reach in and pick up the flowers, thinking they really *do* remind me of Emmy, when I hear a familiar laugh. I glance up and see her, not flipping the store sign, but stepping out the door.

She's not alone.

She's holding the arm of a guy walking out beside her. He's wearing a plaid button down with a gray cardigan with khaki pants and. . .are those loafers?

Without socks?

He's got neatly combed sandy blond hair and no beard. I

slip back into my truck and duck down but lift my phone up and snap a stealthy picture like a stalker.

I send the picture to Mack.

OWEN

Who is this?

MACK

That's Chad Rober! I can't believe she's going out with him and she didn't tell me!

OWEN

Is that really the headline here? I'm sitting outside her store with flowers

I almost just made a complete idiot of myself

MACK

Awwww, you're doing it??!!

Nothing wrong with being a fool for love, big brother <winking emoji>

OWEN

Why did I ever listen to you in the first place?

MACK

Follow them!

We'll go spy!

OWEN

That's a terrible idea.

I'm going home.

And if you want some sunflowers, they're all yours.

MACK

Sunflowers? For Emmy?

That's perfect <heart eyed emoji>

I'll get the scoop on Chad. I don't see this going anywhere. . .

OWEN

No. I don't want the scoop.

This was a dumb idea.

MACK

Please don't give up, Owen. . .

This is a great chance to show her how you feel!

OWEN

I'm not crashing her date.

With CHAD.

MACK

Fine.

But at least throw your hat in the ring and let her decide.

I click off my phone. I'm not going to let Mack bait me.

I watch as the guy—*Chad*—opens the car door for her and she slips inside. Emmy is on a date. With a perfectly respectable looking guy who will probably treat her well. I'm not going to interfere with that.

Before I head home, I drive around the back of Book Smart and see Emmy's car parked in its usual spot. I know she doesn't lock the doors because she claims our city is "one hundred percent safe," something I only half agree with.

Emmy is a little naïve that way.

It's part of her charm.

I pick up the flowers, step out of my truck, and walk around to the passenger side of her car. I open the door and set the flowers on the seat.

I bought them for her.

I want her to have them.

Even if for no other reason than no reason at all.

Chapter Thirty-One

Emmy

My Chad date was. . .fine.

It was perfectly nice.

There is nothing *wrong* with Chad. He's a decent guy. He told me about his job, which was just south of interesting, and then somehow, we got on the topic of *Lord of the Rings*.

We never got off that topic.

He drove me back to my store talking about orcs and elves and the long, winding history of some guy named Celebrimbor.

As Reagan predicted, I was home and in bed by 10 p.m.

There was no fumbling for my keys at the door because I was nervous about a forthcoming kiss, no lingering on the stoop wishing for time to stop, and definitely no sparks or tingles or glances or swoons.

Bonus points for him, though, he did leave a bouquet of sunflowers in my car. I love sunflowers. They're my favorite flower—how in the world did he know that?

They don't counteract the Middle-Earth dissertation, but it definitely checks a romance box.

The next morning, I wake up to find that my parents have taken an impromptu trip out of town.

Again.

Ever since Ellie and I moved out, this is what they do. They jaunt. They're jaunty.

Jaunters?

Jauntpersons?

Jauntalopes?

I giggle at that last one.

And while I'm a firm believer in keeping the romance alive, I'm not sure how I feel about that when it's my parents.

I'm also doing my very best not to think about how my mother recently special ordered a book called *Passion and Fire for the Middle-Aged Couple*.

I'm up early, as usual, and hurry through my routine, aware that the house feels quiet and strange with only me in it. I'm halfway through my shower when out of nowhere, a wave of nausea rolls through my body, making my skin hurt.

It's the kind of nausea that can only mean one thing: I'm getting sick.

Or maybe something I ate last night didn't agree with me.

Or maybe this is food poisoning.

Or maybe this is how I die.

I hurry and finish in the shower, and as I'm getting dressed, another wave hits. This one brings me to my knees, right in front of the toilet.

I grip the cold porcelain sides and thank the Lord that my mom keeps the bathrooms clean.

Definitely not the way I wanted to spend the morning.

I stumble back into my room and pull on a pair of clean pajama pants, dropping back into bed with a thud. I pull out my phone and voice text Reagan, who is surprisingly, my steadiest employee.

"I'm really sick from food, period. Handle the market without me today, question mark." My head is spinning, and there are beads of sweat gathering above my upper lip. It's going to take all of my energy not to throw up all day, I can already tell. "Call someone cover, question mark."

Seconds later, Reagan calls me.

I click the phone on and swallow a wave of nausea back down. "Blech. Hey."

"Whoa. You sound awful."

"I feel awful," I say.

"Your text made no sense, so I needed to make sure you're not delirious."

I glance down at my phone and hit messages. Through squinted eyes I see that it didn't automatically put the punctuation in there, so it reads like I got sick from a food period.

I respond with another groan.

"I know that math teacher didn't give you anything, where'd you pick this up?"

"Might be food poisoning?" I moan. "And he teaches English."

"What did you eat?" Reagan asks.

The thought of last night's tilapia is accompanied by another wave of nausea. "I cannot think about food right now."

"Sorry," she says. "Do you need anything?"

"No, and I don't want to leave you in a—"

"Emmy, it's fine. I got this," she says. "I'll call Jenny. I'm sure she'll come to the market with me."

Jenny might be the nighttime baker, but she's worked the market lots of times. Logically, I know they *will*, in fact, be fine. Reagan is competent. More than competent.

But I still feel like I'm shirking my responsibilities.

But then I feel the nausea coming back around, bubbling

up from my gut and burning my throat. "I gotta—" I drop the phone and rush to the bathroom.

It's going to be a very long day.

Owen

I fell asleep last night trying not to think about Emmy's date.

I'm not one to play things out in my head, nor am I one to worry about what might be instead of what actually is.

But I wonder if he tried to kiss her.

I wonder if she would even let him.

I realized I was clenching my fists, so I tossed off the covers and dropped down to do a series of push-ups, thinking maybe it would help with the nervous energy.

It didn't.

Thinking about Emmy on a date shouldn't bother me this much.

I came home last night convinced I took too long to make up my mind and missed my chance. I even shot off an email to The Hopeful Romantic in my frustration, not that she cares to know I'm sticking with a practical approach when it comes to relationships.

It's weirdly therapeutic.

Now, in the middle of the night and wide awake, I tap the spacebar to wake up the computer.

She wrote back.

Practical,

I'm sorry it didn't work out like you thought—and I know you're looking at this as the final straw, that you're going to stick with practical from now on.

You're thinking that romance just isn't your thing.

It doesn't seem like you gave it a real chance, though, does it? Are you a one-and-done, 50% kind of guy? Or are you a fighter?

Instead of throwing in the towel, I think it's time to double down.

Actions speak way louder than words. ;)
—Hopeful

A fighter. Ha. Maybe she does know me.

And double down? On what, the romance?

What does that even mean?

Like a loser, I'd actually gone back and written out the different romantic things she mentioned on her podcast, but I'm at a complete loss as to what to do next. It's not like I can wait for it to rain, lure her outside, and kiss her in the street.

Strangely, I don't hate that idea.

I should just walk away. Leave her alone. Date someone else to get her out of my head.

There's just one problem: I don't think I can.

I arrive at the Farmer's Market on Saturday morning tired and conflicted. I'm here because I told my mom I'd pick up a couple loaves of sourdough bread for her, and also because I know Emmy will be here.

I reach into my pocket and feel the folded-up romance list in there.

I want to do the right thing, and I know I should try *something*, but what that is or how to go about it? No clue.

I feel utterly out of my league in the romance department.

I told myself not wanting anything serious was because of Lindsay, but now I'm starting to wonder if I was comparing everyone else to Emmy.

She listens, she doesn't judge, she celebrates the little things, she pays attention—all the things a friend would do.

Friend, I think, shaking my head.

Is it wrong that I want more?

In an attempt to act casual, I pick up the sourdough and the homemade jam, and then head over to the Book Smart booth for a cup of coffee. I'm surprised to discover Reagan, not Emmy, is working.

She must see the disappointment on my face because she smirks at me like I have a secret and she knows what it is. "Good morning, firefighter."

"Morning."

"Looking for someone?"

"If that person's name is coffee, then yeah."

"Funny," she says, picking up an empty cup. "I thought maybe you were here for Emmy."

"Nope," I say, hoping my tone sounds casual. "Just coffee."

She nods and fills the cup. "Cream or sugar?"

I shake my head and look around the market.

She puts a lid on the cup and holds it out to me. It takes me a second to notice she's standing there waiting, and I mutter an apology and hand over a five dollar bill.

"This is killing you." Reagan smirks at me as she gives me my change.

"The coffee?" I ask.

"Not knowing where Emmy is." She crosses her arms over her chest. "You're doing a bad job of hiding it."

I level her gaze.

Her smile widens.

"Fine, where is she?"

"Home. She's sick."

I frown. "Like, head cold sick or like throw up sick?"

"The second one," she says. "That or she's had a bad reaction to the boring date she had last night. She'd never miss the market, so she must be really pukey."

Curiosity gets the better of me.

"Her. . .uh. . .date was boring?"

"Looked boring to me." She glances at me. "He was wearing loafers. Without socks.

I noticed that.

"Do you, um," I tap the top of my cup. "Do you think she needs anything?"

Reagan shrugs. "She's alone. Her parents stopped by the shop on their way out of town yesterday. So, maybe?"

I nod halfway through her talking, stop listening, and start surveying the Farmer's Market.

Soup. Bread. Ginger Ale.

Flowers.

Flowers?

Hmm. Maybe not. Maybe just the soup and the. . .

Reagan seems to notice I'm not listening because she waves her hand at me to get my attention. "Hey, you okay? It looks like you've already got a plan, so go, stop wasting time talking to me," she smiles.

I nod and start to walk away.

"Good luck, Romeo," she calls after me.

"We're just friends," I call over my shoulder, but she waves me off.

Does everyone in town think I have feelings for Emmy or what?

I pick up two kinds of chicken soup, one with rice and one with noodles, at the "Just in Thyme" booth, and when I mention it's for Emmy, Susannah, the owner, tells me I need ginger candy. She points a few booths down. "Candy Junction makes their own. It's really good. It'll settle her stomach."

I nod, thank her, and head to Candy Junction. I pick up the

ginger candy, another loaf of bread, and head back to my truck before anyone else stalls me by giving me more advice.

I drive out to her parents' house, turn down the gravel driveway, and park outside behind Emmy's car.

As I reach for the door handle, I stop, suddenly nervous.

What am I doing here?

This might be a really stupid idea.

I shake my head. I really want to make sure she's okay.

I don't have to re-listen to that podcast to know "taking care of her when she's sick" is on the list.

Some sort of rom-com thing, I guess?

And if Emmy really is like The Hopeful Romantic, then I suppose this is a good idea.

Doesn't seem all that romantic to watch someone throw up, but I guess I'm not really an authority. And romance aside, this just seems like the nice thing to do.

I grab the bags and walk up to the door. I knock before I can change my mind but hear nothing inside. Odds are, Emmy is asleep.

I turn a circle on the porch. I should just leave the stuff and go.

But then I turn back and try the door. It's open. Did she really not lock the door last night? I'll have to get on her about that, but in this instance, it works in my favor. I step inside. "Emmy?"

No response.

I take the bags into the kitchen, then slowly, as quietly as possible, walk up the stairs. The Smart house is old and creaky, and it occurs to me that I might scare her. Am I a creep for even being here?

I reach the top of the stairs and realize I have no idea which room is hers. I glance in the first door. No sign of anyone, only of tons of photos taped to the wall. I step over to the next door, and there, dead asleep and holding a large bucket, is Emmy. Her leg is hanging off the side of the bed and her mouth is half-open.

She looks stark white and adorable.

I step inside and gently take the bucket out of her hands. Her eyes flutter open and she tries to focus on me. "Wait. My. . .bucket. . ."

She presses her lips together, then smacks them apart. "Owen?"

"I didn't mean to wake you, go back to sleep."

"Okay." She rolls over, and I pull her blanket up over her shoulders. As I turn to go, I notice there, in the corner, is a small desk, and on it, the microphone and headphones she saved the day after the fire. Both are in professional looking stands, and there's a sleeping laptop next to them. I take a step toward the desk and glance down at the open notebook.

I'm snooping.

And it's rude.

I think about my own journal, in high school, and the wrath I'd unleash if anyone found it and read it without me knowing.

I step away.

But then. . .

The Bell Hooks quote. The same thing said by both the lady on the podcast and Emmy.

She did say she had a date. . .

I look back at the desk.

Why would Emmy, the owner of a bookstore in small town North Carolina, have what looks like a simple recording studio set-up in her childhood bedroom? It could be that Emmy is a fan of *The Hopeful Romantic*. . .or, it could be that she *is* The Hopeful Romantic.

The podcast, in her email, mentioned trying something practical.

That could've been her date last night.

Emmy stirs, and I startle, walking straight out of the room before I get caught.

I can't really do much to help her, but for whatever reason, when I reach the bottom of the stairs, I decide not to leave. Something about seeing her like that sparked something inside me. It makes no sense because honestly, she looks physically worse than I've ever seen her. But the desire to take care of her is so strong, I can't go.

I sit down in the living room and flip on the television, settling on reruns of *The Office*. She might sleep all day, but when she wakes up, I'll be here, just in case.

That's not romantic, it's practical.

Chapter Thirty-Two

Emmy

I can't escape Owen.

Even in my dreams, he's there. And since I'm sick, my dreams are especially vivid.

In the one I just stirred from, I was standing on a long, thin path in a blue bamboo forest, with shifting shafts of light cutting through, mottling the dress I'm wearing.

I look down and realize I'm holding a bucket.

At the end of the path is Owen, wearing loose-fitting white linen pants and no shirt, holding a torch in one hand and, for some reason, a chicken in the other. As I start to move toward him, the rustling of the bamboo creates sounds like wooden chimes, knocking a rhythm that makes my whole body pulse.

Just as I'm about to reach him, reality drags me awake, and it's odd, but I feel certain I've seen him. For real. Here, in my room.

I roll over, and I think maybe I might be feeling a little better. I push myself upright and take a second to check my dizziness and nausea before walking into the bathroom. I splash cold water on my face and brush my teeth, feeling weak and run down.

I hate being sick. When I'm sick, I can't envision a time when I felt well.

I'll never eat tilapia again.

The mental picture of that fish on my plate makes my stomach lurch again.

Blech.

So much for practical romance.

I need to check in with Reagan and see how the market went, though I realize it could still be going on. I have no idea what time it is.

My hair is still damp from the shower, but that means nothing when it comes to measuring time. This thick mane can take hours to dry.

I grab my phone and plod downstairs, taking each step carefully because at any second, I know the sickness could make me stumble. I'm almost to the bottom when I slide open my phone, open my contacts, and find my last message to Reagan.

Looks like I missed a text from her when I was sleeping.

REAGAN

Loverboy was just here looking for you.

I'm not a fan of older dudes, but the firefighter is hot.

Just sayin'.

I would roll my eyes if they hadn't snagged on the first part of her message.

Owen came looking for me?

Why?

I step off the stairs and make the turn toward the kitchen when I hear something or someone in the next room. I freeze.

My parents would've told me if they'd come back early.

Maybe a chipmunk got in—it wouldn't be the first time.

I'm about to take another step when I hear the undeniable sound of a metal kitchen utensil in a metal pot. Frozen, I draw in a breath.

Is someone. . .cooking?

I think back on every scary movie I've ever seen and know that my first mistake was leaving the door unlocked. My second mistake is one I haven't made yet but am about to walking straight toward the sound of an intruder.

Who cooks.

This is how I die. Death by spatula.

At least I'm showered and wearing clean underwear.

I take a step, and the floor underneath my foot lets out an angry, traitorous creak. The sounds in the kitchen come to a halt.

I'm about to dial 9-1-1 when I hear footsteps.

"Hello?" My voice is weak, from either fear or exhaustion.

And then I see a shadow moving toward the door. "Emmy? You up?"

The familiar voice doesn't unfreeze me. Instead, every single nerve ending in my body goes on high alert.

It's Owen.

It's Owen, and I didn't dream it, he's not shirtless in some bamboo forest, he's *in my house.*

Wait. *Is* he shirtless?

Stop it, Emmy.

My hair is loose and wet in spots and unkempt, plus I spent the morning throwing up, so I'm likely two shades paler than Casper. No makeup. No bra. Bunny slippers. Pajamas.

What am I going to do? Run back upstairs?

I don't even have the energy. And my stomach is starting to roll again.

He comes around to the foot of the stairs, and I'm simultaneously relieved and disappointed he's got a shirt on.

"You scared me to death," I say, wishing I had a paper bag to put over my head.

"Sorry," he says, looking slightly shy and out of place. "I uh. . .I brought soup." He half points toward the kitchen.

I look at him and my overactive imagination rumbles to life like a refurbished muscle car, humming and purring with ideas that are turning this entire scene into something it's not. In my mind, I'm more presentable, and I don't feel like I've just traveled through the seven circles of hell. And I'm less gawky than I am in real life.

"Good to see you moving around," he says.

"Barely." I frown. "What are you doing here?"

"Reagan said you were sick," he says, as if this answers my question.

"Yeah." I take a small step, but instantly regret it. The room gets a bit spinny, and my head swims.

I reach out, and he reaches for me, and when his hand connects to my waist my fever spikes.

Or maybe it isn't my fever at all.

"Why don't you come sit down?"

I nod and he leads me into the kitchen where the smell of whatever's cooking on the stove intensifies. "What are you making?"

"Soup," he says again. "And some bread. Do you feel like you can eat?"

I sit down at the table, and instantly want to collapse into a pile on the floor. I'm going to be terrible company, and since this is the first time Owen's come to visit me, I'm a little annoyed about the circumstances. I remember when I announced to my entire podcast audience that having a guy take care of you like Tom Hanks in *You've Got Mail* is such a sweet and romantic thing to do.

I'm rethinking that.

In every fantasy I've ever had about this very trope, I did not look like death warmed over or smell faintly like vomit.

I casually try to sniff myself. *Do I actually smell like vomit?*

Owen stands in the center of the kitchen, looking as out of place as a bobcat in a library.

It dawns on me that this is incredibly sweet of him.

"You look terrible," he says.

"I know." I groan, resting my head down on the tabletop. It feels cool and temporarily nice. "I'm sorry you have to see me like this."

"I'm not."

I peer up at him.

"Not. . .uh. . .sorry to see you. Not happy that you're sick, but, you know. . ." He trails off.

I try to nod. "I know what you're saying," I whisper, but nodding makes my head swim even more. "Maybe you should go, I might. . ."

"I don't think that's a good idea." He walks back over to the stove and stirs the pot. "You shouldn't be alone when you're sick."

I don't have the strength to protest or stay in this chair. "I think I might need to lay back down. And don't hate me, but I don't think I can eat right now."

He drops the spoon, turns off the burner, and rushes back over to me, attentive. "Couch or bed?"

Normally that question would make me blush, but I'm too sick to let it. "Couch." No energy to make it back upstairs.

Owen slips an arm around my waist, and I lean into his body, which smells like a combination of pine trees and heaven. It's the first pleasant moment I've had all day. I lean a good amount of my weight on him because the weak knees are also fully in play.

He leads me into the living room and helps me onto the couch. I try to kick off the slippers but they're just a bit too tight, and he gently takes my foot and removes one. I numbly hold out my foot to him, and he takes the other one off. Then he props a pillow under my head and spreads a throw blanket across my body. "I brought you some ginger candy. The lady at Just in Thyme said it would help."

"Susannah. She's a keeper." She doesn't believe in medicine, so she has all kinds of alternative ways to heal people.

"Would you rather have actual medicine?"

"I'd always rather have candy." I manage a smile, and he disappears as my eyelids close, and all I can think is how nice it is to have him here.

I'm not a person who ever thought I'd enjoy being taken care of. I've spent a lot of time on my own. I *like* being on my own, being independent. I built a business—worked my tail off, really—and convinced myself I didn't need help from anyone else.

But now, here, having someone doing the hard things that I can't do. . .it's everything.

Owen returns with a small brown paper bag of candy and the vase of sunflowers.

At the sight of them, my cheeks flush with embarrassment.

I feel like I'm caught, even though there's no way for him to know they're from Chad. As if he'd care anyway. . .

"Thought they might help you feel better," he says.

He sets them down on the coffee table so carefully, the wall around my heart springs a leak. He pops open the bag of candy and tilts the opening toward me.

I take one, unwrap it, and stick it in my mouth. No idea if it'll actually help, but I'm willing to try.

I sink further into the pillow. It's cold, at least for now, until my face heats it up.

"Do you want to watch something?" he asks, sitting on the opposite end of the couch.

I crack a lid open and peer down at him, certain that from his perspective I've got at least two chins and a lazy eye. "You don't want to spend your day here. I promise I'll be okay."

"Are you trying to get rid of me?" he says, a suspicious grin on his face.

I shift the pillow slightly and look away, smiling. "No."

"Okay, then. Let's watch something."

"Okay, then."

He opens Netflix and since it's my account, most of the recommendations are for rom-coms or historical romances. He starts scrolling through them, and I feel a little embarrassed that he can see my watch history. Maybe he won't notice.

"All of these title slides are of people kissing," he says.

So much for that theory.

"I like romance," I say.

"Okay, so what's your favorite?"

I close my eyes. "Can't pick just one."

"Top six, then."

I open both eyes. "Top six? That's random."

He shrugs. "Top six is better. It gives you one more to add to your list that should be in a top five but is left out."

That actually makes sense. I would have a hard time pinning my top five movies down. . .but if I had an extra one that made it into the mix, that makes it somehow easier.

Top Six. Practical. I'll have to remember that.

I stare at the screen. "Pride and Prejudice for sure."

He scrolls over to it and hovers. "This one?"

I nod. "Unpopular opinion, but I prefer the Keira Knightley version to the BBC miniseries with Colin Firth."

"I have no idea who any of those people are, but do you want to watch this?"

"You're going to sit through *Pride and Prejudice*?" I'm back to my lazy-eyed peering at him.

"If it's one of your favorites, sure," he says, then clicks the remote to select the movie. "I want to know what things you like."

I want to ask him why, but I don't. I'm in a dreamy bubble right now and I don't want it to pop.

The familiar soundtrack begins to play, and I sink a little deeper into the couch. By the time Lizzie is shunned by Mr. Darcy at the party, I'm fully invested and have completely forgotten to feel awkward or self-conscious about how I'm watching my beloved favorite romance movie with Owen.

And then he reaches over and takes my feet and puts them on the pillow on his lap.

I freeze.

Every muscle in my body tenses.

I forget to *awww* over the way Mr. Bingley looks at Jane, like she's the only person in the room. Also, why doesn't Mr. Bingley get more love? Mr. Darcy is all brooding and serious and secretly kind, but Bingley is *adorable*!

But that's not what I'm thinking about. Not when Owen is rubbing small circles into the centers of my feet.

Owen is massaging my feet.

I zero in on the way his thumbs press with the exact right amount of force, and the screen in front of me becomes a blur. I wonder how it would feel to do this every night, to have Owen's hands at my disposal, to be able to rope him in to watching *You've Got Mail* and *The Proposal* and *Sense and Sensibility* and *When Harry Met Sally*. To reenact my favorite moments from those movies from the meet-cutes, to the grand gestures, to the long awaited, much anticipated kisses. . .

"Wait, did her cousin just propose to her?"

The words startle me from my runaway imagination, and I pull my feet away and sit up.

"You okay? You need something?"

"Definitely," I say. "Hungry now, I think." I'm not hungry. But if I don't put some distance between me and Owen, I'm done for. A goner. A dead woman.

My phone buzzes on the table to Owen's left. I pause the movie, and he picks it up and hands it to me, doing his best not to look at it, but fully seeing that it's Chad calling.

I stare at the screen, as if I'm trying to decide whether or not to answer when really all I'm thinking is: *Strike three. He's a phone talker.*

Everyone knows phones are exclusively for texting.

I click it off and set the phone down, eyes drifting to the flowers.

Owen doesn't say anything. Instead, he stands and walks out of the room. I hear him click on the stove, and my heart warms like it's on the burner.

When he returns, he's carrying a tray with a bowl and a piece of bread next to it. "I really hope this doesn't make your stomach worse."

"It'll be good," I say, taking the tray. "Thank you."

He nods, but he doesn't sit back down. Instead, he stuffs his hands in his pockets and puts on his version of a smile. Which is to say, not really a smile at all.

"You okay?" I ask.

"Yeah," he says. "I think I'm going to head out."

The phone call.

"Right, of course," I say. "You've been here a long time. . ." My voice trails off.

He glances at my phone. "You should call him back."

I look at my phone, as if I don't know who he's talking about. "No, it's not—"

"Mack said he's a nice guy," Owen says. "You deserve that."

Deserve? Maybe. Want? *Nope.*

I *want* romance. I want a secret code and inside jokes and speaking a private language. I want to be able to read his face, whether he says anything or not. I want moonlit kisses in cool mountain air and someone to take care of me when I'm si—

I stop.

I do a quick check, and unlike Chad, I find sparkles and tingles and glances and swooning just by looking at Owen.

Owen is wrong for me. He's *always* been wrong for me.

Swoons can't be trusted.

But isn't that *exactly* what romantic gestures are supposed to conjure?

Does it matter *how* the swoons show up? Whether it's from gestures or actions or simply from being in the same room as the person?

Wait. My head is a jumbled mess.

I can't think straight, and I don't know if it's the foot massage or the food poisoning or both.

Is it possible for us to be a wrong fit and still be. . .right?

Images swim around in my mind's eye.

He saved me from the fire.

He organized the clean-up at my house.

He walked me to my car.

He danced with me between the shelves.

He may not be a romantic, but aren't those things romantic? And even if they aren't, don't they *feel* romantic because of the way I feel about him?

"You okay? You look a little green."

The assault on my mind has my insides in a knot. Not just

any knot, either, the kind a boy scout would tie to get his merit badge.

"Yep. All good." My voice is squeaky. It's squeaky because I'm trying really hard not to admit to myself what I am in the process of admitting.

And since he's standing here, I fear he can see my thoughts on my face.

Owen picks up his keys and nods at me. "The flowers are nice."

I glance at them, then back at him. "Sunflowers are my favorite."

"Really?" His face brightens, then goes neutral. "Cool." He looks around, then nods at me again. "See ya later."

He's almost out the door when I stop him with a quiet "Hey."

He turns back and looks at me. "Yeah?"

"Thank you," I say.

"Of course," he says. "That's what friends are for, right?"

I hold his gaze. I don't want him to go. I don't want to look away.

My confession is right on the tip of my tongue.

Again.

And then I remember the last time I told him how I felt.

And how he turned and walked away.

And after a "Hope you feel better," he repeats the same exit as eight years ago.

The door shuts behind him, and I'm alone. In the quiet.

It's been eight years, and after a few weeks of seeing him, I'm right back in the same hopeless place.

I look down at the food on the tray. How is it possible to miss someone three seconds after they leave?

My phone lights up again, and again, I ignore the calls,

choosing instead to text Chad like any decent human being would do.

EMMY

Hey—so sorry I can't talk...I think I got food poisoning last night, it's pretty bad :(

I hope you're having a good day!

CHAD

My mom just brought home proofs of the new fireman's calendar.

You didn't mention you were in it.

Periods at the ends of both of those texts.

Is he mad?

EMMY

You didn't mention you lived with your mom.

I erase that before I send it, but you better believe I was thinking it. Instead, I text:

EMMY

Oh, yeah, they asked me to be a part of it.

Goodwill for the fire department.

CHAD

Oh.

It looks like the cover of one of those trashy romance novels.

I frown. I haven't seen the photo, but there's no way it looks like the cover of a trashy anything. I think I would know. But the bigger issue here is, why does he care?

CHAD

I'm sorry but I don't think we should see each other again.

I'm confused. He's upset that I'm in the calendar? I run through a list of things I could text back. They range from simple:

K.

To snarky:

Yeah, loafers without socks are a red flag for me, so. . .

To sarcastic:

Thanks for the food poisoning!

To gracious, which is ultimately what I choose:

EMMY

I agree we'd be better off as friends.

Thank you for a nice night.

After that, I put my phone away so I can think pleasant thoughts, mostly about Owen.

And I also wonder how I can get my hands on that photo.

Chapter Thirty-Three

Owen

So far, I've intentionally tried two things on *The Hopeful Romantic's* list.

And so far, neither has worked out.

First, the flowers. She doesn't even know they're from me.

Second, taking care of her when she's sick. Totally interrupted by the guy from her date.

Chad.

He's probably a decent guy.

He probably makes sense for Emmy.

I don't want either of those things to actually be true.

The best thing I can do is keep my head down and go back to my original plan where Emmy is concerned: friends only. I can do that, right?

I'm headed back to the station, on shift, and when I walk in, the captain points at me with two fingers and motions for me to follow him.

He doesn't look happy.

I walk back to his office, as he sits down at his desk. "Heard you had a little trouble with Lawrence a few days ago."

I stay quiet, stewing a little.

"I hear everything, Larrabee," he says. "Everything. Including what Lawrence said to you. Listen, I'm not going to condone fighting, but his personality is not what I'm looking for in a lieutenant."

I stand a little straighter.

"But I'm not looking for someone who can't control his temper either."

I give him a nod. "Understood, Captain."

He holds my attention for a few long seconds, then picks up a large, white envelope and hands it to me. "Your study materials."

Instantly, something inside me twists, but I take the packet.

"This packet has been specially prepared for you. There are three phases to the lieutenant test. I don't think you'll have a problem with the tactical exercises or even the oral board exam. The closed book multiple choice is what could trip you up. So, I've arranged for this test to be administered orally. And privately."

"Sir, I—"

"I want you to pass, Larrabee," he interrupts. "And I know you can. I think you'll make an excellent lieutenant, and frankly, I need more guys like you."

It's hard for me not to burst out and thank him. I just grit my teeth and keep it in—but it feels pretty darn good.

The chief leans back in his chair. "Study those materials. There are flashcards online and practice tests inside." He nods at the packet. "There's a study group or you can find a study partner, someone to quiz you on this stuff so you know it better than you know your own name. Most guys study six months to a year, but I don't think you'll need that long. You let me know when you're ready, and we'll get the test set up." He eyes me. "With accommodations."

I turn the packet over in my hand, feeling the weight of gratitude. It's exponential because it feels so undeserved.

I hesitate, then speak up. "Sir, if I can ask. . ." I pause, fiddling with the flap on the envelope. "Why are you doing this? Most people in authority, well. . ." I take a breath. "In my experience most people wouldn't care enough to do all this."

The captain smirks at me. "I think I see a little of myself in you, Larrabee. Hot-headed. Stubborn." He looks off to the left, and with an exaggerated tone, adds, "Ruggedly handsome."

I chuckle.

"I was a wreck till Liz got her hands on me. She calmed me down."

My thoughts turn to Emmy.

"The love of a good woman cannot be underestimated." He laughs.

"Even a woman you don't deserve?"

His expression changes and his eyebrows shoot up.

"Oh! Not talking about you and Liz, sir."

He pauses, then realizes. "Ah. You're talking about that bookstore owner."

I frown.

"Liz is a sucker for a love story," he says. "Said you two got awfully cozy during your photo shoot."

I shake my head. "Emmy is. . .a friend."

"Yeah, I said that about Liz once upon a time." He smirks. "You aren't exactly an open book, but you sure do look miserable."

I ignore the comment. "Thanks for the packet."

"Get to work."

I nod, and as I'm about to walk out the door, the captain says my name again. I turn.

"The other reason I want to see you succeed?"

I go still.

"My kid." He folds his hands on his desk. "He's seventeen, and I want him to know that his learning differences don't have to hold him back."

"I'm nobody's role model, sir."

"I know that." He laughs. "But maybe you will be. . .someday."

I walk out of the office with the study packet and more food for thought.

Moving back here isn't just changing the way I think about Emmy, it's changing the way I think about myself.

I stash my bag in my room, then head downstairs to the day room where most of the guys on shift are gathered around a table. I walk over to the coffee pot and pour myself a cup, and when I turn around, I see Emmy standing in the doorway, holding a white box, looking awkward and unsure.

Jace glances up and sees her, then looks at me. The others quiet down.

She smiles, and the room gets brighter.

The buzzing inside of me calms just being in the same room as her.

"Bookshop Girl!" Levi calls out. He picks something up off the table and walks over to her, looking at what he's holding, then up at her. "It's a different look for you than the photo, but. . ." he indicates from her head to her feet, ". . .this works too." He gives her a once-over, and my blood starts to boil.

Exactly what he was hoping for, I'm sure.

Emmy takes a step away as Levi reaches her. He drapes an arm around her and holds the photo up in front of her. "What do you think?" He looks at me. "I think Larrabee looks a little bored." He looks at her. "Which is weird, because this picture has got my imagination working overtime."

Emmy's face turns pink, then I see her expression brighten, then change, becoming determined.

She straightens.

"Levi, you're the human version of period cramps."

There's a pause, then a collective *Ohhhh!!* from the rest of the guys.

Levi steps back, as shocked as I am, and tries to play it off. "Ooh, she's got spunk, I like that!"

Emmy puts a hand on her hip. "You have the rest of your life to be an idiot. Can't you just take today off?"

Another round of *Ohhh!!!* and a few "*She got you, son!*" and "*Quit while you're ahead*!"

Levi holds up his hands in surrender. "Okay, okay, I give up!"

Emmy strides past him, pausing beside him only to say, "In my mind, you're buried in cement up to your neck. . .no, up to your nose." She puts a hand on his shoulder and loudly whispers, "*It's quieter that way*."

She plucks the photo from his frozen fingers and grins at me.

Emaline Smart can handle herself.

It's shocking, and impressive, and really, *really* hot.

"Owen? Can I talk to you for a second outside?"

In my dumbfounded state, I don't answer right away, and the guys chime in with catcalls and whoops, breaking my stupor.

"Uh, yeah. Yeah, sure, no problem."

Levi walks back to the couch, embarrassed and angrily shoving the guys away while they continue to pile on.

His face says it all.

Emmy just put him square in his place.

That was better than a fist, any day.

Chapter Thirty-Four

Emmy

Did I just do that?

I'm standing outside the fire station holding a small box of oatmeal butterscotch cookies and the photo I nabbed from Levi, nerves crackling with electricity and out of breath from what just happened.

People don't realize that classic romance novels are all kinds of swoony, but they pack some pretty clever insults in there as well.

Thank you, Edward Albee and Agatha Christie!

I'm still feeling like I'm having an out-of-body experience when the door opens and Owen steps out.

"Is everything okay?" I ask.

"Are you serious?" He steps right in front of me. "That. . .that was. . ."

He shakes his head and laughs. For real.

"That was amazing."

"It was, wasn't it?" I grin. "I can't believe I did that!" I'm still clutching the box in my hands.

"The guys in there aren't going to let him forget that for

months," he chuckles. "That was brilliant."

It's nice to see Owen smile. I'm starting to come off of the high of that confrontation, but I'm still nervous about what brought me here in the first place.

"You look better." He's still smiling.

I made Owen smile.

"Better than half-dead?" I laugh. "Thank you."

"That was rough, huh?"

"That's what I get for going out with a controlling mama's boy. My own personal sign to never do *that* again."

His face shifts. He looks. . .relieved?

"Loafer guy?"

"Oh my gosh, *yes*," I laugh. "No socks."

There's a lull.

"He's controlling?" Owen straightens again.

I hold up a hand. "Listen, I know I'm like a little sister to you, but I think I just proved in there that I really can take care of myself."

"I don't think of you as—" He looks away, then smiles softly. "Yeah, I'd say you can handle yourself."

"Good." I smile. "I brought you these to thank you for taking care of me yesterday." I hold out the box.

He takes it and opens it, and when he sees what's inside, he cracks the slightest smile. "Oatmeal butterscotch?"

"O.L. oatmeal butterscotch." I can feel my cheeks heat at the admission.

He meets my eyes. "O.L.?"

I shrug. "They always were your favorite." I desperately look around for something—anything—to help me change the subject. I'm dangerously close to another bold confession.

Thankfully, Owen just nods and says, "You didn't have to do that." He picks up a cookie and takes a bite. "But I'm glad you did."

"It was really nice of you to make sure I was okay," I say. "And I did eat the soup after you left. And I kept it down. It was good, so thank you."

He nods as he chews and swallows. "Good."

"So. . ." I wave the picture in front of him. "The photo proofs are out."

He stops chewing.

"I didn't really get a good look," he says.

"Neither did I. Want to look at it together?"

I move to stand beside him and hold it up.

There's a chance my fingers are going to ignite.

Somehow, a photographer named after fancy chocolate turned a simple photoshoot in a bookstore into something magical. Like something out of a fairytale. She must've put some sort of special effect on it because she'd transformed the aisle of books into a moody, romantic destination, and there, at the center of the image, are me and Owen.

Or, more specifically, me in Owen's arms.

My one arm is draped around his neck, and the other is down, dancer-like, holding a book.

I'm looking down, artistic and dreamy, and he is looking at me.

Not just casually looking either, he's *looking*. Like he's the big bad wolf and I'm Little Red Riding Hood.

I thought I'd imagined the sparks between us that day, but unless Owen is a very good actor, they were real. Very real.

And I want to recreate it.

Over and over again.

How am I ever going to shelve books in that aisle again? *Thrilling romance*, indeed.

He clears his throat. "Uh. . .wow."

I swallow. "Yeah."

He pauses, then asks, "Do you like it?"

My eyes flick to his, and I see something hopeful there. "I do."

"Me too."

"We look, uh. . ."

"Yeah, we look. . ."

I swallow. "Yeah."

I don't look away. I want to let myself feel whatever this is, this cord of electricity humming between us.

I remember the day I told Owen how I felt. I didn't think it was possible, but those feelings have only multiplied. My high school feelings pale in comparison to these grown-up ones.

"I. . .uh," he stammers, and he moves closer.

My breath hitches.

"I. . .really should get back to work," he says, breaking eye contact and the spell.

I blink, shaking my head clear, thinking that will help. "Right. Right, of course," I say.

"And I should probably return the photo."

You mean I don't get to keep this for my private collection?

I hand it back and he takes it, and for a moment we're both holding it at the same time.

He looks at it, and I wonder what he sees. "It's a cool shot."

I nod and let go.

There's a pause.

"Thanks again for these." He holds up the cookies.

"You're welcome," I hear myself say. "I'll, uh, talk to you later then." I'm lingering. Again. And I don't even have keys to fumble with.

"Yeah, that'd be good."

I turn and start back toward my car. My parents are still gone, so no Sunday dinner today, but that gives me time to catch up on podcast things and keep daydreaming about Owen.

I'm halfway to my car when something hits me.

Wait.

I never told Owen about the loafers.

I turn around as I'm saying— "How do you know—"

But he's already back inside.

And I am full of questions.

Monday, after an uneventful day at work, a long phone call with the restoration company, and a not so sneaky drive by the fire station *just in case* Owen was, I don't know, outside washing the engine. Shirtless. In October. I come home to find my mom working in the yard.

She stands when she sees me pull in. I grab my things from the back seat and get out, meeting her in the yard.

"Chili for dinner tonight," she says.

"Corn bread?"

"Of course." She smiles.

"Nice!" Mom's corn bread is the stuff of legends. If she was around back then, her recipe would've canceled that old Hatfield and McCoy disagreement.

"Did you and dad have fun on your weekend away?" I ask. "Where did you go? The Biltmore Hotel?"

"Yes, and it was lovely. I had the best steak, and we ate breakfast in bed and—"

"I'm going to stop you right there," I say. "There's only so much of this story I need to know."

"You look tired," she says. "Are you feeling back to normal?" She starts walking toward the house, and I fall into step beside her.

How do I tell her that it's not the food poisoning that has me feeling off? "I'm good."

"Peggy said you went on a date Friday?" Mom asks.

I groan. "Peggy needs a hobby."

"She has one, dear. It's getting into everyone else's business." Mom grins as she pulls the door open, and we walk inside through the side door. I can smell the chili cooking on the stove.

"So, what was wrong with this one?" Mom tosses her gardening gloves into a basket by the door and takes off her boots.

"You say that like I make a practice of finding things that are wrong with people."

"Not all people," she says. "Just the ones you go on dates with." She walks over to the stove and stirs the pot of chili.

"Can we eat now?" I ask. "I'm starving."

"We have to wait for your dad," she says. "He's on his way."

I sit down at the counter across from where she's standing. "You think I'm too picky?"

Mom turns. "I think you're holding out for something that maybe doesn't exist."

I frown. "You don't want me to have high standards?"

"Of course, I do," she says. "It's just, sometimes I wonder if you're being a tiny bit unrealistic. With the romance thing."

I make a face. "The 'romance thing?'"

"Oh, you know what I'm talking about. It's like you have this list of things a guy has to do in order to prove he really loves you. Not all great love stories start with grand gestures."

I feel compelled to remind her that it was *her* novels on *her* bookshelf that fed me these ideas in the first place.

But I don't.

"I mean, look at your father and me." She smiles.

"No offense, Mom, but Dad is about the least romantic person we know."

"Oh, that's where you're wrong, sweetheart," she says. "Your father is one of the *most* romantic people we know."

"*My* father? The man who speaks in grunts and football analogies?"

"Sure! I mean, he's never going to be the one to serenade me in public, but he does make sure my car is filled up with gas every weekend. He handles most of the laundry, and he makes sure the garbage is taken out every single week."

Practical. Now where have I heard *that* one before?

"Household chores aren't romance, Mom."

"Honey, he is speaking my language. Being thoughtful. Doing things that will show me he loves me. It doesn't matter what the gesture is, if the intent behind it is to show someone you care, then it can be romantic." She slices into the warm corn bread. I can smell it from where I'm sitting, and my mouth waters.

"I just think there's a difference between being thoughtful and being romantic," I say, and then point. "I'm gonna need a piece of that."

"Not before dinner."

I harrumph like a child being told it's time to leave the water park.

"And you're right, one *could* argue that romance will fade. But. . ." she points a butter knife at me, "if a person is thoughtful, that sticks. Doesn't that matter more? Just because someone is good at being sappy or thinking up romantic gestures, that doesn't mean they're worthy of your love." She levels my gaze. "And just because they *aren't* good at those things doesn't mean they aren't."

I narrow my eyes. "Why do I feel you're not speaking hypothetically anymore?"

She holds up her hands and feigns innocence. "Did I mention any names?"

"Somehow I don't think you're talking about the guy I went on the date with."

Mom flicks a hand in the air. "No, Peggy said he's a snooze fest. She and Meg have another match in mind for you." Mom waggles her eyebrows and shimmies her shoulders.

"This is about Owen," I say. Even mentioning his name makes my insides flutter.

"If you want it to be." She serves me a surprise slice of the corn bread—which is the best kind of corn bread. "Here, this should tide you over."

"I don't want it to be," I lie. "Owen is a good guy. He's just not *my* guy."

"Because he's not romantic enough?" Mom asks dryly.

"No, because we're just. . .*wrong* for each other." I take a bite. I swear I could eat this whole pan. "But yeah, maybe because he's not romantic. I mean, I love romance. What's wrong with waiting for someone who gets that?"

"Nothing." Mom takes a bite of her own piece of bread. "If you don't mind waiting forever."

I roll my eyes. "You're not very encouraging."

"What? I like him. He's grown up. He saved your life. He's a good guy now."

"He was always a good guy," I tell her. "Just really misunderstood."

"Fine," she says. "Though I'm sure we can say Owen is at least a little romantic. He did buy you your favorite flowers." She nods at the vase of sunflowers, which have been moved from the living room into the kitchen.

"Those were not from Owen," I say, taking another bite. "They were from my date. Chad. He left them on the seat of my car."

She goes still. "Those flowers are from Owen Larrabee."

Now I freeze. "No, they are not."

She tilts her head down at me. "Honey, *yes they are.*"

"How would you know something like that? You weren't

even in town."

"How do you think?" Mom walks back over to the chili and stirs. "Peggy told me. Meg was in the flower shop when he came in. She works there now. She tried grilling Owen to find out who he was buying them for, but he was very tightlipped about the whole thing."

I frown. "That tracks."

Owen bought me flowers? And not just any flowers —*sun*flowers. But then, how did they even get in my car?

"He is the only person who bought sunflowers that day. Peggy made sure of it."

I pause, but eventually wave her off. "That's a nice theory, Mom, but Owen really does not think of me that way. And he certainly doesn't buy flowers."

I think of the way he looked when he brought the vase into the living room yesterday when I was sick on the couch. He seemed happy when I told him they were my favorite flower.

"Are you sure?" Mom asks. "Because it was also *awfully* nice of him to organize a whole day to help you with the cleanup in your house. And Susannah told me he bought you chicken soup yesterday when you were sick. I saw it in the refrigerator."

"He was being friendly."

"He was being *thoughtful.*" She nods. "And I don't know about you, but to me, that reads a lot like romance."

My dad walks through the door, takes a deep breath and smiles. "Chili!"

"Your favorite," Mom says.

They go through their *get home from work* ritual, which includes way too much over-fifty kissing, so I make myself scarce to avoid having to talk to my therapist about more than just the fire.

That also leaves me to stew about what my mother said.

Surely, she's wrong about all of it.

This crush has always been one-sided, and I don't think that's changed.

But why would Owen buy me flowers and not say anything?

For absolutely no reason?

I think back on the thoughtful things he's done since he got back. Kind things. Little things. The way he pulled me aside during my panic attack so nobody else would see me break down. The way he insisted on walking me to my car. The way he showed up here when he heard I was sick.

They were simple things. The kind of things a friend would do for another friend.

But is my mother right? Are they also romantic?

I look up and find my parents, thankfully not playing tonsil hockey, each moving around the kitchen in a quiet choreography. He pulls three bowls down from the cupboard and sets them next to the pot on the stove where she's cooking. As he passes by her on the way to get spoons from the silverware drawer, his hand grazes her back, not in an amorous way, just in a way that lets her know he's there.

It's always been like that. Her being there for him. Him being there for her.

They live with an unspoken, coded language that nobody else understands. I thought they were boring, but now, I see they're anything but.

How had I missed it before?

Maybe I *have* been holding out for the wrong things.

My mother walks over to the opposite side of the counter and stands in front of me. She reaches out and quietly readjusts the sunflowers, smiling directly at me, and says, "Time to eat!"

And then she walks over to the table, and I'm still standing here, trying to sort through all of my many confusing thoughts.

Chapter Thirty-Five

Emmy

"He might not be practically perfect in every way, Floundering in Florida, but there's room to hope! It sounds like he's open to trying new things, and that, I believe, is worth keeping an open mind."

I click the Stop button.

I'm recording a new episode. I'm off-schedule, but I have the time. I make sure to pick questions that will not veer off into any real-life feelings, and by the time I'm finished, I'm feeling restless.

I scroll over to my inbox and find a notification on something I've never used before.

Chat.

It's right there, right under "Mail," with a "1" in a red circle.

Should I click on it? This feels way more. . .I don't know, *close*. . .than just regular email.

Curiosity gets the best of me.

It's from Practical in Poughkeepsie.

Practical:
How'd your attempt at practical romance go?

It shows a time stamp on it, next to a blue circle icon with a capital P in it.

8 min.

He wrote this eight minutes ago. Is he still on? How do I. . .

There's a green dot next to his email in the chat list on the left-hand side.

He's still logged on.

I feel a sudden rush of excitement. What do I do? Do I respond? How do I make sure to stay anonymous? Wait. Does he see *my* green dot? If so, will he. . .

A new message pops up.

Practical:
Sorry, maybe picking chat was a bit bold. We can stick to email.

He sees my green dot.

My mind randomly flashes to the ball scene in Tolstoy's *Anna Karenina*. I've read it so many times I could recite it. Poor Kitty, dancing in the arms of someone she doesn't care about, watching her love, Count Vronsky, begin to fall for the beautiful, passionate Anna. It's crushing to see her heart break in that scene, hearing her realize that whatever she and Vronsky had was over after that dance.

Then, something dawns on me.

Kitty ends up with Levin. Not Vronsky.

He's the practical one. He's the realist. He's the farmer.

Levin's love for Kitty is patient. Their relationship is complicated, even contentious at times. She denies his initial proposal because she's holding out for someone else, something else that doesn't work out. He's turned down flat, but still he waited. And after they've grown, after they find each other again, they forgive and love each other more easily than Anna and Vronsky ever do.

Levin and Kitty don't have the bombastic romantic roller-coaster of Anna and Vronsky. . . but their love is powerful and true, nonetheless.

With this revelation, I type.

Hopeful:
Bold, yes. But it's okay.
My date hardly talked, and when he did, it was random knowledge about a fantasy movie.

Practical:
I'm guessing you like romance movies better?

I smile as I type the next sentence:

Hopeful:
Let's just say Pride and Prejudice is in my top six.

I see three tiny dots appear then disappear at the bottom of the chat box. Oddly, I don't want him to leave the conversation yet, so I keep going.

Hopeful:
You still swearing off romance? After one little defeat?
I hope she's worth fighting for!

Practical:
It was pretty humiliating. But no, I'm not giving up quite yet.
She absolutely is worth it. What do you think I should do?

With my mother's words swirling around in my head, Kitty's almost missing lifelong love because she was holding out for something she thought was better, my thoughts turn to Owen.

And it hits me.

I wouldn't care one bit if he chose skywriting or a quiet, simple moment where it was just us two. I would just want to hear the words. And I would want to hear them as soon as possible.

This poor guy has been holding his feelings in because he's trying to find the right way to tell the woman he loves that he loves her. But I see it now. He was right in the first place. The *how* he tells her shouldn't matter.

The romance is in the words, not the way.

Hopeful:
I think you should tell her how you feel.

Practical:
Just like that?

Hopeful:
Just like that.

Practical:
What about the romance? The grand gesture?

Hopeful:
I'm starting to think that working up the courage to say how you feel is the grand gesture.

Practical:
But that sounds. . .almost practical.

Hopeful:
Yeah, it does, doesn't it?

Practical:
But you just said the practical guy didn't work for you.

Hopeful:
He definitely didn't. But. . .there's the hope of someone else. Someday.

Practical:
Huh. Interesting.
So, what should I say?

Hopeful:
Well, I'd start with how you feel.
Maybe add in a little bit of what makes her special and end with how you want your relationship to go or change.

Practical:
And you think that's enough?

Again, I think of Owen. If he were going to profess his love for me, I think he could tell me in three words, and I'd turn into a melted marshmallow. Maybe it doesn't need to be fancy or flowery or Jane Austen-esque. Maybe it just needs to be honest.

Hopeful:
Just tell her. Don't overthink it.
Forget I said anything about the romance because I'm starting to see that's not what matters.
What matters is that you're honest.
And thoughtful.

And good.
It sounds like you really care about this girl.
And that is its own kind of romance!

Wow. I really do believe that.

Practical:
All right. Wish me luck.

Hopeful:
Report back!
And I'm sending over a Zoom link for our interview.
We'll keep the video off, but I think it'll be a great conversation.

Practical:
Great.
And hey. . .thanks.

Hopeful:
Anytime.

Owen

I sit back from the laptop on the desk in my small room at the station, rereading the conversation.

Pride and Prejudice is in my top six.

Emmy *is* The Hopeful Romantic.

Chapter Thirty-Six

Emmy

Friday morning, I learn that Owen still has a key to my house.

I head straight over to meet the restoration company before work. When I arrive, I see Owen's truck parked outside and the inside door to my house is open.

My heart flip flops.

My feelings for him are tug-of-warring inside of me.

Tug-of-warring? More like tug-of-warning.

Having him back in town pretty much ensures that I'm going to be single for the rest of my life. Because unfortunately, these feelings, I'm realizing, aren't the kind that ever fully go away.

And his, it seems, will never start.

I don't know what to do with that. I want to be Cosette, and I'm Eponine.

I just hope I don't end up dead on some French barricade.

I get out of the car and walk up to the door, and when I walk inside I see. . .and smell. . .progress. It's starting to look and feel like my house again. If they can wipe away every trace of fire in my place, maybe I can live here without the threat of anxiety over what I went through.

Maybe.

I've scheduled out two months of regular therapy sessions with my therapist. The first ones have gone well—and I'm hoping the rest will help me avoid freezing up and breaking down with panic again.

I hear two male voices, one of them Owen's, downstairs. I head to the basement and find them standing in my office. They're over by the sitting area, next to the breaker box that I hid behind a large canvas painting of tiny, abstract people on the beach.

They're talking about the wiring in the whole house, and when I step inside the room, I hear Owen say, "Can we just rewire the whole thing? I want to make absolutely sure nothing like this ever happens again."

I freeze. *Thoughtful.*

He looks over and I'm reminded once again that I am a goner. He's wearing his trademark serious expression, but the second his eyes meet mine, it softens into something else. Something I can't read. Something I don't want to misinterpret.

Dickenson told us the heart wants what the heart wants, or else it does not care.

But why does *my* heart only ever seem to want *this* man?

"Hey, Emmy." My name sounds so good on his lips.

Play it cool, Emaline Rose. I'm using my best internal stern voice and my full name, but even that's wavering.

I don't think I can speak logic to myself right now. Not when he's standing here in my basement, a welcome trespasser in my home and in my heart.

"I hope you don't mind. I used the key your mom gave me to let Ed in."

Ed gives me a nod. "Morning, Miss Smart."

When I don't say anything because my tongue is tied into a thousand knots, Owen frowns. "Emmy? You okay?"

"Sorry," I say. "I'm fine. What did I miss?"

"We were looking at the progress so far. Another week or so, barring any rewiring, and I think you'll be able to move back in."

Ed is holding a clipboard. "I was just telling Owen, I can have my electrician come through and double check all the electrical. Old house, old wiring. We might need to replace a few things. Just to be safe. Do you want me to show you what we've done so far?"

No, I want you to leave so I can stare at Owen without an audience.

"Sure."

Ed walks me through the house, updating me on the progress, telling me what they've found, but I'm only half-listening. Mostly, I'm trying not to keep my imagination from running away with a romantic scenario.

Like in Hannah Grim's *Love on Commission,* when the main character falls for a real estate developer, and there's a scene where she angles herself so her hand brushes up against his while walking through a condo with his business partner.

I glance at Owen's hand. It's a good ten feet away, but I could maybe trip or something, subtly slide over there. . .

Stop it.

Must. Stay. Grounded.

I'm half-hearing Owen talk to Ed, the questions he asks, the way he seems intent on ensuring *my* safety and *my* comfort. . .

My mother was right about his thoughtfulness.

It's in a romantic class all its own.

By the time we finish the walk-through, I realize I have no idea what's been done in my house, only that it's looking better, and I can move back in soon and, thanks to Owen, I have every confidence it will be safe.

When we've finished, Owen walks Ed to the door, like he's the one who owns this house, and darn if I don't love it. I hang back in the living room, trying to find something to occupy myself when all I really want to do is stare at Owen.

My plan to put him out of my mind is failing, and I'm not even sure I care anymore.

He closes the door behind Ed and turns to me.

"Hey." He points to my hands.

Yes, I'll hold your hand.

I clear my throat. "What?"

He smiles. "No fists. No panic. You're back here and you're okay."

I didn't even realize it.

"Yeah. It's. . .it's better. Helps that it doesn't smell like smoke anymore," I half-heartedly laugh.

He looks at me intently. "I'm glad you're doing better."

"It's a process." I shift under the weight of his gaze. "You didn't have to do all this, you know," I say. "I could've figured it out."

He quirks a brow. "How much of that conversation did you listen to?"

I look away, shrugging like a kid at the front of the class faking her way through a report on a book she didn't read.

He chuckles. "Yeah, I thought so. It's a lot, and I'm happy to do it. I want to make sure they're doing everything to make the house safe again."

"But why?" The words are out before I can stop them. "I mean. . ." *oh, boy* ". . .why do you care?"

He stuffs his hands in his pockets and looks down.

I'm expecting a shrug and a grunt, but he looks back up at me.

"Because it's you, Emmy."

That phrase cartwheels straight into my heart.

Even though I know he doesn't mean for it to, it sounds like he's saying *it's me.* As in *it's me* who he loves. *Me* who he wants. *Me* who he can't live without.

"I mean, I care about you, that you're. . .you know, safe." And it's a good thing he clarifies that because I had us on the way to the altar.

"Thank you, Owen. It's really nice of you," I say. "You're a. . ." *why am I saying this?* "A great friend."

He goes still. And then he takes his hands out of his pockets and walks over to me. He stands there, just looking at me, as if trying to find something to say and failing.

Me, I'm trying not to fall—hard—into those beautiful eyes, and I'm failing too.

All at once I have a whole list of words I'd love to hear tumbling out of that mouth. Words like *love.* And *not just as a friend.* And *'til death do us part.*

I might be getting ahead of myself.

I'd settle for *Do you want to try dating? See where this goes? See if you were onto something all those years ago with your ill-timed confession that you were in love with me?*

Or even *Aw, shoot, now look. . .I'm the one in love with you.*

But Owen doesn't say any of those things.

True to form, he doesn't say anything. Instead, he pushes a hand through his hair and looks away. I can see the muscles in his cheeks flex, gritting his teeth, frustrated about. . .what, exactly?

And then he walks into the kitchen.

He leaves me standing here, in the living room, trying to catch my breath.

It seemingly left the room with him.

And if he can steal that much oxygen with a wordless stare, I can't even imagine how I'd recover if he ever kissed me.

But I really, really want to find out.

After a moment, I walk into the kitchen and find him inspecting the empty cabinets. Or pretending to. I can't tell what he's doing.

"You okay?"

He faces me. "Yeah, great. All good here." He clears his throat. "You?"

I nod. "All good here too."

"Good." He nods.

"Yep."

A pause. He hits the counter a few times with his palm, then looks around.

It's the physical representation of that awkward "Soooo, . . .how 'bout them Cubs?"

I frown.

"Why are you being weird?" I ask.

"I'm not being weird," he says weirdly.

"You actually are," I say. "And being weird is my job."

He leans back on the counter, and I imagine having permission to walk straight over to him and press my body into his. What would it feel like to finally—finally—have his arms wrapped around me and *not* in a burning building?

I can imagine that scenario without a bit of difficulty. It's a nice fantasy. And naturally, it makes my cheeks flush.

I somehow exercise self-control and take a step back, "I should—"

But at the same time, he says, "Can you help me—"

I stop. "What?"

"Uh, I wondered. . ." He looks away. Is he. . .nervous? "So, I got the study materials for the lieutenant test."

Oh. That explains this behavior.

"Oh, good," I say, smiling. "You're going to do it?"

He nods. "I am." He quickly adds, "At least, I'm going to try."

"I'm really glad to hear it," I tell him. "You're going to be awesome."

Another lull.

"Do you want to. . .would you maybe. . .help me study?"

I smile.

He looks down. It's hard for him to ask for help, because it's admitting he needs it. He hates being thought of as "less than," and just the fact that he's dropping his pride and asking is so, so huge.

"Like, you know, before?"

This is the side no one sees. This is the personality that stays at arm's length.

And this is why I've loved him for years.

"Of course," I say.

"All right," he says. "At the dock?"

"Okay."

He looks relieved. Like a huge weight has been lifted off his shoulders. "Could we start tomorrow night?"

I nod. It's the least I can do after the way he's handled things with my house restoration. "I can be there. Unless you want to go somewhere warmer?"

He shakes his head. "No, it needs to be the dock."

I frown. "You need to study."

"Yeah."

"At the dock."

"Yep." His face gives nothing away. "And dress warm."

I keep frowning.

A pause.

"I'll go now." And with a weird pat on my shoulder, he leaves.

What. The heck. Was that?

After he leaves, I'm alone in my house.

I'm alone in my house for the first time since the fire.

I walk around, aimlessly, aware of the time and the fact that I need to get over to the bookshop. But something draws me back downstairs. Back into my office. Where I was when my whole world went sideways.

I stand at the top of the stairs and wait for the anxiety to roll over me.

None comes.

I take a step down, one step, and wait.

My breathing is fine.

I take a few more, then a few more, until I'm at the basement floor, looking into my office.

I see my desk and the chair, but the large rug is gone, presumably because of smoke damage.

Soon I'll be back to recording episodes right here. If only I felt confident about what I might say.

Nothing seems cut and dry anymore. I used to dole out advice with so much confidence, a romance master who had it all figured out.

Now, I feel like a student all over again.

I'm about to leave when something catches the corner of my eye.

There, on the top of my desk, is a small stack of physical letters.

They're all addressed to *The Hopeful Romantic.*

Sometimes people send their questions via my post office box in Memphis, where my assistant Lily lives. She sends it all on to me from there.

Sometimes they send fan mail or thank you notes. And then I've gotten a few not-so-happy notes from people whose relationships didn't pan out. I usually stash the letters away, but in the craziness of the fire, I must've forgotten.

We barely touched this room on the clean-up day because it wasn't hit very hard.

I look over at the painting covering the breaker box.

I look again at the letters.

There's a chance—a good chance—that Owen saw these when he was in here with Ed.

There's a good chance that Owen knows I'm The Hopeful Romantic.

Chapter Thirty-Seven

Owen

I wasn't snooping.

It's the day after the walk-through of Emmy's house, and I'm at the gym with Jace. It's a good thing because I need to blow off some steam.

We're in the ring, sparring, and I'm wondering if I should move to one of the bags because I feel like I need to hit something and I really don't want it to be Jace.

Yes, I had my suspicions, but the letters on Emmy's desk prove it. She *is* the woman I've been trading emails with. She's the one who told me to tell her how I feel. She just didn't know she was talking to me. And she didn't know we were talking about her.

I pop the focus mitts on Jace's hands, *left-right, left-right.*

The last one I hit *hard.*

"Ow, geez, Owen."

I snap to the present. "Ah. Sorry, Jace."

"What's going on with you?" Jace drops his hands and looks at me. "You're off today. And you're hitting these like Levi's picture's on them."

"Funny," I say. "I've just got a lot on my mind."

"The lieutenant test?" he asks.

No. I wasn't even thinking about that. Not that I don't care, it's just. . .

Emmy.

At my reaction, Jace draws back. "*Not* the lieutenant test."

I shake my head.

"The girl," he says. A statement, not a question.

I nod.

"What's the problem?"

"I think I like her."

Jace laughs. "Finally!" Affecting a Sunday morning preacher's voice, he shouts, "Ladies and gentlemen, he speaks the truth!"

I remain stoic.

"What's the problem? Mack says she's sure Emmy feels the same way about you."

I eye him.

Jace turns sheepish. "About that. . .look man, it just kind of happened, I'm sorry, but she's amazing, and, well. . ."

I wave him off. "Mack can handle herself. And you're a good guy." I straighten. "But if you hurt her, we won't be sparring in here. And you know I can kick your—"

He cuts me off with an upheld hand. "I know." He looks away. "I really like her, man."

"Why?" I chuckle. "She's such a pain. Do you have any idea what you're getting into?"

He smirks. "I've got a pretty good idea, yeah."

"She's going to drive you crazy, you know that, right?"

He slaps the gloves together and motions for me to get back at it. "I'm counting on it."

I shake my head and lift my gloves. It should be that easy.

Easy as saying I like her. Easy as saying my feelings for her have changed. Why isn't it easy?

With Lindsay, she was the one that instigated everything. She was the reason our relationship progressed. Emmy is so different, and I get the sense she holds back a little. Probably because of our history.

Left. Left. Left-right.

"So, are you going to tell her?" Jace asks, swinging the mitt over my head as I duck.

Right, right-left.

"I mean, I think I have to." I shake out my arms, loosening the tightness and fatigue.

I wonder if this is how Emmy felt all those years ago, keeping her feelings bottled up until she blurted them out after the not-wedding.

The timing was terrible, but maybe she just couldn't keep it inside for another second. I get it now.

Looking back, she was the right girl at the wrong time.

Still, she did it. She said it. She put herself out there and it backfired.

No chance she's going to do it again.

If our relationship is going to change, I'm going to have to be the one to change it.

"So, what are you waiting for?" Jace taps his gloves to mine and assumes a fighting stance.

"It's different with Emmy," I say. "She and I have a good relationship. A friendship."

He rolls his eyes. "Don't tell me you're afraid of ruining it. That's crap. Friends make the best lovers anyway. We've already established that she's good for you, so if you aren't telling her, it's only because you're afraid."

I react to that and swing for the fences, cracking the mitt and sending his right hand flying.

He immediately takes the glove off and shakes his hand out. "Thanks for proving my point. . ." he says, wincing.

"Ah. Shoot. Sorry. . .uh, again."

He's one hundred percent correct. There's all this pressure to make certain moments romantic.

And now that I know that Emmy is The Hopeful Romantic, I also know that she's the one who originally told me to "double down" on the romance. Never mind that she also told me to "just tell her." To forget the romance. That saying it out loud *is* the romantic thing. Did she mean it?

Her perfect guy isn't me—but her emails yesterday suggest maybe she's softened her stance. "Listen, I'm no romance expert, but I have binged every episode of that stupid podcast," Jace says. "Trying to figure out how to woo your sister."

I hold up a hand. "First, don't talk to me about my sister. Second, did you just say 'woo?'"

"That's the word she uses, the lady on the podcast" Jace says, innocently, like that's a reason to repeat it.

"I do have an idea," I tell him. "But it might be stupid."

"In love, there's no such thing," he says in a sing-songy voice.

I step out of the ring.

"Oh, we're done?"

"Yeah, I don't fight girls." I chuckle.

"That's cold, man," he says. "Especially since we both know Clemons could take us both out in one round."

I laugh. "You're not wrong."

Jace's expression changes. "One day you'll know how it feels to make an idiot of yourself for a woman."

"Today might be that day." I take off the gloves. "You wanna help me?"

"I'm in." He steps under the ropes. "But if there's a

boombox involved or climbing up some kind of vine-covered balcony, then I'm out."

"No boom box, no balcony" I say. "I've got something else in mind."

Chapter Thirty-Eight

Emmy

The dock. I'm going back to the dock.

I step outside my parents' house, and I breathe in the cool, crisp air. Definitely too cold to study outside at the pond. And yet, on similar nights like this in high school, I powered through, shivering and not feeling my toes for hours afterward, just because I wanted to be around Owen.

Tonight feels like that.

I'm just quizzing Owen so he can memorize firefighter things, but I'm nervous.

I'm nervous because it'll just be the two of us, on our dock, and at some point in the evening, our eyes will meet and my stomach will swoop and there's a slight chance that logic and reason will exit my brain in favor of fantasy.

I'm not even pretending to fight it at this point.

I just want to get down to the pond so I can see him already.

I'm wearing jeans, a long-sleeved T-shirt, and a thick, oversized sweater, but I also grab my favorite plaid down blanket on my way out, just in case the heat I feel around Owen isn't enough.

It will probably be enough.

I start the walk down to the pond, telling myself *It's fine, we're just friends* over and over the entire way. Leaves crunch beneath my feet, and I see my breath wisp around my eyes in the cool air. It's apple pie weather. Pumpkin spice weather.

Cuddling under blankets weather.

As I approach the dock, I see a warm glow surrounding the trees. I stop walking and listen, worried something might be wrong.

Is that. . .music?

The quiet, but undeniable, sound of an instrumental melody echoes through the space above the pond. It's like the soundtrack from *Bridgerton.* Slowed down versions of a pop song I vaguely recognize played by an orchestra.

Something strange is happening.

Slowly, I start to walk again, curious about what is happening at my thinking spot, and when I finally get close enough to see, I still can't make sense of it.

There are white lights strung in the trees behind the dock, and on the dock there's a picnic basket sitting on top of a blanket, surrounded by candles. The flickering glow from the twinkling lights casts a golden hue across the whole scene. It's like something out of a movie.

I step out of the trees and into the clearing around the pond. The music—which I now place as the same song we danced to during our photoshoot—*Can't Help Falling in Love*—plays quietly in the background.

I take another step toward the pond, and when I glance up, I see Owen step out onto the dock. He's holding a small book in his hands, and he's watching me, an expression I can't read on his face.

And then, he smiles. It's slight, but I catch it before it skitters away.

"Hey," he calls out over the water.

"Hey." I watch him. "What is all this?"

I barely make out a smile on his face, but I can hear it in his voice. "You'll see."

I want to freeze and run at the same time. I force myself to play it cool. My heart is racing, and my legs are quaking as I start toward the dock.

Toward him.

He's standing at the land end of the dock when I get there, and he reaches his hand out to me to help me step up. I take it, and once I'm standing next to him, he faces me and sort of smiles. "Hey."

"Hey." I smile. But bigger. "Did you do all this?" I motion to the lights in the trees.

"I had some help," he says. "Jace and Mack."

I quirk a brow. Where is this coming from? And, more importantly, what is *this*?

He holds my gaze for several seconds, then finally says, "Hey," again.

I laugh. "*Hey.*"

He shakes his head and rolls his eyes, in an *I'm a dork* look. "Are you hungry?"

I eye him for a brief moment. "I'm not *not* hungry."

He stops.

"That's a yes, right?"

I nod. "Yes, you bozo. That's a yes."

I'm keenly aware he still has my hand in his.

I'm also curious what's packed in that picnic basket. Picnic baskets aren't friendly. This isn't just thoughtful. I can't help but note there is something decidedly different happening right now.

And it's like something out of one of my dreams.

He drops my hand and walks over to the basket. "Do you want to sit?"

"Sure." I move over to the blanket and sit down, setting my own blanket off to the side. I pull my knees up and wrap my arms around them, facing Owen and trying not to let my questions ruin the moment.

Beside me, Owen sits, pulling the picnic basket over between us. "Before we get into this—" he glances down at the basket. "Can I just say something?"

Every nerve ending in my body is misfiring. My *we're just friends* chant has faded into the dark, black void, and I'm left with nothing but growing, burning feelings for this man.

He's watching me, waiting for my answer, and I don't even remember the question.

"Emmy?"

I clear my throat. "Yeah, of course. You can say anything."

He nods but doesn't speak. It's almost like he's working up the courage to say whatever it is that's on his mind.

What is *on his mind?*

"Back when we were younger, I never would've thought we'd be friends."

"I'm inclined to agree," I say, without thinking.

He smiles. "I was. . ." he winces. "Let's just say I know I was hard to get along with. And hard to get to know."

I nod. I'm afraid if I speak I'll scare him off and he won't keep talking. Or that I'll roll over and fall out of bed only to discover this is all a dream.

"But I got to know you, and you were, you know, cool."

I absolutely wasn't, but okay.

"But. . .I didn't think of you as anything but, you know—"

"Another little sister," I say.

"A friend."

"Right." He'd said that before. No new information so far. Maybe this is him thanking me for being his friend. That would be just my luck.

"I never saw you as anything else," he says. "So. . .when you told me about your feelings? On my wedding day?"

I'm transported to those feelings. They're not far away. "Yeah. I remember."

"Well. . ." he continues, "when you told me that, it threw me off."

My face heats at the mention of that stupid confession. "I know, and I'm sorry—"

He reaches over and takes my hand. "No, Emmy, listen."

I go silent.

I like his hands. He weaves his fingers through mine, and my heart bangs around in my chest like a wild bird in a cage.

"I didn't think of you like that back then because we were friends. Good friends, and I. . .really didn't have a lot of those."

He looks down.

"I didn't have any, really. Not real ones."

He looks back up at me.

"And then there was Lindsay, and, I don't know. . ." He drops my hand and reaches for the book that's now sitting beside him. "So, isn't it kind of strange that I kept this all these years?"

He opens the book and pulls out a gold piece of paper.

No, it's not paper.

My breath catches.

It's an old, flat Twix wrapper.

"Is that. . .?"

"The first night you found me here, you gave me half of your Twix."

"I remember."

"I found it in my desk," he says. "In this old journal." He

turns it over in his hands. "There's actually a lot in here about you."

"About me?"

He nods. "On that night, the night we met, I stuck the wrapper between the pages, and I wrote—" He looks down at the journal. It's too dark to see now, so he moves it closer to a candle and reads. "Had the strangest night with Mack's friend Emmy. She didn't talk. She didn't make me talk. But we sat on the dock at the pond. It was. . .nice. I don't think she's judgy like everyone else around here. I hope she's there the next time I go to the pond."

I can't help it—tears brim in my eyes, and I smile.

"I think a part of me always loved you, Emmy."

Did he just say love?

"You saw something in me that nobody else bothered to see. You're kind. You're. . .patient. You don't keep some list of everything I've done wrong. Because of that, you knew me better than everyone, and I didn't realize that until I moved back here." He reaches over and brushes my hair away from my face. "But I don't really want to be your friend anymore."

I can't think straight. "You. . .don't?"

He shakes his head. "In fact, I can't think of anything I'd rather be less."

Tears cloud my eyes. I've dreamed of this moment for so many years, and now that it's actually happening, I'm afraid I'm going to turn into a blubbering idiot.

I'm going to cry.

I'm going to melt into a puddle and slip through the cracks on this dock and into the pond where I'll be lost forever.

"I want to know everything about you, Emmy. I want to listen to you unload after a bad day. I want to make sure you're safe. I want to be the person you think I am because you see a better version of me than I do. I want to fall asleep on the couch watching stupid romance movies."

I laugh through my tears.

"I get it now. I understand why someone would be a fool for love. That whole 'when you realize you want to spend the rest of your life with someone, you want the rest of your life to start as soon as possible' thing makes sense to me now."

I blink. "Did you just quote *When Harry Met Sally*?"

He smirks. "I might've looked it up."

I'm at a loss for words.

Owen Larrabee, the least romantic person I've ever known, is giving me the most romantic moment of my entire life.

He scoots a little closer. "I tried not to fall for you, I really did. But I can't stop thinking about you. And me. And I've been trying to think of some super romantic way to tell you because I know how you feel about that stuff, but the truth is, I just want you to know. I want you to know that I don't want to spend another day without you. I don't want to keep wondering how it feels to kiss you. I don't want to have to ask for permission to hold your hand or stop over at your house without calling first. I want this—us—to work. And I didn't think I'd ever want that again."

"I feel like I'm dreaming, but if I am, I really don't want to wake up." A tear escapes and streams down my cheek.

He reaches for me, swiping it away as he closes the space between us, stopping just short of pressing his lips to mine. "Are you okay with this?"

"Are you about to kiss me?" I whisper, feeling slightly giddy at the thought.

"I am."

"Then yes," I smile. "I'm very much okay with this."

He lets his hand rest at the nape of my neck, pulling me close and everything goes hazy. I want to remember every single detail of this moment, and I beg my nerves to calm down so I can.

A single second before his lips touch mine, I freeze. "Wait."

He stops. "What's wrong?"

"Are you sure about this?"

"Am I sure I want to kiss you?" he asks, his voice breaking a bit. "Yes."

"Are you sure that you and I are, you know, a good fit?"

"No," he says. "But I'm willing to find out."

I pause, and then, as if only now realizing it, I say, "You like me."

His hand threads up into my hair, and he brushes his thumb across my cheek. "Yeah. I like you. A lot."

I smile. "I like you too."

"I think I might actually love you a little bit."

My heart swells, and I move a little closer. In the soft glow of the twinkling lights, his face is warm and full of promise. "I think I might love you a little bit too."

"Can we stop talking now?" he asks. "So we can—" he waves a finger from me to him to me—"you know. . ."

I nod.

And then, his lips are on mine. They're soft and gentle at first, the revelation of a secret we've both been keeping.

Seconds later, the kiss is firmer, deeper, more intense, setting off fireworks inside of me that I cannot begin to quiet.

I could stay here forever, in the dim light of a hundred floating bulbs, whispering through the trees like even they are cheering us on.

I wrap my arms up around his neck, going up on my knees and pressing myself closer to him, because I *need* to be closer to him. He pulls me close, wrapping both arms around me, and it's still not close enough. I *love* this man. I've always loved this man. Through all my childhood awkwardness to the days and weeks and years I tried to pretend he didn't exist.

If he'd never come back to Harvest Hollow, I would've stayed single forever because I gave away my heart a long time ago, and frankly, I never wanted it back. Even after he left. Even though I was humiliated and ashamed. I fooled myself into believing I didn't love him. I see it all so clearly now.

I never moved on because I couldn't. Not knowing he was still out there. And now, he's here, and I'm in his arms.

I never want this moment to end.

The kiss is better than every romance novel ever said it could be. It's the promise of a future. With Owen. Nothing can top that.

When he finally pulls away, we're both breathless, and somehow I know, this is only the beginning.

He presses a soft kiss to my forehead, then holds me close to him. I sink into his chest, reminded of how I felt in this fireman's arms before I knew it was him.

"So, I told you how I feel." He gently pulls back and levels my gaze. "I told you a few of the things that make you special, though I can think of a lot more. And I told you how I want our relationship to change." He says this pointedly, like there's a double meaning to them. "You said to forget about the romance and just get the words out, but I wanted to at least try and speak your language."

I frown. "Wait, I didn't say—"

He quirks a brow.

I think over what he said. "I said to forget about the romance and just get the words out?"

He doesn't respond.

"I only said that in an email."

He nods. "Which is where I read it."

"You read my emails?" My shoulders straighten. This could be a problem.

He laughs, his gaze falling for a single second, then back to my eyes. "Only the ones that were addressed to me."

Realization washes over me. "You're—"

"Practical in Poughkeepsie." He winces.

My jaw goes slack. "And I'm—"

"The girl I love."

"Owen." My mind spins with memories of the things we said in those emails. All that time, he was talking about me? "I don't know what to say."

"You don't have to say anything," he says. "I thought we could look at stars and eat Twix bars and maybe kiss some more."

I smile. "You have Twix bars?"

He opens the picnic basket. It's overflowing with all my favorite candy.

"Oh my gosh, that's my kind of picnic."

"I thought you might like that."

I reach over and take one.

"Maybe if we're lucky it'll rain, and I can spend a few more hours kissing you and making that fantasy come true too."

"I don't need all of that," I say, meaning it. "I just need you."

"That I can give you," he says. "I'm all yours."

I smile. "All mine."

He nods.

Another kiss. How can I be so off-kilter and so at ease at the same time? I inhale the scent of him and finally set the moment in my memory, forcing myself to zero in on every detail—the way he smells, the way his lips taste, the way his hands feel on my body. I don't want to forget any of it. I want to memorize it all so I can replay it over and over.

We lay back on the blanket, my head on his chest and his arm wrapped around me. Above us, the stars and the tree lights twinkle.

"It's not a pick-up truck, but it'll do," I say quietly.

There's a quiet pause with only the sounds of the great outdoors and the gentle strings of the music coming from the speaker.

It's perfect. He's perfect. We're perfect.

"So, we're not studying tonight, right?" I ask with a grin.

Chapter Thirty-Nine

Owen

Six months later

I'm nervous.

I don't usually get nervous about anything, but I am about this.

It's been months since I took the test. The results are due any day.

Haven't seen them yet.

But I have seen Emmy. A lot.

Ever since the night on the dock, Emmy and I have been nearly inseparable.

Dates at DeLucca's, often with Jace and Mack—weird at first, but pretty normal now. My sister and my best friend are a good match. He doesn't put up with her crap, and somehow, I think he even chills her out.

That last bit sounds familiar.

We've recorded three podcast episodes, Emmy and I.

Practical vs. Hopeful.

And by now, I think we're both seeing there's more than

one version of romance. Or maybe it's just one version with two different sides.

I looked for test results yesterday. Still nothing, email or regular mail.

I'm nervous.

Emmy helped me study for the lieutenant test for weeks, and after just a few months, I felt ready to take it, even if most of our study sessions devolved into studying each other.

It also didn't hurt that I managed to retain a lot of information from when I studied to take the test before I came to Harvest Hollow. That meant I didn't need as long to prepare. But when it comes to taking tests, I'll always worry I didn't study enough.

And yet, everything made sense, thanks to the accommodations.

I had to have passed, right?

We've spent a lot of time house hunting for me, and I moved into my new place a few months ago. An old craftsman, just like I wanted. It's nothing fancy, but it does have Emmy's touches all over it. It's a little bigger than her house, and there's even a room that would be perfect for her home studio.

A place I think someday might be *ours*.

Harvest Hollow has become home all over again. I know that's partly due to the town, but mostly due to Emmy. I've been working on proving myself to the people here, at least the ones who knew me before. It'll take time, I think, for some of them to come around, but I'm committed to this place now. And to Emmy.

It's a normal Tuesday, and when I get off my shift, I get a text.

EMMY

Hey, can you swing by the shop on your way home?

OWEN

I was planning on it.

It's been too long since I've seen you.

EMMY

It's been less than 12 hours.

<laughing face> <heart emoji>

She's turned me into a total sap.

I can't help it. I'm crazy about her.

But I'm still nervous. Same way I've been all week. Somehow it feels like the results are coming soon.

Before I leave, I check again.

Still nothing.

I drive over to Book Smart and as I park, I glance down at the bouquet of no-reason sunflowers on my seat. I love bringing them to her when I know she's not expecting it.

I pick them up, get out of my truck, and when I walk into the shop, I'm met by a loud shout of "Congratulations!"

There's a crowd gathered—Jace, Blister, Turner, Clemons, the Captain and Liz are all in a clump, all holding cups of red punch. My family and Emmy's family are there, along with The Coffin Dodgers, neighbors and friends, and several other people I know from town.

And they're all smiling at me.

"What's going on?" I ask.

Emmy steps out from behind the guys from the firehouse and smiles. She glances over at the captain. "Do you want to tell him?"

Captain Donoho gives her a nod, then steps forward, like

he's the mayor about to make a proclamation. "Well, Owen, we know you're not big on surprises. Or crowds. Or people—" the rest of them laugh. "But we wanted to properly celebrate this milestone." He levels my gaze. "Because it deserves to be celebrated."

My eyes flick to Emmy, who looks like she's about to burst.

"We are pleased to announce that you are all looking at the newest lieutenant of the Harvest Hollow Fire Department."

A cheer erupts through the crowd. People applaud, throwing arms around each other and raising glasses in the air. Even The Coffin Dodgers seem to approve.

I. . .I did it?

I look at Emmy. She holds both hands up to her mouth, trying to hold in her excitement. She nods at me, smiling with her entire body.

Through my shock. . .I nod back and mouth *thank you.*

The people in this town, people I gave no reason to believe in me, are here to celebrate my accomplishment. They're all willing to give me a second chance, and I know I'm going to do my level best to never let them down.

The applause dies down, and everyone is looking at me. No way I'm giving a speech, which Emmy must sense because she steps forward. "Thank you everyone for coming out to help us celebrate this huge accomplishment." She slips her hand in mine. "We're all so proud of you, Owen."

The words wrap themselves around my heart like a hug, and I squeeze her hand. "Thanks, Em."

She goes up on her tiptoes, gives me a quick kiss, and grins. "You're welcome, Lieutenant."

I smile down at her, handing her the flowers and thinking that as much as I love that everyone is here celebrating, I'm going to be really happy when we're alone.

Emmy turns back to the crowd. "After we take a few pictures, you're all encouraged to eat lots of cake."

The chatter kicks up again, and I take the opportunity to focus on Emmy. "This is next level. How did you pull this off?"

She gives a knowing shrug. "I asked the captain to notify me immediately when your results came in, put everyone on high alert, and made all the arrangements for a 'date to be determined.'" She smiles. "Everyone is so excited to be here, supporting you."

The door to the shop opens, and Chief Fisk walks in. He makes eye contact with the captain and waves. "The chief is here?"

Emmy glances toward the door. "Oh, I'm so glad he made it! I wasn't sure he could come!"

I watch as the man glances around the room—and I'm surprised when he doesn't walk over to the firefighters, but instead, heads straight for The Coffin Dodgers. He reaches them, and Marco steps out from the group and shakes his hand.

Like they're old friends.

"Huh," Emmy says. "I guess he knows Marco."

My mind spins back to the day the chief called me over. The conversation I had with him echoes back—it was the day he told me someone called to tell him I'd shown great leadership potential.

I look at Marco.

There's no way.

He glances at me and when we make eye contact, he stops talking and raises a brow, so slightly I almost miss it.

And then, he nods. A nod, it seems, of approval.

I nod back, hoping to convey my thanks, and he goes back to talking to the chief.

"Owen, will you get over here so we can take some pictures?" Liz, bossy as ever.

I give her a little wave, and when Emmy and I step over to the cake, the captain's wife grins at both of us. "I knew the calendar wouldn't be the last time I got to take a photo of the two of you. Now, scoot together."

The photos are a lot less awkward this time around.

I spend the next five minutes posing for photos with various groups—my family (who are all quick to convey how proud they are of me, a feeling I'm not sure how to process), the guys from the station, the chief and the captain, Emmy and her family, just Emmy, and even Marco and the other Coffin Dodgers.

Finally, Ernie says what everyone is thinking, "Can we just cut the cake already!?"

A laugh ripples through the crowd, and we spend the rest of the evening there, celebrating something I'd done right.

It feels good.

After the crowd has dwindled, I pull Emmy over into the *thrilling romance* aisle of the bookshop and plant a kiss on her lips so fully it should come with a PG-13 rating.

When I pull back, I search her eyes and find nothing but joy. "You're amazing, you know that?"

She grins. "I do know that."

"I'm serious," I tell her. "Nobody's ever done something like this for me." I pause. "I never gave anyone very many reasons to celebrate, I guess."

"But look at you now," she says.

I nod. "Look at me now."

I think back to what the captain said about Liz grounding him, calming him, and I see how that happens. Things that seemed to matter before Emmy just don't anymore.

I face her, about to attempt a new way of telling her how much I love her when something out the window catches my eye.

Emmy frowns up at me. "What's wrong?"

"Come with me."

It's dark by now, and the spring air outside is cool, but not cold.

We step out onto the street and instantly, cool drops of rain wet my face.

"Owen, what in the world. . .?"

I give Emmy's hand a tug, over under the streaming light of the streetlamp in front of Book Smart. "I've been wanting to do this for months."

She laughs. "You've been waiting to act like a crazy person?"

I shake my head, offering her my hand, bowing ever so slightly like a prince in one of her fairy tales. "May I have this dance?"

She goes still, watching me. "You want to dance in the rain?"

I smile. She slips her hand in mine, and I pull her close, placing my other hand on the small of her back, exactly the way Liz posed us the day of the photoshoot.

"I don't need romance, Owen," she says, resting her free hand on my shoulder. "All I need is you."

I lean down and kiss her. "Well, that's good, because you're stuck with me now."

She rests her head on my chest, and we dance in the rain, right in the middle of Maple Street.

And even I can admit, there's something to it. Something sort of magical. So, while she may not need romance, I'm still going to find ways to give it to her.

Because love really does make fools of us all.

And I'll be happy to be a fool for Emmy for the rest of my life.

THE END

A Love Letter
From the Author

Dear Reader,

Writing is such a solitary journey. There's no water cooler. No across the office chatting about the latest episode of The Bachelor (side note: I've never seen a single episode of that show. . .) There are very few opportunities to feel like you're a part of a community or a group.

Which is maybe what made this project so special.

It started as a sort of "Oh, yeah, we should do that. . ." and grew from there. Once our team was assembled, the fun started, and I'm SO glad I got to be a part of it.

Fall is my favorite time of year, and writing about a handsome, hunky and troubled firefighter seemed like a major win-win. Sprinkle in a bookish heroine, and I'm a goner.

I had a blast writing about Owen and Emmy, and adding a few things to the collaborative town of Harvest Hollow. And I genuinely hope you'll spend the chilly autumn months under a warm blanket with a cozy cup of hot coffee reading all of the books in this series.

Thank you for reading *Can't Help Falling*. If you liked it,

I'd be honored if you took a minute to review it. I know you have millions of choices when it comes to books, so the fact that you picked up one of mine means the world to me. Truly.

I hope you'll check out more of my work and please don't hesitate to catch up with me via email: courtney@courtneywalshwrites.com or find me on Instagram or Facebook. I love to chat with my readers & make new friends!

With my utmost gratitude,

Courtney

About the Author

Courtney Walsh is the Carol award-winning author of eighteen novels and two novellas. Her debut novel, *A Sweethaven Summer*, was a *New York Times* and *USA Today* e-book best-seller and a Carol Award finalist in the debut author category. In addition, she has written two craft books and several full-length musicals. Courtney lives with her husband and three children in Illinois, where she co-owns a performing arts studio and youth theatre with her business partner and best friend—her husband.

Visit her online at www.courtneywalshwrites.com

About the Author

Made in United States
Troutdale, OR
10/26/2023